KEEPING WARM

KEEPING WARM

MARY GARDNER

ATHENEUM   New York   1987

"Loving Her Was Easier Than Anything I'll Ever Do Again"
by Kris Kristofferson

Copyright © 1970 by Combine Music Corporation. All rights reserved. International copyright secured. Reprinted by permission.

Library of Congress Cataloging-in-Publication Data

Gardner, Mary.
  Keeping warm.

  I. Title.
PS3557.A7142K4   1987   813'.54   86-47688
ISBN 0-689-11841-4

Copyright © 1987 by Mary Gardner
All rights reserved
Published simultaneously in Canada by Collier Macmillan Canada, Inc.
Composition by Heritage Printers, Inc., Charlotte, North Carolina
Manufactured by Fairfield Graphics, Fairfield, Pennsylvania
Designed by Laura Rohrer
First Edition

With love to Russ

Beccy *and* Mark

Martha

Ben

KEEPING WARM

1

I USED TO THINK cowboys lived forever, and maybe I would too, that the prairies would never be plowed and that the great trail rides up the Chisholm would roll on and on. That my gums would never recede. That the empty lots I rode make-believe when I was a kid in Wisconsin, a tough little tomboy, would never have houses built on them, and that Gene Autry and Roy Rogers would prance across the silver screen for my children to see. I wouldn't be their natural mother, of course, because I'd be out on the range too much. But I could always adopt some little Cherokees if I wanted.

All the singing cowboys started dying at the same time, though, and their music disappeared like childhood. First it was Tex Ritter, January 2, 1974, hardly into the new year. I'd had an old Victor album of his songs that I'd worn into scratches, but when my mother died, it disappeared somewhere among the carpet rags and *Geographics* from the 1940s. I still regret not having it at home with me in Fargo, safe like mittens on a string, cozy in the record rack with Billy Calloway on one side and Willie Nelson on the other. Even if Jeff would threaten divorce or suicide if I played it.

The next one to go was Bob Wills. His Texas Playboys band kept touring around for a while afterwards, getting slower and thicker, but the real heart of Texas swing was gone. He had been an old man, winding down; friends in the business used to play concerts in his honor while he bobbed his head and got teary-eyed. It was almost a relief when he finally let go.

Then Lefty Frizzell got it, smashed up in a plane crash. No, that was Jim Reeves, ten years earlier. Once you're dead, you all sound alike.

That was my first dream. That they were all still alive. That I danced with them all, one by one, and Jeff just watched and smiled. That I danced with Waylon too, and Merle Haggard, and Willie, and Billy Calloway, the handsomest of them all, and each one swept off in the next figure of the square dance, his guitar cocked tactfully in front of his privates, after he'd handed me on. It was like chocolate cake with orange frosting for breakfast, especially Billy, because he was so tall I spun right under his arm. When I woke up, grabbing my pillow so hard I was slicing it down the middle like yesterday's pot roast, I couldn't believe Jeff wouldn't be able to read my mind. But he just yanked the pillow back where it belonged and said, "If I required those adolescents to copy something in their sketch tablets, do you think they'd make a bigger mess of Picasso or Cezanne?"

Jeff never had learned to play the guitar, or anything else either. All his colors came in his paintings, through his eyes and out on the canvas. But nobody can make a living being an artist, at least not in Wisconsin, so after we graduated from Eau Claire State, we got married and moved to Des Moines all in one week so he could accept a position teaching high school art. That's where Lisa was born, in 1967, tearing out between my legs with bloodied hair that dried to cornsilk even before she learned to suck. I know it hurt, but all I can remember now is how those yellow tufts, soft as goose down, stuck up between my fingers when I rolled my hand back and forth

1

I USED TO THINK cowboys lived forever, and maybe I would too, that the prairies would never be plowed and that the great trail rides up the Chisholm would roll on and on. That my gums would never recede. That the empty lots I rode make-believe when I was a kid in Wisconsin, a tough little tomboy, would never have houses built on them, and that Gene Autry and Roy Rogers would prance across the silver screen for my children to see. I wouldn't be their natural mother, of course, because I'd be out on the range too much. But I could always adopt some little Cherokees if I wanted.

All the singing cowboys started dying at the same time, though, and their music disappeared like childhood. First it was Tex Ritter, January 2, 1974, hardly into the new year. I'd had an old Victor album of his songs that I'd worn into scratches, but when my mother died, it disappeared somewhere among the carpet rags and *Geographics* from the 1940s. I still regret not having it at home with me in Fargo, safe like mittens on a string, cozy in the record rack with Billy Calloway on one side and Willie Nelson on the other. Even if Jeff would threaten divorce or suicide if I played it.

The next one to go was Bob Wills. His Texas Playboys band kept touring around for a while afterwards, getting slower and thicker, but the real heart of Texas swing was gone. He had been an old man, winding down; friends in the business used to play concerts in his honor while he bobbed his head and got teary-eyed. It was almost a relief when he finally let go.

Then Lefty Frizzell got it, smashed up in a plane crash. No, that was Jim Reeves, ten years earlier. Once you're dead, you all sound alike.

That was my first dream. That they were all still alive. That I danced with them all, one by one, and Jeff just watched and smiled. That I danced with Waylon too, and Merle Haggard, and Willie, and Billy Calloway, the handsomest of them all, and each one swept off in the next figure of the square dance, his guitar cocked tactfully in front of his privates, after he'd handed me on. It was like chocolate cake with orange frosting for breakfast, especially Billy, because he was so tall I spun right under his arm. When I woke up, grabbing my pillow so hard I was slicing it down the middle like yesterday's pot roast, I couldn't believe Jeff wouldn't be able to read my mind. But he just yanked the pillow back where it belonged and said, "If I required those adolescents to copy something in their sketch tablets, do you think they'd make a bigger mess of Picasso or Cezanne?"

Jeff never had learned to play the guitar, or anything else either. All his colors came in his paintings, through his eyes and out on the canvas. But nobody can make a living being an artist, at least not in Wisconsin, so after we graduated from Eau Claire State, we got married and moved to Des Moines all in one week so he could accept a position teaching high school art. That's where Lisa was born, in 1967, tearing out between my legs with bloodied hair that dried to cornsilk even before she learned to suck. I know it hurt, but all I can remember now is how those yellow tufts, soft as goose down, stuck up between my fingers when I rolled my hand back and forth like a boat over the round hard sea of her head.

We lived in Iowa for another two years, then moved east with Lisa clinging goggle-eyed to the heap of bedding and books in the back seat of our Chevy. By this time Jeff had done some graduate work and had a job in a second-rate junior college outside Washington, D.C. I plopped Lisa with our neighbor while I went to graduate school two days a week. I guess I'd decided to integrate Chaucer and cowboys, but I had to coerce those Texas voices out of my head before I could concentrate on being a grown-up scholar.

In our real lives, we didn't have enough money to take trips, but I explored what I could reach on my own. On the days I wasn't taking history of the English language or something just as petrified, I used to wind Lisa into the Chevy's one remaining passenger seat belt and set out. Only three miles from our apartment there was an old graveyard with ticky-tacky development houses tight at its edges. I'd haul Lisa out, wedge her into her collapsible stroller, and thunder with her through the overgrown grass inside the gates. Then she'd run from marker to marker, patting the stone lambs, pulling off her sneakers every chance she got and hiding them so she could lure me into the quest. When I thought of it beforehand, I'd pack a can of tuna fish with an opener and plastic forks; we'd eat it together, squeezing the meat tight against the tin and letting the juice dribble into the dried-out grass. Afterwards Lisa would climb into my lap, bare feet straddling, anchored on my thighs, and kiss me mouth-to-mouth with our noses contesting for space. Even when she'd grown into a stringy sixth grader, her kisses always seemed to taste of tuna to me.

It took me three years to get my master's degree in English, riding through the reference books, dancing with Texans in the margins. Then Jeff said he couldn't stand one more East Coast freshman, so we moved back to the Midwest. Lisa went to kindergarten in Marshall, Minnesota, and to first grade in Fargo, North Dakota, a twig among Scandinavian oaks already built for linebacking at five and six. Jeff taught part-time at the local high schools and colleges, as well as giving private lessons, grinding his teeth at night from the inanities of his students. In the summers he would pick up a few hundred dollars working on a combining crew. At first he didn't like me to watch him in the fields, as if I were eating popcorn at some agricultural documentary, but after the first week of the second year, he let me bring his lunches in the Chevy, by then just marginally functioning, driving out from town and down whatever dirt road he was on, his position marked by the clouds of dry topsoil that surged into the sky from the cutting. He usually didn't say anything much, not even thank you, but one day when the rest of the crew was watching, he called me his "redneck girl" and gave me a slap on my rear as I started back to the choking Chevy. I hadn't dared turn off the ignition for fear it wouldn't start again. Lisa was watching out the front passenger window, a serious seven, and as we drove back to town, she said, "Is it your birthday, Mama?"

"You know my birthday's in the spring," I answered back, gentling my foot down on the gas pedal so the car could accelerate without strain. Every time the Chevy survived a trip of more than three miles, I promised it a treat: pansies in a loveknot on the dashboard, chocolate chip cookies arranged like cow pies on the radiator. It was all just a mental bribe; I was too sophisticated to actually do it.

"Then why did Daddy spank you?" The tip of her tongue dusted her upper lip.

"That wasn't a spank."

"It was too."

"No it wasn't." Spanking wasn't in Jeff's repertoire; his hand must have slipped. Even his lovemaking pulled away from body contact.

"Daddy spanked *me* last week, Mama," Lisa said proudly. She reached out her hand and put it on the steering wheel next to mine. "I don't think Daddy likes being a farmer," she announced.

"He's really a painter." I counted her fingers, then put her hand back into her lap. The car gagged, swallowed, took a breath. I turned on the radio, searching for a friendly voice. KFGO was playing something with mandolins, all alohas and palm trees. I must have been getting out of touch.

"Are all those pictures in my closet his?"

"Yes, but he did those a long time ago." And we dragged them across country, Lisa, like defective foster children, only to store them in your closet because there wasn't any other place to put them.

"I'm going to hang them all when I get a house of my own." Lisa had her face against the side window with both hands spread out in fans on the glass. "People can come to see them then. By invitation." She got every syllable right. "You can make chocolate cake."

"I don't have any baking chocolate at home," I gritted out, back in the present, thinking about Jeff's paintings and how their bulk crowded her dresses into a colored wad in one corner of the closet. KFGO announced its slate of two-timers, pairs of songs by country's finest. First Patsy Cline, then Johnny Cash. Then Billy Calloway, but we'd be home before that. They were his old songs; I knew them by heart anyway.

"I don't mean today." She skated her hand over her hair, *Cosmopolitan*-style. "I mean when the people come, so we can serve it." The car choked again. I jiggled the accelerator, promising fudge frosting on the battery terminals. Chocolate was my pacifier: cake, pudding, cocoa. Maybe I should freeze a Devil's Delight layer for Lisa's grand opening, even if I'd rather do something else. But what?

That was the second dream. I could still see to drive, but in the middle of the windshield, as if on a movie screen, I was playing the piano in Billy Calloway's Range Riders band, my hands big enough to span an octave plus two. Billy was singing "Low-Down Lady," and Johnny Cash jumped up over the footlights from the audience to join him. When we brought it on home, the people screamed so much that Billy swung over and lifted me right off the piano bench, his hands under my arms like crutch tops. I was playing cowboys in Wisconsin again, riding the Great Palomino through the empty lots next to my home, only not make-believe this time. Billy's face was shadowed under his hat, but his hands were bright as silver. The color ran down my sides as he held me.

"Mama," Lisa whispered, and I came back. Sweat beaded her forehead like transparent fever blisters.

"What?" The Chevy hacked terminally, then subsided into a grating hum. We kept going forward.

She licked her upper lip. "Mama, I would like a sister."

Under the fat pads of my palms, the steering wheel rebounded. "I guess we sort of thought you were enough, Lisa," I explained decorously, even though we hadn't thought about it very much at all.

"If there were two of us, then we could both hang Daddy's pictures when we grew up."

"Daddy will have to hang his own pictures," I said through my teeth, expanding the chocolate frosting to the cylinder heads, whatever they were. It was no use. As chocolate and paintings burst into pyrotechnics in my head, the Chevy bellied up conveniently at the driveway to the EXXON station two blocks from our house.

"Jesus Christ!" I moaned, losing it.

"Mama!"

I grabbed the "sh-" of "shut up" as it whistled over my lower lip and turned it into "shame." "Shame it happened on such a hot day," I pontificated, trying the ignition with a fierce thrust of the key. Nothing.

Lisa opened the door and bounced barefoot onto the cement. "Ouch!" she roared, a furnace of indignation. She launched herself backward into the seat again.

"It's hot," I said, organizing the universe. An ancient gas jockey moved toward us, mirage waves circling his Cenex cap. He was new; I didn't know him. Maybe he would adopt me as his daughter and take the cost of repairs out of my inheritance. My bangs stuck to my damp forehead. If he gave me a bargain rate, it wouldn't be out of infatuation with my looks.

"Problems?"

"It just quit."

"Vapor lock?" He unlatched the hood and bent inside. Lisa was rubbing the soles of both feet on the dashboard, muttering.

"Maybe. But it's had trouble before. And the key doesn't even catch now."

He didn't engage in repartee. Something hissed, then clattered like little feet. Lisa poked her finger in her nose, planting herself sideways so I could have a good view. I wished for a horse—bay, chestnut, anything. Jeff would spit. I didn't belong in this age of four-wheeled transportation.

"You got bad wiring in here," a voice came, so detached from the man's legs on the pavement that for a moment I couldn't trace its source. "Current's not getting through." I waited for the price tag, victimized and grateful at once. Bad wiring was worse than running out of gas, but not in the category of motor disintegration. "I'll just tape it together for now until you can get home," his voice came again. "Have your husband bring it in soon as he can so's we can do a good job on it."

I reached around and yanked Lisa's finger out of her nose, then nodded humbly out the window at where his head had emerged. His cheeks had little puffballs in them, like a chipmunk's. Gray bristles decorated their centers. "Thank you," I articulated. "I don't know if I have enough money."

"Bring it in anytime," he replied, serious as a bank president. The honest Scandinavians. "Try it out now."

I did, walking on water with perfect faith. The car surged forward. Lisa put a different finger in her nose, and we drove on home, where I pulled the Chevy into our driveway, gently edging its grille up to the wall of what should have been the garage but was the kitchen wall instead. Without a garage, Jeff and I were always shoveling the car out in the winter, and we had to keep it plugged in with an extension cord snaking from its block heater to the front hall receptacle, letting in every draft under the door.

But it was summer, with its own dilemmas. Lisa squirmed down and out around the house, heading for the sandbox Jeff had built her in the backyard. Sand weaseled its way out through the crooked corners in little drifts of gray. We had to refill it every spring.

So she wanted a sister. I edged up the steps, my thighs squelching together. She was lucky she hadn't gotten two or three by this time, birth control being the chancy thing it was for me because I was afraid of the pill or the loop and couldn't get the diaphragm in right even with a compact mirror held between my legs, squirming myself up against the sink in our tiny downstairs bathroom. The block was full of siblings whom I'd hardly noticed, even the Khymer triplets on the corner. Jeff and I didn't discuss more children, but why? Money? Midwestern reticence? I didn't know. We didn't quarrel much either. All his passion went into his painting.

Through the kitchen window, Lisa's hair was a fuzzy golden halo. She was rearranging the drifts around the edges of the sandbox. As I leaned on the sink, my elbows wobbled in their sockets. Lisa turned and waved at me, her fingers twinkling.

That was the third dream. We were in bed together, not making love, just cuddled up under the comforter like children so Jeff couldn't possibly be mad if he came home and noticed. Billy's beard prickled along my forehead because he had my head tucked under his chin, and when I giggled, he laughed too and pinched me gently in the ribs. It was really more a tickle than a pinch. When I moved so my hand wouldn't go to sleep underneath him, I knocked over his blue guitar, his trademark, which had been leaning against the bed. "Don't worry, baby," he said. He sounded just like his records, all Texas.

2

"JEFF?"

He was drawing.

"Jeff?" The charcoal blurs on the rice paper looked like smoke.

"What?" He smeared the smoke around with his finger tips.

"The Chevy is sick."

"What else is new?" He took a new piece of paper, ripping it off the tablet so hard a corner tore loose. "Damn it," he said, but not about the car.

"You're supposed to bring it in so they can do a decent job fixing the wires. They're just taped now." Wheat dust was caught inside his right ear, a little carpet on the shelf over the lobe. I licked my finger, then wiped it dry on my shorts.

"You can do it tomorrow while I'm out there heaving bales."

"He said my husband should do it."

"What's he know?" He made three circles, overlapping, then smeared through their middles.

Upstairs, Lisa was singing to her teddy, a high line of notes like a spring mosquito. I listened, one ear on her voice, one on the charcoal scratching. The sounds moved toward each other in my head, feinted, interlocked. Then I did something I hadn't done for months, maybe a year. I slid up to Jeff on the sofa, ran my fingers down the chaff scratches on his arm, and asked him to go dancing with me after Lisa was asleep.

"You're crazy."

"Come on. We won't stay long." Lisa's song paused, then spun on. "We'll go to the N.P. They'll have a band, even if it's awful. We could polka."

"God."

"I promise we won't stay late."

"I hate dancing. Especially on a week night."

"No you don't." I touched his arm again. "I can call the oldest Khymer girl to sit."

He was quiet. I thought I'd won. Then he dropped the charcoal next to the rice paper and watched it roll onto the carpet. "If I have to be Mr. Farmer all day to earn enough cash to keep my family fed, I don't think you have any right to ask me to play one of your cowboy heroes at night," he said, flexing his hand.

That hurt. Lisa's song had died, and I replaced it with my own voice. "Then I'll go myself," I jolted out, and I got up from the sofa so abruptly that I flattened the charcoal under my foot.

"You'll what?"

"I'll go myself." I could wear my Mexican skirt. "That way we won't have to get a sitter." In the closet, my skirt was wadded over a hanger, and when I dragged it out, the front was patterned with wrinkles.

"Kay, I regard that as blackmail." When he put his hands around my upper arms, the charcoal left two lines of gray dots like tattoos. "I have no intention of letting you go off and flirt with some crazy cowboy. You're acting like a child."

"I'd rather be what I am than what you are," I snapped. I hated soap opera scenes, and as I struggled angrily to shake out my wrinkled skirt, I shrugged his fingers loose. The band at the N.P. would probably be from Dilworth or Glyndon, not big-time even by Fargo standards. Without the college kids, now gone home for the summer, I'd be the only one under forty there. Couldn't be under thirty anymore, could I? I slid out of my shorts in the hall by the closet door and then pulled the skirt up over my bare legs. Jeff turned away, rubbing his hand along his eyebrows.

We went dancing at the N.P. I thought Jeff was still mad at me, but he quietly sketched a few pictures at the table, squinting in the dim light from the Miller High Life sign above the bar. One of the sketches was my profile. The band had an old-time Norwegian accordion player, and Jeff was good at the polka, but he danced a few slow numbers with me too, and on the last one he let his chin sink down against my forehead. It was so unlike him that I pulled back to see if I was dancing with the right person. I knew I was, of course, because he didn't have a beard. Even with all that field work in the sun, his skin was smoother than mine.

When we got home, Jeff plopped into bed before I'd even brushed my teeth. I took a long time in the bathroom, working the dental floss both ways, pretending it was a task I was being graded for. As I trotted through the house afterwards, checking Lisa, checking locks, I thought about listening to the record player, very quietly, maybe joining Billy on his *Lone Man on the Road* album for a song or two. I wasn't really tired. But even if I kept the volume low, I might bother Jeff. He had to work tomorrow, and he had gone dancing after all.

Jeff looked hard asleep when I joined him on the margin of the crease we'd worn into the old mattress. If he'd been awake, I might have talked to him about what Lisa had said and how I felt about more babies. Like Banquo's descendants, a row of infants stretched out along the prairie in my head. We could have another child if we wanted; all our systems were still go. We didn't have much money, but we still had the old baby clothes boxed in the attic. I'd even painted Lisa's crib before I hid it away.

Then Jeff's breathing picked up a little. Maybe he'd read my mind. I didn't dare touch him; if he was still asleep after all, he'd shoot up out of the bed and be mad. The night table light pooled on the side of his forehead toward me. "Are you asleep?" I asked.

"No."

"It wasn't so bad tonight."

"No, it wasn't."

"How much longer on the combining?" I balanced my tight body straight out on the brink of the crease.

"Four more days, if it doesn't rain." His skin was so tan along his smooth jaw that the cleft in his chin chalked it in two.

"Do you mind?"

"Make your bed, lie in it." He shut his lips and the line disappeared.

"I guess so." My hand flexed, then caught in my nightgown tie when I stretched it toward him. Carefully I worked it loose, but by then he had turned his head away.

Oh, if I could have done it then, I would have stretched the four bedroom walls in canvas, covered right over the windows and door, stretched them professionally tight, and stripped the carpet off the floor so every paint tube could ooze and no one would care. I would have sliced through the ceiling so the good light would blossom, and then I would have left Jeff with every color in Fargo to flame out his universe with and be happy. I would have, yes I would, and I wouldn't even have put Waylon or Willie or the Hag or Billy Calloway on the stereo. Maybe Glenn Campbell; Jeff didn't mind him so much. Then I would have strictured myself into a modeling dummy, polished wood with every joint movable, no longer shy of my funny body with its breasts like poached eggs, and given myself to him to move whatever way he needed for his art, all jointed under his hand. When I came alive on the canvas, I would be a Vermeer lady, sleek and blue, or a Rubens with pink toes sweet as Hershey kisses.

When I finally got to sleep that night, the painting room came into my dreams, and I teetered for hours on a stepladder, Jeff's staple gun in my hand, bracing the canvas against the plaster, fastening, fastening, while all the corners hung loose and swung over me like shrouds. My mother was floating against the ceiling, making little noises. I swatted her away whenever she bumped against me. When I woke up some time in the middle of the night with Jeff's body on mine, his breath quickening as he pushed against me, I couldn't exchange the dream anxiety for pleasure even though he was holding himself back so I could catch up. I slid in and out of sleep, the diaphragm hovering on the edge of my mind.

Later, in my next life, when they held Jake up in the delivery room, his cord still anchored up in me like a lifeboat line, I fought through the narcotic to see him clear, saying words the doctor teased me about every time I went back for my yearly checkup. Had he expected Emily Dickinson? Jake's head had a halo around it from the fluorescent lights on the ceiling, and he was purple with rage. Jeff had been with me right to the end, rubbing my back faithfully in all the wrong places, but when I had to push I'd squeezed his fingers together so tightly he'd choked and run out. The doctor teased me about that too, but it wasn't Jeff's fault; he needed his hands intact. I couldn't help it either, of course; I don't feel guilty. When I finally got to hold Jake, with him lying under my chin, his hands splaying out convulsively every time I caught my breath, I tried to extend his spot of warmth down my nakedness where the useless hospital gown spread away from my flesh like oversized wings. They couldn't get the placenta out, and the head nurse thumped on my sagging stomach until I screamed, but I wouldn't let go of Jake then either. Lisa was home dreaming of the sister she never got; Jeff was in the hall trying to look back at me through the little window, rubbing his fingers; I was crying. None of us could help it.

The memorial service for Jeffrey Jacob Lombard, 36, Fargo, N.D., will be held at 2 P.M. Tuesday at the North Dakota State University Festival Hall. He died Saturday after a brief illness. Mr. Lombard was born Feb. 27, 1943, at Black River Falls, WI. He attended college at Eau Claire State College in Wisconsin and later taught art in Des Moines, IA, Rockville, MD, Marshall, MN, and Fargo. He married Kay Christianson June 4, 1965. He is survived by his wife; a daughter, Lisa Marie, and a son, Jacob Edward, both at home; his parents, Robert and Elizabeth Lombard, of Black River Falls, WI; a brother, Thomas, of Boscobel, WI; and two sisters, Louise Smithies and Rachel Lombard, both of Ashland, WI.

In lieu of flowers, donations to the American Cancer Society are requested.

3

A BRIEF ILLNESS was a cold, I'd always thought. Or the flu, or strep throat at the most. A long illness was the measles, if your mother made you stay in bed in a dark room. I guess time pushed in or pulled out like an accordion, depending. A brief illness.

We took Jake home from the hospital and went back to living. When my vagina healed, we made love again, sometimes. Jeff got a job teaching full-time in a special college program for adult students, so we had a little more money. After two years we bought a better car, my choice, a Plymouth Trail Duster. We took a real trip. Lisa won a prize for handwriting in fifth grade and got her copy of the Gettysburg Address put up on the wall of the Fargo Post Office next to the money order window. We filled the sandbox with new sand from Acme Sand and Gravel every spring.

He got tired. I thought it was just in contrast to me, flowering with energy once Jake got toilet-trained and I didn't have to inhale all that urine. Then I thought it was spring fever, because Fargo was having a real spring that year, even with crocuses. That summer Jeff went combining like he always did, but he quit halfway through his biggest job. He wouldn't talk about it. He mostly stayed in the backyard, sitting with his legs on either side of the frayed canvas lawn chair, drawing flowers. He'd get up, pick one, come back, sit down, draw it, using his colored pencils imported from Italy. I'd peel things at the kitchen counter, humming Marty Robbins, and then suddenly find myself simmering with anger because Jeff wasn't fixing the rotted windowsill or sitting inside at the table talking to me. Jake piled saucepans on the floor at my feet and kissed my knees when I tried to move. Lisa said the only country music she could stand was Elton John, and looked to see if I'd laugh.

In September he started teaching again. He hadn't tanned as much that summer, so he got pale quicker as the daylight dwindled with our northern fall. Then the college instituted an all-faculty life insurance program that required everyone to have a checkup. Jeff waited until the final week, and he wouldn't have gone then if I hadn't lost my temper, the worst I'd ever done, and driven him down to the clinic myself, so angry my foot shook on the accelerator, and the car jerked like those crash cars on the rink outside of town.

He had leukemia. It didn't seem to mean very much; the doctors all said they could treat it, and the health insurance plan covered everything. He didn't even lose all his hair from the chemotherapy, just the part around his ears, which stood out like rubber cookies on the sides of his head. I told Lisa what was going on, sort of; Jake was too young.

Then around Valentine's Day things got better. His white blood count went up. No, it was the white one that went down. I can't keep them straight. He did two big paintings of the prairie, slashing in each grass blade over foot after foot of canvas until it looked like green fire propped up against the wall. In March when the weather started to break (we were having another early spring), he came home one day from class, dropped his portfolio, and drove away without telling me where he was going. When he came back for supper, his hair was tousled from the wind and he had what he used to call his egg-sucking grin as he sat down and ate macaroni casserole with us. After the kids went upstairs, he told me he'd bought a gun and been target shooting, something he hadn't done since he was a kid. The gun seemed awfully heavy for anything so small, and he laughed when my wrist tensed as I hoisted it. After that he went out to the target range at least once a week. I made him wear earplugs.

We slid into summer without looking around. Billy Calloway and his Range Riders band had a concert scheduled at the downtown auditorium, and Jeff suggested we go without my even hinting. I ordered two of the most expensive tickets. Lisa went to day camp at the Y and filled the house with more useless crafts than I would have believed possible. Jeff's sister sent Jake a collection of plastic horses, red and green. He spent hours with them in the sandbox, saying he was playing cowboys, and he was too young for me to argue about definitions. Jeff and I bought an air conditioner for our bedroom, silly for Fargo's three weeks of summer heat, but it did make sleeping easier. We started to make love more often, not saying anything when we reached out for each other. At first I thought he was getting fat on my cooking when I felt the lump in his belly.

That was July. He died August 13. None of the drugs worked the second time. When I knew he'd have to go to the hospital again, I went and had my tubes tied in that new Band-Aid procedure. The doctor thought I was crazy. Billy Calloway's concert was on August 2, and Jeff said I should go anyway. Lisa was with her friends, so I took Jake on the second ticket. I'd been with Jeff all day and hadn't listened to the radio, or I would have known that the Calloway bus with its big blue guitar on the side had broken down near the Montana border and the concert had to be canceled. Instead I stood for almost an hour on the brick walk in front of the auditorium, while Jake sat in the grass and rubbed handfuls of it on his T-shirt, before I finally got my head together enough to ask someone why the doors weren't being opened. I didn't tell Jeff what had happened.

The last week I stayed with him every afternoon, one to six, but I went home then because I was worried about the kids. Margaret across the street was taking care of Jake; her son, Brian, was Jake's best playmate. I had given her a list of every possible number to call: our doctor, the police, the fire department, even the long-distance numbers like Jeff's parents. Jeff hardly ever talked, and I wore my watch with its face turned around to the inside of my wrist so I could hold my hand in my lap and peek at the time without his knowing. In case he did happen to be looking. On Tuesday afternoon he opened his eyes and said, "Bring me my gun," so naturally that I thought it was part of his dream. When I asked him why he wanted it, he lifted the hand that wasn't fastened to the IV and then let it drop down on the sheet beside him. Of course I didn't bring it.

When I got home that night, after I got the kids fed and put to bed, I sat on the floor exactly in the middle between the two stereo speakers and played Billy Calloway albums until two in the morning. I pulled the phone over with me along with some paper and a pencil and made more lists of people to call, only my people this time: my mother's old number before she'd died, the one graduate school teacher I'd liked, Waylon Jennings, old Ernest Tubb, the boy I used to play cowboys with, Merle Haggard, Hank Williams, Johnny Cash. It was amazing how many people, even famous ones, had their numbers listed and available through the information operator. I didn't dare ask for Billy's. Then I crawled up on the sofa, dragged the afghan over me, and finally went to sleep. In the bedroom I kept the comforter pulled up over the sheets Jeff and I had used in July; I just couldn't put them in the wash or sleep on them either.

That last week they let Lisa in to see him twice, and she

brought him a clay elephant she'd made in camp, its legs so uneven that it could stand up only if you rested it against its trunk. It was on his bedstand until an aide knocked it off when she was washing him. By then he didn't even know the difference.

4

SPRING IN FARGO, and the Red River still rising. In 1980 it was flooding so high that the Traffic Department closed off the street bordering it alongside the scooped-out valley where the golf course was. Not that anyone would have driven on it anyway, because it was under water for about three hundred feet, great slate-gray waves slamming against the retaining wall next to the fairway, water already oozing over around the greens. People who lived on the other side of town drove over in a steady stream, turned at the corner by the clubhouse, and then eased along to the parking area where the river lapped at the yellow barricades, white blurred faces as near the window glass as they could get. Nine point two feet over flood stage and the ice jam at Breckenridge still unmelted, although even where the plow had packed snowbanks by our front curb, they had dwindled to lacy borders.

In other springs I'd taken the kids down to look at the river at its peak, and even the year I was pregnant with Jake, I'd waddled down a day after the crest, holding Lisa's hand a little distance from my side because my belly was so big. But this April of 1980 I was just too busy to go down, dealing with student papers, faculty meetings, colleagues, teenagers, all pressing in on me, asking for grades, crying about tests, papering my desk with mimeographed forms. I had started teaching composition at the State University when their second quarter began just before Christmas. So Lisa took Jake the day before the river crested, walking down with Margaret and Brian from across the street, while I sat at the dining room table and evaluated test scores, the stereo on low. Cowboy music pounded my thinking mind too much; I had to listen to instrumentals like Gordon Jenkins. I had the scores about half figured out when I heard my family at the door again.

"Was it fun?" I caught myself. Nothing about that flooded river was fun.

"That thing is *big*, Mom," said Lisa as she waved to Margaret and Brian, splashing through spring puddles on their trek back across the street. "Come on, Jake." They both stood damply in the front hall, moisture outlining their shoes on the linoleum. It was chilly for spring, despite the overwhelming thaw. I rubbed my hands in the armpits of my sweater, then pulled them out to catch the kids' jackets as they discarded them on the hall floor. Any other day I would have nagged, but they were back safe; the river hadn't swept them away. Damp and pink-cheeked, dripping on the slippery linoleum, they seemed precious.

"Any homework?" That was a question for Lisa; in nursery school, Jake was seldom burdened, though he liked to feel he was in an academic pattern too.

"Just my English. And copying over my essay about North Dakota pioneers." Lisa put her fingers in the corners of her mouth and pulled. "All those fat Norwegians. Yuck. I'm glad I'm French."

"Well, you're not all French," I said, thinking of the one-eighth Norwegian she got from me, but not reminding her.

"Mostly I am!" She tore upstairs, followed by Jake, panting.

I was nervous that night. First of all, I didn't have all my tests corrected yet. Then the radio kept reporting on the rising waters, predicting a crest around three a.m., although the weather forecaster wasn't sure, because the Breckenridge ice dam was still blocking the water. I knew we wouldn't be flooded or anything; Fargo—all the Red River Valley—was as flat as a pancake griddle, not a real valley at all, so one inch of river overflow would have distributed itself in a film over hundreds of square miles. The worst that happened was always when the crest began to pass us, sucked up by the cloudless, faceless sky not even a child's fantasy could populate, rolling north to Lake Winnipeg with its muddy layer of tires and condoms. The water would retreat from the golf course basin, leaving dying carp with scales like translucent tiles stuck gasping in the bottom foot of the chain-link fence. That had happened only in 1975, though, the year of my heavy walk with Lisa, and I'd moved so naturally between the fence and her as we'd walked by, lighter on my feet than I'd have thought possible with Jake an undigested brick in my belly, that she'd never even seen them.

The kids were quiet that night at supper. Lisa had three pages of mindless English punctuation to fill in and check, and since she insisted on going over every sentence with me, it took forever. Jake had brought home some rolled sheets of newsprint from nursery school on which he was supposed to draw fruit. "Fruit?" I asked, thinking he'd gotten it wrong.

"Yup," he said, digging for his favorite stub of black crayon in his battered box. "One on each, Mom." He laid out a backbone of magazines on the living room carpet and cornered his first sheet on it, then flopped down at the bottom end, his hard little rear punching against his brown corduroys. With a magnificent sweep he drew a black circle, overlapping at the top. "That's my orange," he said, and set it aside. The circle on the second sheet was slightly elongated. "Banana," he said, adding one small black spot at its midsection.

"Why don't you color them in, Jake?" The third sheet had crumpled corners.

"I like them this way," he answered, his voice dropping. "I *like* them this way, Mom." With his free hand he smoothed at the crumples, then drew.

His third fruit was tiny, a marble-sized circle in the center of the creamy expanse. I had to come up close to see. "What's that?" I asked, genuinely curious. It was his last sheet.

"That's a pit, Mom." He stood up. "My teacher will like these a *lot*." Under his swatch of hair, the dark brown of his eyes widened like an ink wash. "They don't do them this good even in *kindergarten*." He stuffed his crayon back into the tattered Crayola box and went upstairs pridefully. Lisa, who had been prettying up her grammar pages, gave me a quick nose tap on the cheek as she followed him.

Maybe it was the river. Its swollen rise just three blocks away, documented by the compulsive KFGO weathermongers, bordered my evening, and I couldn't get sleepy. Tea didn't help; neither did cocoa. For the first time in a while I let myself think about Billy Calloway, wishing I'd known him when we were both kids, playing cowboys. Maybe we could have built a raft together. KFGO revised the crest for one a.m.; the Breckenridge ice dam had broken earlier than they'd thought. I played an old Hank Williams record, made from a live performance, and then put on Billy's earliest album. As the guitar began, one thin line of high notes like water-glass music, I sat down on the sofa, afghan over my lap, and looked hard at his publicity shot on the cover. He was leaning on a wooden fence, shoulders hunched so that his head stuck out straight at the viewer. It looked like he was squinting against the sun, or maybe his eyes were really that narrow. His shirt was open halfway down. On this shot his face was smooth, though he'd grown a beard sometime in the seventies. Then, without realizing it at first, my hand was rubbing against the synthetic velvet of the sofa, and before I could yank my arm back, Jeff's skin came alive in my palm, terribly smooth, so smooth that even when he hadn't shaved, the prickles seemed like they'd been sprinkled on from outside. I looked at my hand, expecting to see it marked, but of course it wasn't. Like a metal clamp, my shoulders pulled around as if they were trying to join in a circle in front of my collarbone; I had to fight to keep my own body from crushing me. The album cover slid to the floor.

Then Jake screamed. I thought he must be dying. His voice tore through the house, high and grating, with no words, not even "Mama," just a great shriek from his throat as if all the breath he had were being pushed out through his mouth. I ran to the stairs, but my legs gave out and I had to go up on my hands and knees. All the time I was crawling, that voice from another world swept down around me.

When I got to the upstairs hall I could hardly stand, but I scuttled as fast as I could along the carpet to Jake's door. In the dim flare of his nightlight I didn't even look at him, but instead for whatever gremlin figure could have sucked the breath out of a little boy so he would have to scream like that to stay alive.

There wasn't anyone. The screaming stopped. Jake sat up sobbing in his bed, arms wrapped around himself as if his insides were falling out. I dropped down beside him and took him into my arms.

"Sweetheart." I was shaking so hard I couldn't get his pajama top unbuttoned so he could get more air. Then, as my eyes adjusted to the dark, I realized he had it on backwards anyway, so I gave up and just held him some more. After a little while he untangled his arms and put them around my back.

"Were you dreaming?" He didn't answer, just burrowed into my neck. "Were you dreaming, Jake? It was only a dream." There was no phantom in the world that I would let near him. "Don't be scared."

He was so quiet against me that I thought he'd gone back to sleep. I waited until my own heart slowed down, until it wasn't pounding into his ribs with every beat, and then I started to lay him back on his pillow. He didn't resist, but his voice came out so softly that at first I thought the words were inside my own head. Then I felt the tiny puffs of air, damp with April and his own liquid breath, against my cheek.

"The river took him away," he said. "The river took him away. That big river." I thought he was done because his arms loosened, but then he pulled tight again, wrenching the stubs of my neck hair under his grasping fingers. "I can't swim," he whispered. "I'm scared of that river."

All that came to my mind were simplistic solutions, even though I knew better. Should he take swimming classes at the Y? Should I teach him myself next summer? Before I even had a chance to turn down my own silly suggestions, his head flopped back and he was asleep in my arms. I slid him back down in bed and let him be.

Then I went down the stairs, upright. Through the hall and the front door. Outside the moon was shining as if it had been hired to reflect in the spring's overflowing waters. I didn't even need a winter jacket. Fifth Street was a white chalk strip between black lawns, soggy, heavy with midnight. I didn't lock the door. Even though my legs were short, they were longer than Jake's, and I reached the overlook in ten minutes. No one else was there, of course. Fargoans slept through their midnights.

Whether or not the river had crested, I had no way of knowing. Looking down in the dark, with the moon doubled by the mirror the water made for it, I didn't feel as if I were looking at the river at all, but rather some twisted creature churning along beneath me. It had worked itself over the golf course bank and half filled the bowl; the carp must be searching the edges for their freedom and finding their wire rectangles of death. Was there any music at the end except the sloshing of the water? All the guitars and husky voices were beating inside my skull, and Billy Calloway might as well have been pushing me down with his hands on my shoulders, he felt so close. But I shook him off. I shook them all off. That dragon river could eat the land, could wash all North Dakota into Canada and spread its alluvial soil over the provinces as far as Saskatchewan, and I would hang onto the golf course fence like the carp, only alive, clutching Jake and Lisa against me, sprouting arms like an Indian god to keep them safe, because I was all they had now, damn it, and longing wasn't going to do me any good, Billy Calloway, nor sweet guitars either, nor looking back. Nothing was going to do me any good except staying away from that river and keeping my children dry beside me.

1309 Fifth St.
Fargo, ND 58102
Oct. 29, 1980

Mr. Billy Calloway
Blue Guitar Productions, Inc.
3750 Sedgewick Blvd.
Austin, TX   78710

Dear Mr. Calloway,

In the midst of getting ready to carve the Halloween pumpkin, I just felt an inspiration to write to you and tell you how much I appreciated your new album. Bring It On Home seems to me one of the best things you've done, especially the two songs you wrote about being a child in Texas. I've just about worn out Side B playing them.

I'm primarily a housewife, mother, and college teacher, but I've liked country-western music since I was a child. Thanks for the pleasure you've given me over the years.

Sincerely,

Mrs. Kay Lombard

5

"MOM, I HATE IT. I hate it. It's a dumb, stupid assignment, and if old Pruneface had thought about it for half a minute, she'd have known that nobody was going to do it anyway. I don't care if I get a B for the class, I don't care if I get a C. She can *flunk* me. I don't know any celebrities; there aren't any in Fargo to begin with. Nobody famous would live here."

I should never have asked, but the asking had become a ritual. Lisa usually narrated her assignment list without fuss, then went off to do it. She'd been a straight A student all her life; I never had anything to complain about.

"It can't be that bad."

"It's worse!" Lisa was stomping around the dining room table. "Interview someone who did something important or is a celebrity. Ask him why he is the person he is." She had thrust her voice into a nasal whine like, I assumed, old Pruneface. "A guinea pig is about the most famous person in Fargo. Right up on top."

"Well, you could interview Antigone." Lisa had gotten two

guinea pigs for Christmas, Antigone and Electra, though we weren't at all sure about their sex. They lived in the tiny bedroom upstairs that was really a cedar closet with a window, and they chittered whenever they heard footsteps. Their appetites were infamous, though they seemed content with newspaper when we ran out of lettuce scraps.

Before the next explosion, the phone rang. Margaret wanted to know if I had an extra shovel, because her husband was doing the walk and Brian was helping him. Then the phone rang again, and it was Emily, who taught with me, asking for the address where she was supposed to send her English teachers' conference registration form. Then Lisa called her friend Rebecca to complain in a new key. Then Jake called Brian, who had gone in early from shoveling. Meanwhile I shoved aside my own needs, scrambling around inside my head for persuasive resources, sorely tempted to let Lisa beg off this one time.

"Mom?" Jake had edged up next to me.

"What?" I had a half inch of papers left to correct.

"Can I go sledding?"

"*What?*" It was already dark and nearing bedtime.

"Brian and his dad are going, Mom. Just for a bit. Down by the golf course. Because Brian worked so hard shoveling." He made percussive sputters at the ends of all his sentences, whether they were complete or not. "Can I go, huh?"

Be generous, Kay. I ran my thumb over the edge of the paper pile. "I suppose. Wear your double mittens, OK? Are they picking you up?"

"I'm going over," said Jake, already bundling himself up in the front hall. Both the thumbs in his outer mittens were frayed from being chewed, but the inner ones were intact. "Bye, Mom. I'll be careful." I hadn't even shown any anxiety.

Ever since my childhood, I'd hated sledding. In my dreams it was the ankles that got me, because lots of people dragged their legs along the sides of the sled, digging in with their heels to brake the downhill plunge, and I always thought that if I tried that, or even if my feet slid off the sled accidentally, my ankles would get crunched, bent back, folded the wrong way. Crazy. It couldn't happen to Jake, I knew.

I did a quarter inch of papers. They were three paragraph narrations about a favorite Christmas present out of the past, a topic of desperation. The boys expounded about guns, pistols, deer rifles, occasionally drums. Noise seemed to matter. Girls preferred jewelry of various sorts. They could have been Lisa's age, bless them, or even Jake's, except that some of them could type. My own favorite Christmas present had been a subscription to *Country Song*, a tacky newsprint magazine that came out of Nashville every month. Jeff had bought it for me our first Christmas in Fargo, but I had had to tell him what I wanted, so it wasn't as if he'd come up with the idea himself.

February blew in, Jake with him. His cold cheeks were frosting; the rest of him was straight from the oven. He went up to bed with good cheer, leaving his snow-filled boots melting by the coatrack. I finished the last quarter inch of papers.

Somehow in the February night I'd stopped thinking about Lisa and the celebrity assignment, so when it came back to me, I startled, as if I hadn't turned off the bedroom light or turned down the heat. Unfinished business. But Lisa was fourteen, just, her birthday two weeks before celebrated by a monumental sleepover, with all the curly blondes from the eighth grade wound together in their sleeping bags on the living room floor. I should leave her alone. If she didn't do her assignment, then that was her responsibility. And Pruneface was an old martinet, damn it, everything I was never going to be as a teacher. You couldn't expect a fourteen-year-old (just) to work with someone like that and do it cooperatively.

Eleven-ten. I had office hours the next day. After neatening the corners of my papers in a pile on the table, I put them into my briefcase, all its fake leather corners stubbed from where I'd miscalculated doors and walls as I swung through my professional life. I checked upstairs to put the house to bed. Jake was asleep, holding Rachel Bear spread-eagled right on top of him, raggedy front paws laid out along his own arms. Lisa's door was shut, no crack of invitation, and I didn't want to intrude, now that I was thinking about my role and her role and how I wasn't doing anyone any favors by stirring them together. I touched her knob with one finger, then put my foot on the stairway going down.

No scream this time, but something. Inside her room, fabric was rasping against fabric. The friction stopped, and I tuned my ear toward the sound, waiting. Maybe she was dreaming, though Lisa usually slept solidly through the night. Then the sound came up again, coupled with a tiny whimper. Did she have Antigone in with her, sharing her bed? Unlikely.

I knocked, very softly, with my knuckles barely curved. "Mom?" came her voice. She didn't invite me in, but the rising question stayed in the air even after my "It's me." I gently opened the door.

Lisa was sitting up in her bed, notebooks and binder paper splashed across her knees. She was biting her lower lip so hard that when she opened her mouth a broken red line laced across her chin, whitened, disappeared. "I am trying to make something *up* for that assignment, Mom, but I *just can't*." She spread her hands among the papers and flurried them to each side, then angrily wrenched a page out of her spiral notebook. "See? I wrote a few dumb things like Senator Burdick was saying them, but I don't even know what he *thinks*."

"Not much," I said, not meaning to be ironic. "Look, if this one assignment didn't get done, the world wouldn't end."

Lisa was not accepting consolation. "I am not going to let that woman *beat* me," she muttered. Then she started shredding the spiral bindings off her paper, wadding every few into a ball between her thumb and index finger before secreting them in a curve of her quilt. Lisa the saver—she still had her first grade drawings piled on the shelf of her closet.

"Look, it's late and getting later." No response, just more

paper balls. "Could you write an essay about a regular person, with the idea that we're *all* celebrities in this world?" And if you're so clever, Kay, why can't you come up with these brilliant ideas for your own students?

Lisa grabbed her pillow from under her head and thumped it down on the debris spreading across the quilt. "No!" she roared, that piercing voice wobbling her epiglottis as it tore out. "I can't do anything! I have to write this thing RIGHT NOW! And I can't make it up!" I was afraid she'd wake Jake. Underneath her nightgown, her bony chest contracted and expanded in rage. It was midnight. I had to go to school the next day. So did she.

"All right!" That was *me*. "Get up from there. We'll go downstairs to the phone and call Billy Calloway."

"*What?*"

"We'll call Billy Calloway. He's certainly a celebrity. You can ask him whatever you want and write it down. Then you'll have your paper."

"*Mom!*" She had both hands in her hair above her ears, tormenting her curls.

"Get up, Lisa. I mean this." Then, inspired, "If he isn't home, you can tell old Pruneface you couldn't get in touch with him, but you sure tried. Perfect excuse."

"Mom, you're crazy." She shoved the papers down toward the foot of the bed and wiggled her feet under the quilt. "You don't know Billy Calloway. You don't know where he lives, even. You don't know anything but those stupid songs of his. I can't believe my own mother is doing this."

"Well, she is. And that's not true. I don't know him personally, but I know he lives in Austin. I wrote him a letter there." And I have a list of phone numbers you wouldn't believe, daughter. I'll bet we can get one more.

"You did what?" Her nightgown came just below her knees when she stood up. When had she started to grow so fast?

"I wrote him a letter telling him how much I liked his music. *Who's Who* gave his business address as Austin, so he

35

must be there too. We'll call information." With our shoulders matched together, neither of us allowing the other to go first, we marched down the stairs.

"Maybe his number is unlisted. Maybe he lives in Nashville and commutes to Austin. Mom, you're *crazy*."

Now, I was not a crazy person. I am not a crazy person. Calling a country-western singer at midnight might have *seemed* crazy (all this was racing through my head as I separated those worn instruction pages in the front of the phone book, stuck together along the edges with some residue of a Jake Lombard project), but this was the obvious solution, wasn't it, to appease Pruneface, encourage Lisa, gain control? Even if it didn't work, I'd have lost nothing. I had always wanted to talk to Billy Calloway anyway, and if I did it for my daughter, then I wouldn't even be embarrassed. Lisa had sat herself with her feet up on a kitchen chair, nightgown wrapped around her legs. If she was going to model herself after me, and daughters were supposed to do that, then she might as well have a good act to follow.

"OK, this is the area code. 512. Now, do you think he's William or Bill? Or Billy? Or could he use initials?" I had my fingers in the reassuring holes of the old black phone. "Lisa, do you have a pencil? Because when I get this number, I want you to write it down when I tell it to you. Hurry *up*." Already the phone was ringing in some distant operator's switchboard, alerting her to our crusade. Maybe computers did it all, but I preferred to think there would be a person on the other end of the line.

"Mom, they won't have his number. You might as well call Liberace. Or the President."

"I am calling Billy Calloway, who is a better singer than either one of them." And who leans on wooden fences with panache, I thought, but didn't say, because I wasn't sure how to pronounce "panache," having only read it in books. "Shhh. Stop it, Lisa." She was shaking her finger at me as if I were a misbehaving Girl Scout. "Get that pencil ready. Here comes the operator."

When I heard that metallic "What town, please?" and then "What name?" I jerked tight inside for a moment. After all, I could blame only so much on old Pruneface. But, with an exploding rocket of freedom, I didn't care. What did I have to lose?

"There are four William Calloways in Austin, ma'am," came the voice. "Do you know the street address?"

"No, I don't. Could you just read me the list?" I'd go eeny, meeny, and pick whatever one I landed on.

"We are only allowed to give two numbers at a time, ma'am," replied the Bell Lady, the edge of exasperation in her voice.

Roadblock. I kicked free. "Well then, try Billy Calloway," I said.

"*M*illy Calloway?" came the voice.

"No, *B*illy. B as in . . ." I couldn't think of any words that began with B. Plunging through my shelves of vocabulary, I came up with "breast." "B as in breast," I sent back over the phone wires, enunciating clearly.

"*Breast?*" Her tone indicated that she was no computer.

"Yup." Ride the trail you pick, sleep in the bed you make. I started humming. Lisa was making screwing motions with her forefinger next to her left ear, but she had a pencil in her right hand and a pad from the insurance broker on the kitchen table.

"773-8965." Now that I had it, I couldn't absorb it, and suddenly I was frantic that the operator would dissolve and I'd never get the number again. "Could you repeat that, operator?" I asked, my hand freezing to the phone.

"773-8965," said the distant voice, already slipping away. I repeated it after her. Lisa copied it down, her thumbnail cutting into her second finger as she dug the pencil into the tablet. I hung up.

"Do you think that could be *him*?"

"Well, it's the only Billy Calloway in Austin. There can't be many people with that name. Unless he *is* a William in the directory."

"It's going to cost a lot to call, Mom."

"Not now. It's after eleven. And anyway, you don't have to talk long."

"*I'm* not talking!"

"What do you mean, you're not talking? This is your report."

"But calling him was your idea!" Then she grinned, and I gave up.

So I dialed. I hadn't the faintest idea what to ask him, and Lisa wasn't going to be any help, especially since she was now lying on the kitchen floor with the top of her head pressed against the refrigerator, kicking her feet up and down and beating her fists in mock spasms against the linoleum. But I could cope. Hello, Central, give me heaven, I thought, as I spun the last number. I sorted out my fingers and rearranged them on the phone. My ear was hot from being ground into the plastic circle. Then the phone rang, and it sounded nearer than the hospital, nearer than Jake's school, nearer than Eau Claire, Wisconsin, and the house where I didn't live anymore and which didn't even belong to me. No distance at all. From the spaced-out skies of West Texas, that arrow of sound arched against the midnight blue right into my chest. No, shoulder. Cowboys always got it in the shoulder.

Somebody picked up the phone but didn't say anything. Then there was a crack as if the whole machine had been dropped on the floor. For a moment I thought *I'd* dropped it, but when I checked, my hand was still tight around the mouthpiece. On the other end of the line came a series of thumps, alternating with scrapes on something hard. "Shit," came a voice, so faint I thought perhaps the lines were crossed, but I couldn't imagine with whom. Then a man's heavy voice, stunningly familiar, all Texas, plunged through the wires as if it were running their tunnel. "Hello!" said Billy Calloway.

I was dumbstruck. On the floor, Lisa had stopped beating her fists, and her toes were suspended in midair. "Is he there, Mom?" she whispered. "Say something. Say something, Mom."

"Hello," I said, my mind washed clean of everything. Waves of chill from the linoleum were climbing my calves. I tried the other ear, just to see if they were both still connected by the highway through my head.

"Goddamnit, who is this?" The phone crashed again, but not quite as far. "Tweeter, is that you messin' around? Shit, I told you I was bushed after them goddamn shows in Galveston. Leave me be."

"Mr. Calloway?" Who was Tweeter? "Mr. Calloway? I'm calling from North Dakota." I sorted out my shelves of words. "Could I ask you a few questions?"

"North Dakota? Where the hell's that? Jesus Christ, I can't keep ahold of this goddamn phone! Hang on." Like a whitewash, silence stretched across the other end of the wire with a few swishes very far in the background. Lisa was standing next to me, holding her hair back from her ear, which was competing with mine for the little black circle of the phone.

"Mom, did you really get him?" Her mouth circled up tight, then flew apart in a rampant grin. "Mom, you are wild and crazy. You are a beautiful woman!" She flung her arms around me so hard I fumbled with the phone myself.

But he was back. "Alright. Had t' git my pants on." That was a Texas voice for sure. "Now who the hell is this? You wanna ask me some questions? You ain't one of them goddamn magazines, are you? Shit, I figgered they let you alone once you was in bed, leastways."

His profanity cauterized my brain like bleach. I liked it. All the color-coded wires in the telephone were dancing behind my eyes. What was I supposed to say now? The truth, Kay, tell the truth. "My daughter is writing an article," I said. Article sounded better than paper and still wasn't a lie. "She needs to know why you are the person you are." Good Lord, Pruneface couldn't have meant anyone to take that idiotic question seriously. "I mean, she needs to know what kind of a person you are, and how being a celebrity affects you." I was sweating, but pridefully. My honor was being upheld.

"Shit, I ain't no kind of a *person*," came the voice. "I mean, I'm a *picker*. I always been that, ain't no diff'rent now." Lisa and I were breathing so hard and so near together that the mouthpiece of the phone was damp. "Your *daughter* is writin' this article? What *you* doin', callin' me like this? Shit, it's so goddamn late I can't figger out what's goin' on."

If someone had been interviewing me, asking me what kind of a person I was and what my most outstanding characteristic had been, up until that moment I would have said truthfulness. Honest Kay. But without any contradiction, betraying my whole past life as casually as I would have dusted my night table, I replied, "Well, she's in the hospital." My own words came back to me like an echo, but I was already launched on the next betrayal. "She's very sick, so I'm helping her with it. So she won't lose her job." Meanwhile, Lisa had flung herself bent over on her knees next to the stove, her forehead rubbing the linoleum. Her whole back was rippling in seizures of laughter.

"Jesus Christ." Silence, both of us breathing heavily. He yawned loudly into the phone. Then, "She got a good doctor? Some of them ain't worth shit, all they care about is money." Silence again. "Ain't no fun, bein' sick, you kin bet on that. Me, I'd rather jest shuffle off and git it done with."

It was like he had pulled the plug in the bottom of my brain. I had nothing more to say. Lisa rotated her head toward me from the floor, mouthing words I couldn't translate.

"You there?" His voice was gruff.

"Yes."

"Jesus, you sound funny." Silence again, then a burble of melody. He was humming into the phone.

"Ask him how long he's played the guitar, Mom," Lisa

whispered as she rolled up from the linoleum. "Ask him how much money he makes. Ask him . . . what color hair he likes women to have." She choked with bravado and plunged down to the floor again.

At first I really thought I was going to. The humming held off as if he knew the question was coming. "Are you in love?" said a voice from somewhere that by the process of elimination had to be mine.

"Shit!" A great eruption into the earpiece. "You're askin' me *what*?"

"Do you love anyone?" English teachers could rephrase any question six ways.

"You mean like my mama?"

"Not exactly."

"You mean like *wimmen*?"

"*One* woman."

"Jesus." His whistle hit my eardrum like a tornado warning. "You better git yourself ready for a goddamn *list*."

But you only get one, I thought, although I knew perfectly well that if that were true, all those country-western fan magazines would go out of business. You only get one. That's what's hard. I thought my face had begun to sweat, but that wasn't it. That wasn't it at all.

Lisa was looking at me as if she'd come across me in an art gallery, hung on some obscure wall. I put the phone back on the receiver. He didn't know who he'd been talking to anyway, and if he didn't know my name, then this conversation hadn't been real, had it? He couldn't catch me and make fun. He didn't even know where North Dakota was.

6

DURING THE WEEK I didn't read the Fargo *Eagle*, our local paper, at all, just the headlines on the front page and Ann Landers, who wasn't regional. But on Sunday mornings I gave in. All those Norwegians never did much beyond farming and thinking about farming; still, their lives seemed more exciting than mine. Even the sprouting of May, robins giddy with protein on the front lawn, tulips flopping their petals with every gust, didn't seem like much to me. But at least I wasn't shivering anymore. Jake had started to read almost on his own, and his kindergarten teacher had had lunch with me at Sambo's so we could admire each other. Lisa still got straight A's. Her batteries were well charged; she sparked through our lives as if I were the child in the house. My waves of students crested and then crested again, their Scandinavian faces blurring together in a wash of decency. But I liked them. I really could teach. I deserved the indulgence of the *Eagle* on Sundays.

"Read me *that*, Mom." Jake had tromped into the kitchen where I had fixtured myself at the table, cocoa steaming alongside my hand, and was pointing to a brisk sketch of the park board's plans for restructuring the local pool. He edged the paper aside and hefted himself up onto my knee, which was sticking out through the gap between buttons in my bathrobe. "I read good, but not *that* good," he said, smiling. "*Next* year."

"Doesn't look very interesting to me, kid." I flipped the page.

"Me either!" Lisa sat down next to us with a bowl of Grape-Nuts soaking like cement powder in their skim milk bath. "Jake, you know that paper is the dullest thing in Dullsville, North Dakota." As she bent over to stick her spoon in, the damp ends of her hair made lines of water dots on the wood of the tabletop.

"I give up." With an overarm sweep, I handed the paper to Lisa. "Read it yourself and suffer. Jake, I'll do two chapters of *Oz* if you can find the book. OK?"

Jake went off, mission-bound. I drank my cocoa down to the melted fudge at the bottom of the cup. No matter how much I stirred it, it never fully homogenized. I cleaned out the last bits with the tip of my spoon.

Through the kitchen window, the sun was sending spring light in straight transparent vibrations full of churning dust motes. The gas bills had started to go down to the point where they no longer overbalanced the budget. Outside a robin was browsing in the sandbox; her mate watched from the black ash and gave small indications of approval, hardly stopping for breath. The screen let the sound in.

"Mom." Lisa's voice was a husky whisper. "Mom, shut your eyes."

"Why?" I kept them as wide as I could, even hoisting my lids up under my brows.

"Mom! Come on. Shut them." She put one cool hand across my face and twiddled her fingers against my forehead. "You'll like this."

"If you bite, I'm going to bite back."

"Come *on*. Come on-n-n." She was pleading, her feet drumming the chair legs.

"All right. Tell me when to open." My birthday wasn't until the end of the month, so it couldn't be a spanking or a cake. "What is it? It's dark in here, Lisa. When can I come out?"

"Now! Look, Mom, he's coming!"

Blinking in the sun, I spread my field of focus over the last page of the *Eagle*'s entertainment section, which Lisa had spread out on the table, my cocoa cup making a hump underneath. An obituary border, but inside it was a wide-brimmed hat and beard, open shirt, blue guitar toned gray in newsprint hands. Big black headline: BILLY CALLOWAY TO APPEAR AT KENSINGTON FAIR JULY 10. Lots of details along the sides and underneath, including some quotes praising his Range Riders band. Ticket prices: more than we could afford, eight dollars apiece, all reserved. No special prices for children. Maybe it would be possible to fold Jake up in a picnic basket and smuggle him in.

"Can we go?" She waved her damp curls like dewlaps.

"Do you know how far away Kensington is?" After eight years in this prairie state, I could finally pinpoint a few distances. "Twice as far as Bismarck. We'd have to drive back in the middle of the night. Rather, I'd have to. Or else we'd have to stay over at some motel for more than we can afford. Not to speak of the tickets." With my incomplete sentences, my English teacher mind recording them as they came out of my mouth, I was as bad as Jake. "Besides, you hate Billy Calloway," I concluded, "and if he ever found out we were the ones who called him, I'd curl up and die."

"Mom, he won't find out!" She was hopping around the table. "We'd just be in the audience like everyone else. And I don't hate him *that* much, just his old records with that whining thing in them. What *is* that thing they play?"

"Steel guitar."

"Anyway, it could be your birthday present. And Mother's Day."

"Mother's Day is over, Lisa." And I already had my pot holder and enameled pin shaped like a rosebud.

"Come on."

"No." My voice came out harsher than I meant.

"Mom, *please*."

Oh, why should I be so stubborn, and on a Sunday morning too, with Lisa dancing around me, a spring nymph still damp from her chrysalis, skinny legs bobbing up and down beneath her nightgown? I caught at its folds as she flirted by but only managed to brush my fingers along the fluttering ruffle as she leapt onto a kitchen chair and wiggled her little bottom like a go-go girl. Not such a little bottom really, not anymore. Her body had caught up with the reckless curls tumbling across her face, catching in her eyelashes as she swept them back.

"We can drive out in the morning early and go on the midway before the concert starts, Mom. I know you're scared of the Ferris wheel, but that's OK. We can ride the merry-go-round. We can see the horses. Maybe there'll be cowboys!" Knowing my every weakness, she spun to the record player, grabbed up one of Billy's albums, and danced across the room with it pressed passionately to her chest. Jake, bedroom slippers on the wrong feet, *Oz* under his arm, watched entranced from the bottom of the staircase. "Come and dance, Jake," she squealed, twisting her hips in a succulent oval. Embarrassed, Jake hunched over as far as he could, looking up his crotch. She pinched the back of his neck. He collapsed on the floor, thrashing mightily on the hall linoleum with his hands over his eyes. She sat on him.

"Stop it, you two!" I bent over them in the hallway, my bathrobe gaping. Lisa beamed up at me, sure of her victory, reading my eyes before I spoke. "All right," I relented. "I give in. The price of those tickets will kill me, though. I'm not as rich as Croesus."

"Crocus?" Jake had noticed them for the first time this spring and had dug up several in his enthusiasm. He jabbed at Lisa to make her roll off him.

"No, somebody else, honey," I said, and slid down next to them.

Lisa reached over and kissed me under my ear, but in the pride of her victory she kept on talking. "Someday you'll grow up and like rock 'n' roll, Mom," she teased, "but country-western is OK too. And Billy Calloway has a good backup group." She checked to see how far she could go. "Even if he sounds like a creaky door."

"Shush, you monster." The paper was still caught in my hand, and I looked down at the ad again. How many nights have you spent, my golden Lisa, listening to those songs, moving around their centers like the records on the turntable, feeling no bad news could ever come on the phone or stretch itself across some doctor's desk as long as the guitars kept on?

"We'll get dressed, Mom, and mail the letter." She had hoisted Jake up and stood next to him like a nursemaid.

"What letter?"

"The order for the tickets." She sounded like a nursemaid too.

"All right. I'll write the check even if it bankrupts us. For July tenth. Don't schedule any sleepovers."

"*Mom*." She had a Grape-Nut between her front teeth.

"Well fought, daughter. You've won."

Jake scuffed over and sat on my foot, patting my shoulder with the palms of both hands. "What did we win, Mom?" he asked.

7

JULY HEAT, with the metallic edge that even in the early morning touches the remaining stars. Jake was shriveled into his bed when I woke him, the patchwork quilt matted around his sweaty head. The attic under the second floor eaves, where I hid the things I never wanted to see again, would be ready for spontaneous combustion. Just standing by Jake's bed, I could feel my bra glued to my chest.

"Hey, Jake!"

Silence. Then he convulsed out from under the quilt, pulling at his cowlicks, eyes tight shut. "No, Mom, I don't want it. Go away."

"Come on. We're leaving in less than an hour." I bent over and kissed his nose, still enough of a baby's that its bridge was flat. "On the road with Billy Calloway and the Range Riders. Prairie and antelope. Maybe cotton candy too." I laid out his clean jeans and T-shirt on the bed, then unearthed his sneakers and added them to the pile. Still no luck—his eyes were glued tight. I began unpeeling the covers.

"Mom!" He snatched them back up to his chin. "Go wait in the hall. I can't get up 'cause you're watching me."

That was true, gospel according to Jake. His private parts had disappeared from my claim more than two years ago, and he had never let me watch him dress himself since.

"Go ahead, kid. I'm leaving. Bring it on home quick, though, OK? I'll get your sister moving."

Lisa's room was even hotter, a garret over the kitchen. This morning she was sleeping flat-out naked on top of her bare mattress, all her bedclothes in a tight bundle wadded between her legs, her pillow wedged around her neck like an orthopedic collar. I took a breath and held it against the heat. "Lisa, time to get up."

An explosion sent the bedclothes airborne. Lisa scrunched herself under them as they fell. "Oh darn it, I set the alarm, I must have pushed the wrong button, what time *is* it? What time are we leaving, are we eating on the road, can I shower?" Like Jake, she kept her eyes shut.

"Come on, daughter. Get moving. You showered last night." I had gone to bed with the pipes humming.

"But my hair will be a *mess!*" Moaning, she rolled out of bed. "Get *out*, Mom!"

Lisa was less modest than Jake, but she wouldn't dress in front of me either. She did leave more signs of her body around than Jake did, though—toenail clippings arranged in a circle on the bathmat, tampon tubes holding one paper clip apiece on her desk. She had a crumpled paper bag on the floor of her closet with all her hair combings in it; she said she was saving them to stuff a pillow for her wedding bed. I had checked them a few times when she was safely out of the house, thoughtfully holding the soft mats in my fingers. Over the years the straw blond had darkened to honey, then almost to the edge of brown.

Hair. While Lisa dressed, I went downstairs and looked at myself in the bathroom mirror, standing on tiptoe, of course. I had been brown-haired forever, chocolate fluff with cowlicks that swirled whenever I looked from one side of a room to the other. Even a poignant thought could send it askew. But it waved by itself and made my narrow face softer, I thought, and my eyes were nice. The smears underneath them were hardly noticeable this morning. With modest vanity, I smiled as if the Range Riders and Billy Calloway were crowding the door. Gums still holding up there, Kay, I muttered, and then laughed at how silly I was, rubbed on a castaway lipstick from behind the Benzedrine, and trotted out to make cocoa.

Despite my efforts, it was almost nine when I finally got the kids into the Trail Duster and midafternoon before we drove into the bumpy field outside the Kensington Fairgrounds. We parked next to a pickup with a WAYLON poster blazoned across its rear window and a bumper sticker that said "Cowboys Make Better Lovers." At the Trail Duster's last surge, Lisa slid her legs off the backseat, leather sandals dragging at her heels. Jake's sleepy head, tossed from her lap, flopped against the upholstery. "We're here," she muttered. "Billy Calloway is here if we're lucky." She poked Jake in the armpit. "Get up, you lump. If you're lucky, they'll give you the Piglet Prize. Wrumpf, wrumpf." She swung herself down into the dust while Jake followed her, whining. At the ramshackle admissions stand, the gatekeeper charged us as one adult and two children while Lisa grimaced, humiliated but unable to refuse the bargain. There were four hours before the concert, three before the stadium opened. The long dusty midway stretched ahead, somnolent, all the colors soaked up by the sun until even the erector set rides were sepia. Not many people yet either.

"Look, kids." They weren't looking, so I tried again. "Look, kids, you go check it all out first, OK? See what you want to do while I stand here running cowboy music through my head. Then come back and we'll calculate time and money needed. I might even invest in the hot dog market."

"Cotton candy, Mom?" Jake had sweet memories.

"Maybe."

"Did you remember the tickets, Mom?"

"Lisa, they've been under my pillow since they came in the mail." They had been too, but I hadn't meant to tell her.

"Come on, Mom, that's gross. You forget everything else, so I just wanted to be sure." She bent down to fasten one sandal tighter around her scuffed heel.

"Can we go on the merry-go-round?" Jake asked.

"*You* are my merry-go-round," I replied as I grabbed him under his arms and swung him in a circle, sneakers straight out, shoelaces flying. Secure in knowing there wouldn't be a single one of her friends there to see her, Lisa pried him loose and started down the midway with him, her fingers making little forages until she finally caught his hand. Dust puffed under their feet, then swirled back down. The farther away they got, the more it drifted around them, until they had disappeared into the little gatherings of people and the haze at the end of the midway.

There used to be a regular October feature in one of the Sunday papers when I was little, the Milwaukee *Journal* or the *Tribune*, I don't remember which. It announced Indian summer in a four-color picture with a little boy looking off at the distance next to an old man pointing out to him the mist of the warm days of autumn. "Those are the Indian spirits dancing," the old man always said as the wisps on the horizon blurred on the newsprint. "Some folks say those are just piles of leaves burning, but you and I know it's the smoke from those old Indian campfires. The Indians are all gone now, but in the fall they come back for a little while. Can you see them dancing?" I used to hover over that drawing, yes I did, and look for the campfires myself every autumn. Just dust, I knew, not smoke. The Indians were gone. The cowboys were pretty much gone too.

Coming out of the eye of the midway, Jake and Lisa reappeared in the distance. A sudden wind sent dust devils along the ground, and one swirled right to them, wrapping them in motion. Lisa stopped and pulled Jake against her, protecting his face with her shirt until the devil passed. Then they finished the race to me.

"We are going to need lots of money, Mom. The rides are wonderful this time. They have *two* Ferris wheels."

"How many allowances do I owe you, truthfully?"

"You really owe me three, Mom. But I think I should get something extra for that drive, maybe a dollar a pound for Jake's head in my lap. Maybe per hour too. I think it should be a *lot*."

"Here is what the Lombard budget allows, you two. Four dollars for Jake, six for you, Lisa. OK? Enough? Maybe I can find a bit more for suppertime nourishment, since you are both growing children." I checked the bills at the back of my billfold.

"Not enough, not enough, notenoughnotenoughnotenough." Lisa was her own dust devil, her own Indian campfire, burning in a dance around me. "I will have to sell my body, Mom. My only choice. Debradation at fourteen." She pulled up her hair and held it in a tangle on the top of her head.

"De*gra*dation. Spare me." I found another three dollars and passed them on. "Food will be cheapest at the Lutheran Ladies' booth. I know they'll have one here; they always do."

"When do we meet you, Mom?" Lisa had her hand on Jake's collar and was yanking him along.

"Say three hours? Two and a half? Where's best?"

"By the pigs, Mom." She giggled. "Then we'll go and bake a cherry pie with Billy. Don't get lost!" Mothering us both, she pushed at Jake, her hand wedged in the small of his back, then got under steam down the midway. Jake clapped his hands above his head and chugged ahead of her.

All right. Three hours. Not too long, but long enough. I started toward the barns, walking past the tilt-a-whirl, its Chicano keeper asleep by the controls in a canvas lawn chair, braced upright by his hard little belly. No one tilting today, at least not yet. A little farther down the midway, Ferris wheel seats were swaying in the wind, and although I glanced up at them from as far away as I could get, their back-and-forth touched me right below my ribs. Two teenagers were looking at them, nudging each other with their hips while the boy moved his hand up and down under the girl's blouse. Lisa in two years, Jake in a millennium. As I passed at a safe distance, she reached up and ran her hand over his forehead, wiping off something I couldn't see, then whispered a few words into his ear, holding his head down to hers. He shrugged and pointed, then turned back to the Ferris wheel. She walked off.

I didn't feel much like the barns anymore. All the sheep were the same anyway, underneath their wool blankets. Instead I started to trot down the midway, cutting perilously close to the Ferris wheel, jogging as if I were the kind of person who jogged, which I wasn't. Someone whistled. The first time I thought it was part of the equipment creaking in the wind, metal on metal. The second time when I glanced back, the boy was looking at me, hands on his hips. He was the only person around. When he saw that I had noticed him, he lifted both hands up under where his breasts would have been if he'd been a woman and jiggled them up and down. Then he whistled again, stretching it out. If he'd been in one of my classes, I could have given him a D and written a humiliating comment on his paper, but here I had no power over him or his straight-leg jeans, or his silky green shirt with the sleeves rolled up.

Now I really didn't want to see the barns, sheep or cattle either. Instead I set my goal for the end of the midway where the 4-H exhibit booths clustered in the old frame building, paint blistered gray, that had been the heart of the fair since the Depression. I could look at the crocheted doilies and embroidered blouses. They were safe.

Once I got to the 4-H building, however, I couldn't go in there either. Instead I slipped around the side, through the patches of yellowing worn-down grass, and headed on out.

Here at the edge of the fairground the midway ran down like a forgotten clock, and beyond it was the prairie. Housing developments hadn't touched this side of Kensington; it was flat grass for miles. As soon as I passed the back of the 4-H building, I was out with Willa Cather, watching the hawks wheel. Under my sneakers flowed acres of two-foot-high grass, some of it headed out like renegade wheat, all of it a dusty green, all of it lying curved back like a greaser hair style when the wind passed over it. Down around my feet I could see individual blades, but the farther I looked the more uniform it became, until it was a watercolor smear of green under a wider smear of blue. A few carny folks had parked their mobile homes on the edge of the fairground, but not many, and I was soon past them, walking faster now, cruising through the sea of grass, no anchor, just wind and sail, just prairie. The sun still stuck part way up the round of the sky, but it wasn't high afternoon anymore. When I looked back, a few of the rides had their rigging lights turned on, practicing for the dark. Voices from the loudspeakers pieced out the gaps in the wind; carousel music sprinkled past me, stopped, got loose again, sang in my head. Not cowboy music exactly, but bright and forbidden and sweet. How many fairs did you see in Texas, Billy Calloway, when you were first learning how to pick that blue guitar? How many Ferris wheels did you watch with your hand up some girl's back, stroking her sweaty skin, feeling the down under your fingers, just the lights and the dust devils, the randy guitar music over the loudspeakers, and all the little radio stations beaming their honky-tonk signals into the blue Texas night?

Another noise. There was something in the grass ahead. My heart began to hammer childishly. I didn't want any more surprises in my life, not ever. Rattlesnakes in the prairie, venom and pain. Scorpions. My kids wouldn't know where to find me.

Three steps more. The grass was being flung around contrary to the wind. A muffled exclamation. About twenty feet ahead of me, unafraid of rattlers or scorpions, two people were tangled in the grass making love.

They didn't see me, but they might have if I had made a noise and left. First I stopped and tried not to look, scanning the horizon line. No use. The boy was doing a lot of thrashing around on top, more than seemed necessary, but it had been a long time. The girl, her long hair swathed across the grass and tangled along the sides of her head, made little noises like a sparrow. She had chunks of his blue denim shirt clutched in both hands; her legs, the parts of them I could see, made a perfect V back toward the 4-H building. Had Jake and Lisa been there, I could have saved some breakfast table lectures.

It made me tired. Bored. Cather hadn't written it. At a peak moment I walked back to the fairground, around the campers and the extension cords, past the exhibit doors, on down Barn Row to the Lutheran Ladies, where I bought a bratwurst on a homemade bun with sauerkraut so thick it dangled over the edge and dribbled down my wrist. The Lutheran Ladies and the prairie, symbols of my state.

8

THE KENSINGTON FAIRGROUND grandstand, where the three of us ended up along with dusty shoes and gritty remnants of cotton candy, bisected the midway with a battleship gray wall, checkered from the weather and then painted over, a mesh of wire stretching along the top against the early evening sky. All along the back, the only access route, were campers and concession stands, frayed rubber extension cords, construction cables knotted together in the dust underfoot, tattered signs flapping in what was now a constant wind. Jake and Lisa could lean against it, it was so strong, their hair pushed straight back from their foreheads like wings. Grit crunched in my teeth and coated my tongue; the grains layered down in my hair. Jake mouthed something, his face white and urgent. I bent down so I could hear.

"So loud a song," he said.

"What?" Lisa was looking over the ticket taker.

"So loud a song, Mom. Like the book." He rubbed his nose with the back of a grubby hand.

My mind was as empty as the sky. "You mean Billy Calloway sings loud?" I asked, as I herded him along, tickets in hand.

"*Child's Garden*, Mom," moaned Lisa, as we edged through the gate and past the Billy Girl, her sweat shirts with their embossed blue guitars stacked on the folding table. " 'Oh wind that sings.' He probably thinks he made it up." Sighing an exaggerated sigh, she reached into her shoulder bag and pulled out our family paperback of *Jane Eyre*, holding it under her arm all the while we were scuttling past the turn by the harness raceway where a yellow machine sprinkled down the dirt, past two ushers talking in western twangs, down to where our reserved seats were, three rows from the front. A skinny, middle-aged cowboy, sandy hair cut tight to his head, fringed buckskin jacket hanging open, was checking over some of the electrical equipment on stage. As we settled ourselves, he looked up speculatively at the sky.

"Wow, we got near." Jake had forgotten Robert Louis Stevenson. A piece of stage equipment crashed to the floor somewhere in back. "Whang-bang," said Jake. He pulled at Lisa's arm and leaned over her book. A spot of drool fell in the margin.

Lisa swung around and jabbed him in the shoulder. "You shut up," she said. "I can't read." The wind blew her hair across her lips; she took an irritated nibble before pulling it away.

"Come on, kids, settle down." I didn't want to referee all through the concert, especially not through "Hello, Walls" or "Orange Blossom Special" or any of my other favorites. Especially not through the songs Billy had written.

"Mom?" Lisa had shut *Jane Eyre* and was holding her place with her index finger. She squinted up at the stage, still deserted except for the fringed cowboy, then pulled her shoulders back and looked at me adultly. "Mom, why do you like this stuff? I mean, I know Billy Calloway isn't bad, at least not as bad as Waylon or Willie, but I personally don't think he's worth all that money for tickets."

Arrow in the breast. And who had started this whole thing anyway? "Come on, Lisa, give me a break. *You* were the one who dragged out that newspaper ad and began this. You know I've liked cowboy stuff ever since I was a kid. When Tex Ritter faded away, I went for Johnny Cash. Then Waylon. And nameless others. I forgive *you* your little passions. Billy Calloway got a nice review in the Minneapolis paper just after we moved to Fargo, so I bought his *Cowboy Lovin'* album. By my simple standards, he was a master songwriter and singer."

"He's also big and hairy." Challenging, Lisa nibbled at her bottom lip.

"Look, he doesn't play his guitar with his *hair*."

"Mom!"

"Lay off me, daughter. I mean it. I am the woman who can't follow the beat in Bach. In country-western music, the beat is so strong it's *inside* you. Nothing for me to feel inferior about. And I am fond of his black hat. And vest. Not to speak of that little barroom crack in his voice."

Lisa looked at me creamily. "It's all right, Mom. I know he's sexy. So is Billy Joel. *My* Billy." She giggled and flipped open *Jane Eyre*.

Well, I've told you the truth, my dear, though not necessarily every bit of it, I added in my head. Lisa the straight arrow, the organizer with the hair bag, the one who makes sense of things. Yes, Billy is sexy, like all good cowboys are, like all good English teachers never get a chance to be, and yes, I'm sick of insurance men and estate lawyers and decent people who never do anything dangerous and don't lose their W-2s. Would you like to know my fantasies while you follow Rochester and Jane, eyes sponging the pages? Would you really like to? I want to be raped in some recording studio under the ramped mikes, only not the bad kind of rape that gets the feminists angry, while all the while an incredible steel guitar player is waterfalling notes in the background, and somebody like Billy Calloway is laughing, but gently, while he pulls my blouse open. And I will never say one word

57

of this out loud to you or anyone else, so don't tickle me or wheedle me or sneak into bed with me at night and put your hand in my dreams.

"Mom?" Lisa reached out and tucked a loose piece of my hair behind my ear where the wind could only tweak at it.

"What, honey?"

"Mom, you know something? You're pretty."

I was stunned.

"I know that sounds silly, but you do look nice. Your eyes are really big, and when you smile your whole face lights up."

"You just say that because we look alike. Nothing but self-flattery." I was helpless before a compliment from my daughter, downright embarrassed. While I struggled to come up with another line of repartee, Lisa squeezed my fingers. "I think the show is getting ready to roll, Mom," she said while we beamed at each other like two old bridge partners.

She was right. Things had begun to happen on the stage. The crew had rigged a line of spots on a horizontal bar, and now they were hoisting it up under the red canopy that flapped in the wind. The big speakers were in place, stacked on each other to the right and left of the action like giant fabric doors. Eddying behind them, the Range Riders hauled out their instrument cases, pushing the stage clutter around into more comfortable arrangements. I had to laugh a little when I saw that Billy Calloway's blue guitar had been painted on every available surface, even the side of the piano. If the system held true, he probably had one on the bottom of his cereal bowl, glimmering through the milk as he gobbled down his Grape-Nuts. Or corn flakes.

"Ladies and gentlemen!" The thin man in the buckskin fringes was giving instructions from a hand mike at the side of the stage. "The Calloway bus has just arrived in the fairgrounds, so we are getting ready to roll. Sold-out crowd here tonight, and a big show coming. Get ready for that Texas sound!" The last of his voice still swooping out above our heads, he swung over to the piano player and clapped him on the shoulder, then adjusted the mike jutting out over the keys.

Up above us the blue prairie roof, gold around the edges with dust, was holding still as a stage set. Yet, over the grandstand behind us, over the ramshackle broadcasting booth fastened to its top, a cluster of graying clouds was beginning to rise. The gusting wind seemed to come from behind them, pushing hard, then holding off. But as soon as the gusts had established a rhythm, it broke, and an unexpected blast tore *Jane Eyre*'s pages loose from Lisa's hands. She jerked over against me as she forced the book down into her lap and grabbed it between her thighs. "What a place to live!" she moaned as she hunted for her page again.

The heat was intense, the wind like waves off a gridiron. Above the stage the row of lights rocked in increasing surges. The fringed cowboy and a taller, pony-tailed one conferred in a far corner; then they scrambled through the on-stage chairs and began tying a sheet of blue plastic around the drum set.

But there has to be a concert, I thought. *I'm* here. And Billy's here. I couldn't miss him this time. The dust made me cough, and I felt the spasms all the way down in my chest, though I didn't even have a cold. North Dakota couldn't do this to me. I dug Kleenex from my purse and blew my nose into it, swabbing around my face before I wadded the Kleenex up and put it back. Surely someone who didn't litter didn't deserve to be punished. Would it be his yellow shirt or the blue one tonight? His leather vest? Which album cover would he look like? Lord, I was worse than Lisa!

An intense conference onstage, led by Mr. Fringes. The blue plastic came off. Unswathed, the Range Riders started tuning, while their lead guitarist came down front to tell us they were going to go for it and we should pray for the weather to hold. Cheers and cowboy whoops. Jake looked up blankly, then dropped his head again toward his T-shirt bottom, which he was unraveling. I was never going to take him to anything where the tickets cost more than $2.50 at any time in the future.

First out of the gate was "Blue Suede Shoes," back to the days of rockabilly, a roadhouse beat that you could call the cattle home with. They should hire me to write for *Rolling Stone*, I speculated. The bass guitar player picked with his eyes shut, savoring the music like an erotic dream. They were getting set up for the chief, no doubt about it, and even the withered old honky-tonker on the steel guitar glided out his notes with an anticipatory whine. It was an advantage to be old on the country-western circuit, because everyone honored you for surviving and heard all your past hits in your new mediocrities. Your past failures they forgot. Once Billy stopped being sexy, once he lost his hair, couldn't write a decent song anymore and forgot the words to the ones he had written already, they'd still be backing him up and smiling.

I jabbed Lisa for companionship. "Are you excited?" I asked gratuitously. I had given up on Jake.

"Oh, *Mom.* Don't *tease.*" But she was nodding her head a little to the beat of "All of Me Belongs to You." We might be able to make this a duo if we practiced enough. Smiling to myself, I turned front to see if Billy had snuck on stage while I had been mothering, but of course he hadn't. Probably another three or four numbers before his entrance. I jittered with impatience. Come on, cowboy. Trample that sagebrush. Fan that hammer.

I poked Lisa again. "Do you have an extra page in *Jane Eyre?*"

"Do I have *what*, Mom?" There was a little dusting of sand in the ridges of her collarbone just above her open shirt collar.

"Do you have an extra page in *Jane Eyre?* One you can tear out and give me? I'm going up and getting Billy's autograph after the show."

"Mom, you don't even let me *write* in books!" A great crashing chorus from the Range Riders. "You mean like a blank page at the end? You're crazy!" But she looked and found one. "I'm not going to tear it out, though," she said, shoving the book at me. "You do it." As I ripped, I noticed that Jake was rocking back and forth. If he needed to go to the bathroom, he was going to have to wet his pants right there in the seat.

The microphone up front crackled. "Hey, this is a West Texas wind!" shouted the lead guitarist. "Quite a night out here, but hang on. Dig your heels in!" Behind us, someone young and throaty gave a cowboy yodel. "We'll anchor down up here and bring on Big Billy in just a minute. Don't blow away!"

Don't blow away, huh? Well, we wouldn't. But the kids' hair was being combed back by the wind, and Lisa was shivering. Jake's face was a road map where he'd licked his fingers and run them over his dusty skin. Over the grandstand behind us, the bank of clouds swarmed through the sky, black on gray. Dust filtered through the spots from the lighting booth, wavering yellow. A sudden sweet breath of damp, then thunder.

No stage manager could have planned it better. The thunder rolled like great jaws, and out on the brim of the stage sauntered a tall figure, every country-western cliché, blue shirt pressed and shiny, open way down, bearded face all in shadow under the black felt hat until the spots got located and caught the sweat on his cheekbones. Heavy leather vest. Pressed jeans covering the boots. One of the side men handed him his blue guitar, which had been propped up next to the piano. Already the crowd was yelling, along with that rhythmic clapping like some crazy pagan ritual.

"Alright." A few chords. "Alright now. Wanna do it for me?" Scattered shouts, including one young woman's voice saying "Yeah!" "Wanna join in?" The band had picked up the rhythm. "They say we're in for some weather, boys, but if that ol' grandstand stays anchored down, I reckon I kin." He was picking in a line behind the pattern of his words.

Lisa poked my arm. "Wow, Mom, he really *is*—"

I cut her off. "Yes, he sure is." We turned front like Tweedledum and Tweedledee just as Billy was tossing his head back at the Range Riders, the wind tugging at his hat. Everyone on stage was poised to do whatever he wanted.

"Here's a song I wrote back when I was a lot younger than I am now. Open my mouth and them ladies would turn on." He hoisted the guitar a little and let it balance on its straps back against his belly. "Every goddamn one," he added. The steel player gestured like a schoolteacher shushing an out-of-line student, but Billy had angled himself full front and paid no heed. "Some of 'em still do, boys," he said with a little smile cutting a line of white through his beard. "Some still do." Swinging nearer the mike, he slid his guitar into a series of glancing chords, playing around the beat. When he began to sing, his voice barely touching the tune, the words were like a thread tied around the audience. Then he let the sound out.

Oh, it was silly. It really had nothing to do with cowboys, of course, or being a tomboy, or Tex Ritter, or anything. Nothing at all. But the rhythm hit, the sound rose into the wind, the steel man was sliding down his strings like silver whimpers. Jake had all his fingers from both hands in his mouth, right on top of left. Billy's voice, gravelly and rich, told how it felt when you'd never get her back, never, while the bass player and the drummer underlined. As the repeated chorus thinned out, Billy hummed the last few notes of melody, then raised his hat a little at all of us. "We're so near he could sweat on us," Lisa whispered.

For a moment the wind took a breath. Then it swooped loose and the dust hit us like hail. Billy's mike tottered. He grabbed it with his right hand, the left steadying the neck of his guitar. A blurred "Goddamnittohell" came through the sound system. To the left of the stage, one of the banked black box speakers shook and leaned backwards, arcing on its journey so slowly that I thought it might just rest there on its corner. Two cowboy roadies plunged out from backstage to steady it, but it slid through their hands and crashed to the board floor. A blue flash and crackle. Jake had his hands over his ears, but there was no need because all the sound had gone out too. Next went the lights. Through the dimness, dust spiraled up from around the speaker lying on its back. Someone to the side of us screamed.

"Jesus Christ, watch out! Everybody move back to the grandstand. It's shorting out!" Billy was gone. Most of the people were up and shoving, pushing toward the back, but a few of us diehards stuck to our seats. Kay Diehard Lombard.

"Mom, this is crazy. We'll get hurt." Lisa was waving at me with *Jane Eyre* elevated. "Besides, it's going to pour."

"Never." I pulled Jake into my lap. "They'll have to get us all, pardner."

"Mom!" She didn't want to desert me, however. "Is it all for that stupid autograph? You'll never get it!"

"I will die for that autograph. I will drown. If a fountain pen runs, I will use a ball-point. If that breaks, blood." I yanked her down to her seat. "Hang on, kid."

Like a black curtain against the blackening sky, the rain came. It swept in such a direct line that we could hear it hit the grandstand behind us while we stayed dry a hundred feet up front. It thundered off the wood, the fence, the chairs, and then it hit us in drifts, layering us from above and splashing back on our legs from below. Bending over, I pushed my autograph sheet down inside my blouse. I couldn't even see where the seats next to us had been.

"Lisa!" I had to put my mouth on her ear for her to hear me. "Take my purse with the keys. Run for the car. You know where it is. Watch that Jake doesn't get lost. Wait for me there, OK? I don't care if it's raining Noah's flood. I'm going for that autograph."

The kids plunged into the aisle, Jake running ahead of Lisa, jiggling up and down, his heels flopping out of his sneakers. Lisa had one arm out, though, a ray in the deluge, and was holding onto the tail of his T-shirt to make sure he didn't disappear.

All right, Kay. I was the one who knew how to manage things, wasn't I? This was no big deal. Lots of people got autographs. Loretta Lynn smiled on the steps of her bus for hours while she signed. She expected her fans to love her. Whatever Billy Calloway expected or didn't expect of me, he ought to be able to spare forty-five seconds and a signature on an unwritten page of *Jane Eyre*. All right.

Through the rattling tin sheets of the downpour, the stage was disintegrating as every available roadie, cowboy hanger-on, and band member wrapped and stowed equipment, shirts stuck to their torsos, hair plastered down their foreheads. The skinny man in buckskin was supervising the lowering of the lighting bank in front, showing with his hands just how much leverage to use, then when to pull tight. "Anchor that down," he yelled when one end swayed out over the edge of the stage. It got anchored. Every time the wind gusted, I thought it was blowing him off the edge, but he just widened his stance and held on. All his fringes were pouring water in individual cascades that threatened to melt him completely.

A pause in the wind while the rain drummed. Perhaps ten minutes had passed since the power blew. No, more. The bus must be around in back somewhere, maybe on the raceway embankment. Up by the far side of the stage, the equipment was going into the side of a semi that had been pulled up tight to the platform. Billy wouldn't be riding in that, though. Find the bus, Kay.

I slogged out of the row of seats, so wet that it was a relief not to have to protect anything from the rain. Since most of the activity on the stage was concentrated to the left side, I slid around to the right, edging up against the boards. Someone had a battery-powered spot going, and it cast enough light for me to keep my footing without taking a header over the steel cables and extension cords. Once I got under the edge where the stage floor projected out, I stopped, hanging onto the corner with my left hand while I protected my eyes with my right. And there it was, the boss man's bus with RANGE RIDERS on the side and the blue guitar, glistening black in the rain, painted underneath it, pulled up right behind the stage, angled toward the raceway, motor running, wheels settled into the fairground mud.

Of course I'd hoped somebody would be there, maybe a polite stage manager or maybe even Billy Calloway, just about to step inside, mysteriously not wet yet, not in a hurry, polite, and with a pen already in his hand. Fat chance. The door was shut, bus dark. Above the motor and the rain, now not gusting but just a steady downpouring river, there wasn't a sound. I'd knock, just like a normal afternoon on Fifth Street in Fargo. Just a little friendly knock. Teacups at five. No embarrassing phone conversations. Talk about the kids' schools. See if Margaret would watch Jake while he played with Brian. *Knock.*

I didn't have a chance. The door wrenched open, slamming against the side of the bus and sending the water off it in a spray. Out of the opening plunged a figure, stumbling on the bottom step, landing on his knees in the wet dirt beneath. He missed me by about six feet but didn't even notice I was there. As he sprawled in the mud, he spread his hands to keep from going face down. Water geysered up between his fingers.

"Jesus Christ, Calloway! What in God's name do you expect me to do? I can't pay off the weatherman!" Balancing on one arm, he wiped at his face with the other, smearing his sleeve across his cheek. Something dark spotted it. Blood.

No sound from inside.

"You think you own the whole fucking *sky*? Half price is plenty for what you put in tonight. Goddamn cowboy!" One hand on his face, he hoisted himself to his feet, then slapped the side of the bus. The metal vibrated like a cymbal, sending off another deluge. The man stamped off.

Oh wow. And I thought only my students ever said that. No autograph, but a great story. If I didn't drown on the way back to the Trail Duster or catch pneumonia once I got there.

65

If I got back to the Trail Duster. Because the bus door was still open, and in it was a tall figure, broad shoulders filling all the space just like in the old Gene Autry movies. But my old cowboys didn't travel by bus. They didn't hold pink bath towels either.

"For crissakes, lady, git inside. Gotta flood out there. Last ride, boys. Sure ain't no *music*. Wetter'n a Butte whore, ain't it? Come on *in*, goddamnit."

I came in. Rather, I got lifted in, my sneakers coming loose from the mud like little suction cups. "Jesus Christ, you don't weigh nothin'," Billy Calloway said, handing me the towel. "Dry off before you freeze t' death." Absentmindedly he looked down and started to rub the knuckles on his right hand. "Shit," he muttered.

"Are you all right?" There was no way he could remember my voice. My hair was standing on end in little brown spurts as I ran my hand over it.

"Shoulda knowed better'n t' slug somebody when I gotta pick tomorrow." He swung around past the driver's compartment, and as my eyes followed him, I saw a whole miniature home, kitchen appliances, counter tops, dollhouse living space. He was rummaging in the cupboard over the stove. "Kin never find nothin'," he grumbled, but he came up with a box of Band-Aids and began peeling one, dropping the paper wrapping on the floor. The two adhesive ends stuck to each other before he could spread them out properly.

"Jesus Christ." He sucked at his knuckles. "Gimme a hand, will you?" He handed me the box.

"Do you have any antiseptic?" The puddle around me on the speckled carpeting was spreading, and the water that I hadn't been able to rub out of my bangs was running into my eyes. I felt like the Monday wash. "You don't want to get an infection."

"Christ, if I got a infection every time I did *that*, I sure wouldn't of been 'round t' win no gold records. You sound like my mama." He went back at the cupboard, though, and came up with an ancient bottle of iodine. "This what you want?"

"I haven't seen one of those since I was growing up in Wisconsin," I said, smiling. Lisa will never believe this, I thought, as I took the guitar-picking right hand of Billy Calloway in mine, laid it on the green Formica counter by the stove, pulled the cap out of the iodine, and swabbed a line across the spot on his knuckles where the blood was oozing.

"Shit!" He jerked away, but I hung on. "That goddamn stuff hurts."

"Not that much, for heaven's sake." I held the Band-Aid in my teeth and stripped off the outside coating, then juggled it around into my free hand. "Hold still, because I need both hands for this." I stretched the Band-Aid out flat and flicked the plastic loose with the same motion I used to stick the pad and adhesive across his knuckles. Then I pressed the edges down. His fingers were so big I couldn't imagine how he picked the right strings.

"Alright." He lifted his hand and shut his fingers. The Band-Aid stayed put; I was a pro with Band-Aids. "Thanks." He turned away, dug out a pan, and set it on the stove.

"Awful weather, isn't it?" I folded the towel and put it down on the bench that ran alongside the door. Except for the rain and the idling motor, the bus was absolutely silent. If I listened hard, I could hear the teacups delicately clattering.

"Goddamn right." He was rummaging in the cupboard again. We seemed to be at a conversational impasse.

"It was too bad you couldn't finish the concert tonight." No good. "I'd love to hear a whole one when you get back this way." Shut up, Kay, get your autograph and go. Where was my paper? Inside my blouse, hopefully, cozy and dry. I unbuttoned my collar button and started to reach inside to where I had it tucked, but I could only touch the corner. It must have slipped down. Yanking with my fingers, I pulled my blouse out of my jeans, shivering as the dank denim pressed against my belly. I edged my right hand tentatively up underneath. Where *was* that blasted thing?

"You know, baby, there ain't really time before the boys git back. Not that I don't appreciate."

"What?"

"Besides, you're so goddamn small I'd prob'ly flatten you right out."

"But the paper is flat already. I'm sorry if it's wrinkled." The page had slipped halfway around me and was clinging to my side, but now I had it retrieved and safely in my hand. Billy had his back to me. "Do you have a pen?"

"A what?"

"A pen." Was my language ability disintegrating?

"Well, sure, if you mean what I think you mean. Ain't never heard it called *that*, exactly." As I tried to smooth out the paper, bending over the bench, Billy leaned on the counter and shook his head. "You know it ain't so good when you gotta hurry."

"I'm an English teacher; I can read anything." I was feeling in my jeans pocket. "Oh, it's OK. I've got one of my own." The ball-point was wet in my fingers, but it seemed intact.

Billy spun around. I was holding the paper and pen out. His face was appalled. Could he be a functional illiterate? I certainly wouldn't want to embarrass him, but even most of them could sign their own names.

"Oh Lord." Billy laid his head in his arms on the counter. "Shit. Lady, I am sorry. I ain't thinkin' right." He grabbed the pen and scrawled his name diagonally across the paper. "Anythin' else you want? No, shit, I don't mean that." He clenched his fist and swung it against the cupboard door, which crashed shut. "Ow, goddamnit!" Wincing, he grabbed his knuckles with his other hand, and one end of the Band-Aid flopped loose. For a moment I thought he was going to plunge past me and out into the rain.

Someone knocked and opened the door. It was the skinny

blond man in buckskin, now sodden brown. "We're ready to roll, Billy. Let's head on out. Missoula tomorrow." He walked past me, boots squelching, as if I weren't there.

Billy recovered himself. "OK, Tweeter. Git a towel before you flood this place. Elmer drivin'?"

"Once he gets himself changed." The two of them stood shoulder to shoulder next to the stove, leaning back a little against the counter edge. Billy was sucking his knuckles again.

I hesitated. Neither one even looked at me. "Well, thank you," I said, figuring that all-purpose phrase could never go wrong. "My kids will really appreciate this." Billy nodded from a great distance, then turned on the sink tap. I edged back down the steps and out the door, feeling like a fifth wheel, but already starting to play back the experience in my mind. To my own surprise, a grin popped out between my cheeks as I plowed into the fairground muck, aiming myself through the pounding rain back toward Jake and Lisa and the Trail Duster.

1309 Fifth St.
Fargo, ND   58102
July 17, 1981

Mr. Billy Calloway
Blue Guitar Productions, Inc.
3750 Sedgewick Blvd.
Austin, TX   78710

Dear Mr. Calloway,

I want to thank you for the autograph you
gave me when I went to your bus after the
show that got rained out in Kensington.
My children never believed that I'd get it,
and I think they were rather proud. I really
appreciate your being willing to give it to
me.

I'd like to see a full length concert of yours
if you ever go on tour through the Upper Midwest again. I'll be watching the advertise-
ments.

I hope your hand healed without any problems.

Sincerely,

Kay Lombard

9

WHEN WE GOT BACK, through the rest of July and August, I made a systematic search through all four Fargo record stores for every Billy Calloway album I didn't already have. My Holy Grail summer. I rooted out three I hadn't owned, two of them oldies with his angular twenty-year-old face on the cover, greased-back hair, cigarette hanging like a white slash out of the corner of his mouth. He must have given up smoking since, like all sensible people, even cowboys. The kids listened to them once with me, as if putting in their time waiting for a doctor's appointment, and from then on Billy was mine alone. When I spent part of an afternoon in late August checking the infinitesimal dates at the bottom of the jacket covers so I could label the fronts in the approximate order of recording, Lisa said, "Mom, no one would believe you," as she spurted through the living room on her way to go shopping with Rebecca and Lilibet. Jake pasted labels on all his Matchbox cars in the approximate order of nothing at all.

The Saturday night of the weekend before all our schools started again, I was in bed with my Victorian poets anthology.

No labels there, just feelings encased in metrics. When Lisa trotted into the room and churned up the bed next to me, it took me a moment to oust Robert B. and pay her appropriate heed. Summer had pushed her hair two steps back toward blond, on top at least, but underneath it was still dishwater, darker in the neck. Even through her sweat it smelled of residual shampoo and conditioner. I laid the Victorians open on my chest and let my arms fall to my sides, pointing my toes and trying to look as much like a tomb sculpture as possible. She tickled me.

"Stop it!"

"Say please, Mom."

"Please once, please twice." Her hand tucked itself back into her lap. "If you promise not to pester me, you can stick around and talk." Once she swept off into ninth grade, I would probably have to leave her memos to get any messages through. "Are you looking forward to school?" Innocent enough.

"Yuck. No, wait. It'll be OK." She thumped the empty pillow next to my head; I thought she might have something else to say, but she didn't. When she wasn't smiling, she looked more like Jeff than she did like me, the Jeff from back when I first met him. Nothing in her head came out through her eyes unless she wanted it to.

"Is Jake asleep?" I had left him private in the bathroom, rusting his less-favored Matchbox cars in the tub.

"Sort of. But he's all turned around with his head at the bottom of his bed."

"Probably couldn't tell the difference, the way he played all day. Brian was so tired he fell asleep next to the sandbox."

"I was never that young."

"Want to bet?"

Like a warm cylinder, she rolled herself over crossways on top of me, framing my body with her knees and elbows. "No, I haven't any money because you won't raise my allowance. But I could never have fit in *there*." She poked at my stomach.

"Well, I can't remember any adoption papers."

"You forget everything." She was wadding lumps of comforter into her palms. "Mom?"

"You're about to ask me something I won't want you to do."

"*Mom.* Don't read my mind. Daddy never did that."

"But am I right?"

"Rebecca's going to the lake tomorrow for one last day before school. Her folks are driving out. Can I go too?" Primly, she swung herself up beside me, propped on the extra pillow. Her whole body in profile, she pulled her shoulders back and smiled at me. Yes, she had breasts. Well, no surprise, she'd had them in May too. But then she hadn't noticed, and now she was comfortable with such summer riches.

"Shouldn't you bargain for my approval? What will you give me?"

"My eternal and abiding love."

At fourteen, love could be eternal, I guess, until proven otherwise, especially with breasts newly round. Lord, I should honor her innocence.

"Do you miss him?" At first I thought somebody else had said it, but of course that was impossible.

"You mean Daddy?"

"Yes."

She was dampening down her eyebrows, forefinger wet with spit. "Do you know, I can't remember what color his eyes were."

"Like Jake's. Chocolate." My voice creaked, so I stopped talking.

Lisa dried her eyebrows with her other forefinger. "I remember he painted all the time. And smiled when I got good grades." She disorganized her eyebrows. "Of *course* I remember him, Mom. I've got his picture in my room." She was stretching the toes on her right foot, laying them apart on the comforter like fat toothpicks.

I shifted on my side. "You know it's fine if you go with Rebecca tomorrow."

"I know." She admired her toe design, her curls spilling

down across her face until only the very tip of her nose stuck out. "Mom, do you still have Billy Calloway's autograph?"

"Of course."

"Where is it?"

"In my underwear drawer, on the bottom."

"*Mom*. That's such a dumb place!" She plopped over me again, compressing my stomach down into my spine. "Why there?"

"Get off me before I suffocate, and I'll tell you. Who would think to look in my underwear drawer if he was robbing the house? Who would steal rayon panties? Where better to keep the first tooth you lost or Jake's report card from kindergarten that says 'An unusual child who likes to glue'? It's the treasure casket of my past."

"No caskets for *me!*" The comforter followed her in a great brown wave as she slid to the floor. I wrenched it back. "I'm going to bed, Mom. I'll call Rebecca and tell her we can start early tomorrow. Sleep tight." She kissed the air just short of my cheek and padded out, golden right through until she turned the corner to the stairs and I couldn't see her anymore. I took up with the Victorians again.

When I woke up in the morning that last Sunday before school started, I couldn't untangle myself from my dreaming, but I couldn't get the images molded hard enough to keep them either. The door shut, then a car door in the driveway. Lisa was on her way to the lake. Outside my bedroom window, a mourning dove was saying good-bye to summer, stationed somewhere on the smooth needles of the blue spruce planted so near the house that when our downstairs bedroom had been added, before we even got there, it had taken the tree only a few years to reach out and rub the window whenever there was any wind at all. I arched my feet to the rhythm of her cooing, then held them flexed when she stopped. If I were to rear up, spin around, break the glass, and clutch, could I grab her in my hand, downy feathers, pink feet, startled wings soon complacent when she saw how really tender I was? She couldn't be mating; it was almost fall. We might get frost in a week. The Indian campfires.

I turned over on my stomach and let my dreams loose. A stretch of morning light pushed through the branches and made a square through the window on the brown comforter, still askew from Lisa's departing plunge last night. I knew what hole the light came from. Some of the spruce's inner needles had turned brown and dropped, but the biggest space was where Jake and Brian had stripped the branches off so they could have a secret clubhouse. When they weren't flooding the sandbox in the backyard, they huddled there on the needle-covered ground, crashing Matchbox cars and looking through comics, most of them bloated and warped from having been left out in the rain. They didn't seem to mind.

Last summer weekend. Jake was still asleep. Did he ride the prairie in his dreams the way I used to? Once Jeff had told me he'd heard me humming in my sleep, but when he woke me I couldn't remember. I'd never asked him about his dreams.

I swung out of bed, tossed my nightgown into the dirty clothes hamper in the bathroom, pulled on my shorts and T-shirt, wiped my face with a washcloth. If I couldn't keep my dreams, I'd make something to hold onto. Finish off the summer with a keepsake. Something to add to the album in the bookcase, with time left over to paste in the old pictures I'd stuffed loose between the pages. There'd be time to take photographs this morning, bright sun, summer of '81, sleeping son. Enough words. I was worded out.

The camera, an old Kodak I'd had since Lisa was tiny, was right where it had been since the Christmas before, wedged in the corner of the kitchen drawer where I kept the Scotch tape, the string, the shoe polish. Did I have any film? If I didn't, I'd have to go buy some, and Jake would wake up before I got back. But I was lucky, because the camera had a roll in it with seven exposures left. I wouldn't need that many. Already the dew was being soaked up off the front lawn. I stepped through the door, shutting it quietly behind me, camera in my hand.

OK. First the sandbox. I walked around to the back of the house where it sat under the plum tree. Jake's latest flood had receded in the sandy valleys, and the pebble houses he had become passionate about building were still sitting just inside the gray board frame, each one with a stick in its top. A flag? A TV antenna? A scepter? He probably didn't know himself. I knelt down on the spotty lawn where hidden roots sucked all the nourishment from the grass, focused, and shot. It might not look like much, but I would know.

Next. The sun was getting higher, and all the yard vegetation was becoming photogenic. But I didn't want landscapes. Instead I walked around the corner of the house toward the front. The spruce? I could never get it all in the picture unless I stationed myself across the street, and in this Norwegian neighborhood, I'd be too conspicuous. Grass was boring. The lilac clump on the border had no individuality. The Trail Duster.

Picture Number Two. I climbed up quickly to the front porch and looked through the viewfinder at the car, my own prehistoric monster in my own driveway. Four years old, not Jeff's kind of car at all, but mine. The salesman had started to laugh when it was my turn to try it out, but then had swallowed and given me a boost up. "You can buy a running board for these things," he'd said, but we'd never gotten one. Still in good shape, the old range rider, still able to get us to Billy Calloway and home again. In winter I didn't even have to shovel the driveway unless we had more than a foot of snow; instead I'd just back it out, churning through the drifts, packing them down under the four-wheel drive. I snapped the picture head-on.

One more. An inside shot. What should I make immortal now that immortality was within my power? I walked through the kitchen, rejecting everything. No kitchen utensil deserved preservation. Not the plants in the dining room, not even my one African violet. Not the sofa. I hated that sofa, stiff and velvety. If it hadn't been a bargain, we never would have bought it. Not the fireplace, which we couldn't afford to use much because it pulled more heat out of the house than it sent in. Not any of those things.

I stopped in the doorway of the downstairs bathroom. All right. Lisa's shampoo and hair conditioner bottles stood on the edge of the tub, half empty. Sticky residues ran down their sides like little lava flows. What could be more typical? The blond would be brown in winter whether she liked it or not, but she would die before she let it get dirty. I opened the bathroom door all the way so a little more light from the hall could fall in, enough so the snapshot wouldn't come out gray. Then I took the picture.

Dear Billy,

I would never send this letter in a million years, and since I'm not going to, it doesn't matter whether I use a formal salutation, does it? Do you actually know anything about the prairie? When I listen to your records on the stereo in my living room or play them over in my head while I'm driving, I know they must be all hype and recording studio deception, produced one place, mixed another, hardly a natural breath drawn. It's a job, like mine. But then why do I keep playing them over and over, pretending I'm watching you singing, hanging on to the sofa arm so I won't float away?

I wish I'd paid more attention when I was holding your hand. I've been a mother so long that all I could think of was making that stupid Band-Aid lie flat.

Kay Lombard

10

"Mrs. Lombard, your box is full. And the Payroll Office needs this form before tomorrow." Lucille, the English Department secretary, whose patience with me was limited at the best of times, handed me the vital sheet as I walked by her desk, barely far enough into the quarter to be sure even where my appointment book was. Her hair was beauty parlor red, set in plowed waves down the back of her skull. I had detested her ever since I had been hired.

"Well, Lucille, if I sign it today, even in the passive hands of faculty mail it should trickle over to Payroll by tomorrow." I grubbed in my purse for a pen and brought up my old friend from the fair. It wouldn't write beyond my first name. While I turned it around in my fingers, trying a different angle, Lucille watched. Sneered. Would it go into my faculty evaluation folder if I couldn't persuade the ball-point to finish my signature?

"Do you have your keys, Mrs. Lombard? The janitor didn't get your office unlocked yet."

And why not, when I come in at noon every Wednesday? Of course I didn't have my keys. When they had last been seen, Jake was transporting them across his bedroom in a Matchbox truck, Number 37. "No, I don't have my keys. Could you lend me yours for a second?"

"Bring them right back, though, would you please?" She held out the silver ring and I took it despairingly. The ritual of humiliation. Down the hall to my door. The unlocking. I brought them back in less than a minute, then scurried back to the safety of my office, just cozily bigger than I was. I liked that little room better than I usually admitted, because I had a window that real light came through. Across the hall Emily had a window too, but hers faced the university smokestack so nearby that belches of cinders from the last coal-burning furnace in a North Dakota state university smeared the outside of the panes. I was in better shape; my window, while it didn't open, faced into a little atrium big enough for a table of aloes from Botany and one medium-sized birch tree. The sun came through the top in the early afternoon, real sun, not a fluorescent substitute.

Wednesday was my afternoon for office hours, so I didn't have to plan classes, a blessing. Through persistence I had managed to get my teaching hours scheduled only on Tuesdays and Thursdays, when I taught the freshmen about writing until we all staggered home exhausted. On Wednesdays the freshmen came to me, dropping in to complain, to bless, to seek help, to cry. There usually weren't many; they found academics too painful to visit a teacher often. I did whatever I could to make it easier: pictures on the wall, Kleenex, as much of a smile as I could muster. If I ever bought a tape deck, I was going to bring it along with two or three Billy Calloway tapes and play them reassuringly in the background.

"Hi, Kay:" Emily stuck her head out from across the hall. She taught English too. "In the groove yet?"

"Barely. But surviving. Any crises among the troops?"

"Few, but mighty. We nearly lost one yesterday. Did anyone tell you about it?"

"Guess not." I checked my appointment calendar, which had turned up under the telephone. Judy was due any moment, according to what she had phoned in on Monday, assuming that Lucille hadn't messed up the message. Judy had essay attacks as regularly as her periods and came faithfully to me for help.

"One of the sophomores in Engineering got upset after he failed his first exam and tried to do himself in." Emily, who in her quiet way kept a biographical file on everyone, looked at me quickly, then went on. "Sleeping pills. They found him in time, though. There's a huge mess in the department about it, as well there should be. Engineering drives students to an early death anyway."

I opened my top drawer and began to check my pencils. All but one needed sharpening. Erasers were OK, paper clips, rubber bands, staples, ditto sheets, typing paper, college memos. "Emily, is there anyone lingering out there in the hall? One of mine is due."

Emily, who had retreated to the doorway of her own office, craned around the entrance. "Not a soul. No, wait. Is it someone who looks worried? A girl?"

"You've got it. Perfect description."

"She's coming right now. Have fun." Emily smiled and slipped back to her desk, shutting her door.

Footsteps. I pushed my top drawer closed. "Mrs. Lombard?" Flushed and anxious-looking, her heavy sweater buttoned all the way up, Judy hesitated at my office threshold. "I thought I was going to be late. I'm having trouble with this paper, Mrs. Lombard, that's what I called about. It's for Political Science, and that teacher doesn't like me anyway." She chewed at her lipstick. "I can't get it ended right," she mumbled.

"Well, that's better than not getting it started, Judy. Have a seat and let's look at it." I reached out for the yellow folder she was clutching and captured all but a corner, to which she still clung. She edged down into the student chair by my desk. "This isn't a subject I'm expert on, you know, so let's just try for a decent overall structure."

"I think I know how to paragraph pretty well."

"I mean the big structure." I flipped through to the final page. "See, here you're building up to what sounds like a powerful conclusion, but nothing much happens. Can you summarize more generally?"

"But I thought I did that already!" She was bending the corner of the folder back and forth, putting a permanent crease in the plastic. "There isn't much more to say." Her voice was raspy.

"Oh, there's always more to say if you try." Ease off, Kay. "Or a better way to say it. Look, if you could just switch these paragraphs around, you could finish off with a sentence about the new age of unity." I made a gentle mark along the margin with my one sharp pencil.

Judy looked at me, lips pale, eyes dampening. But she got control and took the paper back. "I guess I can do some of those things if I try." She twitched in the chair and then got up. "Thanks, Mrs. Lombard. Is there anything else?" She was checking her sweater buttons.

Oh, change the color of your folder, Judy, and try being really late so I know you're human. Buy an indelible lipstick. Put both your buttocks on the chair instead of teetering on that one little fat pad like a tightrope sitter. "No, Judy, nothing else. Read it through a few more times before you type it over. Have a good day."

Judy left, stopping just outside the door to make a twist in her hair, then tuck it down the neck of her sweater. Fragile but indestructible like them all. They couldn't even count sleeping pills correctly. Their bodies betrayed them every day—errant teeth on lipstick, a bulge in the pants that *Great American Poets* open in the lap couldn't hide, the flu, the migraines, the strep throats, the mono, all at exam time or just before a paper was due. But out of this stew of physical disasters would come a witty dialogue, effervescence, a paper with no typing errors, two six-footers in down jackets shoving Emily's Honda out of its blocked parking space during a snowstorm.

"Mrs. Lombard?" No lipstick this time. I stood up behind my desk and stepped to its corner so I could see into the hall just a little. Blue ski jacket with a fraying eagle appliquéd to the back. Straight black hair. He was looking over his shoulder toward my door, ready for retreat if it didn't work out. Dennis.

"Hi, Dennis. Come on in. I'm not busy." The door was still open, but I gave it a little extra push against the wall for complete hospitality. Dennis was a very young military man who had spent two years guarding North Dakota missile silos at night until his guard dog had bitten him. Then he'd started college on his disability payments, supplemented by tending bar around town. He'd written this all in his first English essay for me last fall, but when I'd given him a C-minus, he'd dropped the class. Not me, however. He still came around to chat. I would have been nervous if he hadn't been so fundamentally shy; the first time he'd looked me in the eye was when I had been hunting for another student's essay while he was visiting and had yanked my file drawer right out of the desk and onto his foot. He still preferred to gaze at my pictures on the wall or stare out the window.

Today Dennis had a piece of blue electrical tape patching the right arm of his jacket. He approached the student chair, paused for acknowledged permission, sat down. "How're things?" he asked, his eyes sliding outside to the aloes.

"Not too bad. My freshmen are doing all right, but they usually are three weeks into the quarter. What are you taking this time around, Dennis?"

"English with Dr. Rogers. He comes in late every day and makes us write about our mothers." Silence, and communion with the aloes. Despite his past experience, he stretched his feet in their combat boots toward my file drawer.

"Are you doing anything else?"

"Working." He almost looked at me. "There's one good

thing coming up, though. The Rodeo Association's got a big dance at the Nite Hawk Lounge just before Focal Problems Day right after Halloween. I'm in charge of tickets."

"Have you got a good group to play?" The Rodeo Association could be counted on for pure North Dakota country, no pink hair or shaved heads.

"We're working on it. There's a bunch of guys from Linton we can book, and they're supposed to be the best. One of them goes to school here. They're all cousins." Dennis looked happier than usual. "Teachers can come too," he said, as he humped his ski jacket higher on his shoulders and started out the door. "Bye, Mrs. Lombard. I gotta go. Nice talking to you."

I had to go too. Jake would be home from school in half an hour, morosely picking mortar out of our brick front steps as he waited for me to come and let him in. Morosely wasn't the right word. Speculatively. That was it. He had to go inside to get his bedroom slippers, which he would wear over to Brian's, where he would play until supper. He had his own house key but wouldn't wear it on a string around his neck like other children of working mothers. "No necklace, Mom!" he had shouted.

Out past Lucille's desk, where she was reading a paperback and ignoring her typing. To the parking lot. Late September gold, cutting down from where the sun pierced the slot between the English building and the gym. I held my hands out to catch the warmth, but there wasn't any, just the deceptive color. Already the air had turned toward the next season. In my beige poplin jacket I was shivering, as if a prairie wind were blowing. Was it? Somewhere it must have been. I climbed into the Trail Duster and started home, gently easing the car out of the college driveway.

The drive home was about fifteen minutes' worth, less if I didn't hit Fargo's tiny rush hour. Surely no other community was so polite that cars waited graciously at all the four-way stops, anxious not to be pushy and leap into the intersection first. When we moved here, it had seemed sweetly quaint. Later on, Jeff hadn't been as sunshiny about it; he'd had a theory that people in towns like Fargo were polite to outsiders because they were going to boil in Hell anyway. Only the locals would be saved. I hadn't argued, because he'd had his first treatments by then, and I don't suppose anything seemed natural to him.

Jake was just coming up the walk when I got home, and we negotiated the Bedroom Slipper Ritual with grace. I dropped my briefcase, made tea, looked for the mail in the box and then threw it out—all ads and notices of things I'd never go to. The living room carpet with its tweedy design waved psychedelically under my feet, making me register how badly it needed vacuuming, but when I had the vacuum yanked out of the closet, I remembered that the belt was broken. I tried to think about my teaching for the next day, but my mind wouldn't focus. It was too early in the week to be this tired. Heavy-footed, I put Billy's *Cowboy Lovin'* album on the stereo, then noticed the needle was thick with lint. When I reached out my fingers to strip it clean, they were shaking so hard I was afraid I'd break the stylus. Even though it was only four thirty, with Lisa not home yet, I felt my way into the bedroom and let myself down on the comforter. It was like sinking into the tar pits, and I was gone before I could even get my last leg pulled up off the floor.

The next thing I knew I was in a tunnel like a marble aqueduct. It seemed to be leading downward because I felt the balls of my feet press as I kept walking, but I couldn't really tell. I heard a twanging noise, the same note over and over, awful guitar music. No, a sitar or one of those other Indian things. I had to hurry, but my feet were getting smaller, my sneakers those dime store miniatures. When they were gone, what would I have to walk on? Where were the Linton cousins?

"Mom! You're going to fall on the floor. Wake up." Startled awake, I pulled myself back to the middle of the bed, floating on the brown comforter. Lisa was wrenching blouses out of my closet. "What were you dreaming, Mom? It isn't even night yet. It's just suppertime."

"What are you doing in my closet?" My voice sounded like radio static, the words distorted and crackly. "I was tired when I got home. I let Jake in and then I took a nap."

"He's home again now, Mom, crying because Brian used his bedroom slipper to float in the sandbox."

"Is he still wearing it or is it beyond repair?" I felt weighted with responsibility: their heads, their feet, their garments.

"Of course he's still wearing it." Lisa began to line up my blouses on their hangers, pushing the rest of my clothes to one side. "It's leaving smears of mud all over the kitchen. He's making Ragu for supper and the water is boiling for the spaghetti. Why don't you get up, Mom? Where's your yellow blouse with the little saddles on it? I want to wear it to the game tonight."

Oh, Lisa. You hate games, as far as I can tell, and won't buy an activity ticket at school, but you go to every one your friends go to and make a point of sneaking by the ticket taker in a confused bouquet of fourteen- and fifteen-year-olds, all of whom look just like you. The triumph colors your evening. Rebecca, Roni, Rachel, Lisa, Louise, Lilibet, all pushing and giggling through the gate, then crowding into the bleachers to jab shoulders together and squeal when the boys run out. If you ever had to be alone, you'd wither away.

"That blouse is in the clothes hamper because it's dirty. Dig it out if you think you can salvage it. I'm getting up. Tell Jake he can drop the spaghetti in."

I slid out of bed and stood up, dizzy but whole. When I was growing up, sleeping during the day had been the nearest danger to dying. I had avoided it violently, struggling up from waves of boredom and exhaustion on car trips, on long visits with relatives, wetting my eyelids with spit, then blinking until my vision blurred with moisture. At night it was all right to let go; I could turn the bed lamp off, I could let the hall light glow like the center of a pulse, dim and bright. I was getting old; I slept during the day. Things got mixed up.

"Mom, it's ready. I cooked, Mom." Steam rose from the sink where Jake was draining spaghetti in a flowerpot, the water pouring through the little hole in the bottom. A few strands of spaghetti hung over the red clay edge, wisps of steam rising from them. A row of Jake's stuffed animals watched from the counter.

"Jake, where's the colander? You can't drain spaghetti in a clay pot!" I grabbed him by the shoulders, but my shake was feeble. "I just hope the miserable thing is clean."

"I washed it out with the sponge, Mom." My counter-top sponge. "And then I rinsed it. Did you read your letter?"

"What letter? We didn't get any real mail today." I reached out to help pour the spaghetti into the blue bowl, but Jake was doing it himself. He transported it to the table, knuckles white with concentration, and dumped a gob onto my plate.

"Your letter, Mom. It was in the big bush."

"Is the mailman now delivering to the big bush?" I struggled to get the first installment of spaghetti up to my mouth. Lisa was still shuffling around in the bathroom hamper.

"It was there when I came from Brian's, Mom. I think the wind blew it." He smiled, the right side of his mouth stretched up so it caught a tiny well of spit. All his portals caught the light. Since he'd outgrown his crib, he'd even slept at night with a slit of white gleaming under his stretched-down eyelids. Like a werewolf, Lisa said, suspecting all innocence.

"Jake, come on. No mysteries. Where's my letter?"

"Under your plate, Mom." Spaghetti hung down his chin. "It was a surprise for you."

Gently I lifted my plate and removed a long white envelope, pre-stamped. No return address. I ripped it open with my thumb. Two pieces inside, one a newspaper clipping with a picture. Big black hat and beard. CALLOWAY HALLOWEEN CONCERT IN ST. PAUL, with details. The picture went down to his waist, vest flaring, guitar hoisted. Better than the one in the Fargo paper.

I unfolded the second piece. It was a letter, printed stiffly in pencil on lined paper, very short. No return address, no date:

Dear Kay Lombard:

My hand is OK. We are
playing St. Paul for
Halloween see clipping.

There was a signature, but it was impossible to read. Never mind. English teachers can read anything.

Halloween. I must have said it out loud.

"I'm going to be Flash Gordon, with boots," Jake said. "Brian has boots. Lisa says she's too big to dress up this year, so maybe she'll hand out candy in our house, Mom. Last year we didn't have enough Sugar Babies." Sugar Babies were Jake's favorite. "Brian is going to be a cowboy."

"Sounds good to me, Jake. I may be one too."

"I guess nobody's ever really too big, Mom," Jake said philosophically.

11

IT MADE NO SENSE to go to St. Paul, what with gas, ticket expenses, the five-hour drive there and then back again. I made up my mind not to. After all, I had the autograph, two of them now, though the second one was even harder to read than the first. I didn't have anyone to go with me either, because to whom could I have confessed my addiction to begin with? Jake and Lisa simply refused. "I'll go if you'll tell him where you keep his first autograph, Mom," Lisa teased.

Since I wasn't going to the concert, I listened to Billy's albums more, correcting themes in the living room, playing my favorite songs over and over, although I knew that would eventually damage the records. The albums with their silly titles I knew better than Shakespeare's tragedies stayed lined up on the carpet next to the record rack: *End of the Trail, Cowboy Lovin', Lone Man on the Road,* the earlier ones like *Magic* and *Starting Over.* From looking up from whatever I was doing and passing my eyes over the album covers, I had that craggy Texas face memorized. Lisa and Jake were very gracious about it all, and they even left me in peace when I changed my mind and wrote a formal request for a ticket to the St. Paul Civic Auditorium office. Then I got caught up in lesson planning at school and forgot to mail it. But the Civic was an enormous pit, even if they closed off the balcony for small-draw country-western shows. There'd be seats.

The day before the concert, I checked across the street with Margaret to make sure she'd keep an eye on the kids. She came to the door in a fitted sweater and A-line skirt, the college girl we had both been a long time ago. Walking up Margaret's straight front path from the street always made me feel as if my shoes needed tying, and her appearance just confirmed that. She was like one of those casually planned photographs in the Living Section of the *Times*.

"Hi, Kay. Brian is picking up the family room. Then he'll come play with Jake."

"I figured. Margaret, I'm driving to the Cities tomorrow for a concert in St. Paul. The kids can manage by themselves, but I just wanted you to know so you could keep your eyes open for kidnappers, white slavers, and the like." Margaret always drove me to ridiculous exaggeration.

"You're driving out by yourself?"

"Not a whole lot of choice."

"Well, at least it's too early for blizzards. Or we can hope so." We'd both experienced storms that lined I-94 with abandoned cars and jackknifed semis.

"The kids will have to handle trick-or-treat by themselves. Lisa is staying home to distribute. Can Jake go with Brian?"

"I think they've already planned their route. He can sleep over afterwards if he wants to." Margaret ran her hand down the side of the door, checking for flaking paint. Smooth as a cheek.

"Thanks, Margaret. I probably won't be back until the wee hours, maybe even dawn. It's a good five-hour drive, and the concert isn't likely to be over until ten thirty or so."

"Who are you hearing?" Her steady gaze followed me as I started down the walk.

"I'd be ashamed to tell you. One of my deepest flaws."

Back across the street in the next country, Jake and Lisa were waiting for me in the living room, and Billy Calloway was there too, soft on the phonograph. I was being set up for something. "Look at Jake's costume, Mom," Lisa insisted, springing up off the couch to corner me before I could exit anywhere else. "We haven't got it finished yet, but once I get the shirt right, he'll be so cute. I'm making his boots out of that old leather in the trunk in the attic. If I just fasten them on the tops of his sneakers, he can still walk in them, but they'll look like real boots." She ran a passionate hand through her hair and tugged at Jake as if he were a mannequin. He was sucking his thumb.

"Stop it, Jake. You outgrew that." Wrong thing to say. If he sucked, then he needed to suck. However, Jake took his thumb out obligingly, looking at it as if it had just visited his hand for a day or two. He wiped the spit off on his cape.

"Mom, after the trick-or-treaters stop coming here tomorrow, I'm going to a game with Rebecca, OK? I need extra money if we go out for Cokes afterwards. Can Jake stay with Brian?"

"It's already set up. They're going out to pillage the neighborhood together, then he's sleeping over." I went to get my purse from the hall shelf and handed Lisa my billfold. "Take what you need. Not more than three dollars."

"I'll get home by midnight, Mom."

"You know I won't be back until really late? Or really early Sunday morning, to be accurate." I wrenched my mind back to the other issue at hand. "Another game, Lisa? That's three this week. The jocks will be prostrate, and I'm not real happy about it myself."

"Oh, Mom! Come on. They're all different teams. We just have fun." She was pulling the basting stitches out of the felt letters saying FLASH on Jake's front, holding him in place with her other hand. "Halloween is nice, Mom. It gets better as you get older. Seeing the little kids come around will be neat this year."

"Do you remember . . ." But they weren't listening, and I didn't want to ask anyway. Two years ago she and Jake had both been ghosts, covered in sheets like upright cakes with melted white frosting. Their own choice. I had held together while they had scurried up their trick-or-treat bags and their flashlights, and sent them down the steps with all the proper cautions and farewells. Then I had locked the front door and lain down on the sofa, hands over my ears to block out the doorbell. Their pumpkin had flickered in the window, his tormented little face reflected back at me through the glass. But I hadn't cried. .

12

GEOGRAPHICALLY, I knew that the prairie, the real history book prairie with the sod houses and the dust storms, was way out west, past the rich flat soil that marked Fargo and the affluent farms around it. Once you traveled east through Minnesota, toward St. Paul and Minneapolis, the Twin Cities and civilization, it wasn't prairie at all, just decent farmland flatter than most, easier to plow and cultivate, nothing geologically unique. There weren't a whole lot of farmhouses, but if I were to skid the car off the road at night, there would be a light I could reach. The towns—Fergus Falls, New Munich, St. Cloud—were all respectable settlements, with schools and churches, kept-up streets. I just didn't belong to any of them.

I did have the car radio, though, coloring in the fringes. It was like a map, Fargo blurring, another station getting clearer, then fading, the Cities pushing in their signals. Weather was the central news here, always. Even when nothing was happening, weather was happening or getting ready to happen in the Rockies. Flat midwestern voices caught the edge of passion from a particularly good storm raging out of Montana. It was irritating, it was dangerous. It was reassuring. No wonder people stocked up in supermarkets when a blizzard warning went out, grinning at each other in the checkout lines.

Four o'clock. The Cities in an hour and a half. Exit off the 694 bypass and thread my way down to the Civic in St. Paul. It was much too early. I took my foot off the accelerator to coast a bit and changed stations. Commericals from everywhere. Easing the Trail Duster around a graded curve through the fields, plowed and ready for spring, I tried again. OK. Hank Williams, Jr., a new release. He didn't sound like his daddy at all. I waited for the next song. Larry Gatlin and the Gatlin Brothers. I was sick of all that gold in California, so I changed stations. Church announcements and hospital releases, not what I wanted to hear. And I had to go to the bathroom. The Cities suddenly came in clearly; it was Merle Haggard with "Tonight the Bottle Let Me Down." I hadn't heard that song for a long time. Billy should try recording it.

There was a rest stop, trees almost bare around the bathroom shanties and the big map of the Minnesota counties. No cars, no trucks. I parked in the luxury of two slots and slid down. The bathroom was clean and cold, only a lingering smell of urine. No hot water, of course, when I washed my hands, and a brown stain down from the faucet. All the groundwater around here must be packed full of minerals. The little machine on the wall was jammed so solid with paper towels that when I dug for one I got three, all tattered. I tossed them into the empty trash bin as I left.

I was just starting down the narrow walk back to the car when I heard the noise, one sharp crack. Then another. The echo from the first overlapped. A third. I hadn't heard that noise in a long time. They weren't very far away.

I stopped on the sidewalk, buttoning my jacket. My hands were still cold from that water. Somebody was hunting, that was what it was, up in the hills behind the rest stop, up among the maples that were sketching lines against the sky, among the pines that darkened the forest spaces so a hunter could hide, angling his rifle through the needles until only the tip showed. I wasn't all that stuck on being a humanitarian about hunting animals, though I was glad Jeff had been just a target shooter. As I pulled myself up into the driver's seat with my hand on the wheel, I could feel his little pistol against my palm that night he'd laughed when I'd tried to heft it. I gunned the motor before his voice came back too.

On to the Cities. I pulled out of the parking lot and back onto the highway, merging without even having to slow down. Almost no traffic. And then in half an hour a few more cars, also heading toward the Cities. Some of them spun off for the south bypass, down to Minnetonka and the towns along the Wisconsin border. Some of them went right through on I-94, but I was scared of doing that because I hadn't tackled the inner city superhighway for a long time. So I went over the top and then edged down on 35W, city traffic but still not too crowded. At one of the stoplights I checked my map, the engine mumbling and surging. If I turned off two main streets down, I'd be only about a mile away. On Saturday there should be parking. If the box office was open already, I could buy my ticket and then find someplace to get a hamburger and a malt. I wasn't hungry, but if I didn't eat before the concert, I'd have to stop in the middle of the night in rural Minnesota to scavenge up something. No good.

My luck was on, and the street signs corresponded to my city map. Right turn and straight down. It had been so long since I'd seen the Civic that for a moment I couldn't remember what it looked like, but it rose out of the drugstores and going-out-of-business storefronts like a cliffside pueblo. I didn't even have to go past it and circle around, because there was a parking space across the street and down half a block, obviously meant for me.

I parked the Trail Duster and locked up. Down to the pavement with a few subtle knee bends to check against driver's paralysis. Up to the corner and across, with the light changing to green just as I got there. This princess was approaching her castle, and it was opening its arms to her.

Actually the Civic was a little like a castle. A 1920s pile of stone, its front and sides were great rectangular blocks of granite bulging out at the middle, then curving back to the line where the next row of blocks joined. In Fargo, with its lake-bottom silted soil down to subterranean depths, the building would have sunk like the *Titanic*, but here it stood on the bedrock without a tilt. The windows were little slits for boiling oil or aiming crossbows, and the main doors had fake medieval carving from their peaks almost down to the steps. It was an awful place for a country-western concert; only a minnesinger could have been comfortable there. The doors were shut, but when I pulled on the twisted brass handles, one of them creaked open. Once showtime got nearer, they'd have to prop those Middles Ages barricades back against the outside walls. Well, they had more than an hour before anyone with any sense would show up.

The lobby was red and textured, carpet and flocked wallpaper, like a bordello. Some historic-minded person had saved the old chestnut woodwork, and even though it was heavy with layers of darkened varnish, it still looked high class, the moldings around the ceiling, the sweeping stairway to the mezzanine, the backing to the ticket office area. The woodwork made me feel as if jeans and a blouse weren't quite up to the occasion. Silly. I knew what the costume was for a fan from the prairie.

A blurred young man with a vacuum cleaner made a path in front of me, the red carpet turning smooth and liquid in his wake. He stopped. I must have looked more like a vagrant than a princess to him.

"Need something?" Why were his eyes so vague?

"Is someone in the ticket office?" The light was on, but I couldn't see through the bars whether anyone was there or not.

"Yeah, but he's in the john. It shouldn't take long." He shut off the vacuum, which subsided, whooping. "Come for the show tonight?" Until he lowered his voice halfway through the question, I hadn't realized that he had been shouting.

"I guess so." What did I mean? I hadn't driven five hours for a tour of downtown St. Paul, that was for sure.

"The whole band is here already and mostly set up. A bunch of them are out getting something to eat right now. They haul as much equipment as a rock group." Why did he seem to be talking to someone else even when he was looking at me?

"I guess they must need it for the kind of show they give." He was a little older than a student, now that I was really looking at his face up close. I mustn't lecture him.

"Want a toke?"

"What?"

"Toke?" He pulled out a clumsily rolled cigarette from his shirt pocket.

"I don't smoke, thanks." I shook my head, trying to get what he had said into focus.

"Sure makes the time pass." His hands cupped around a match, he lit up. I'd passed through enough student parties to recognize the sweet smell.

"Well, I guess I'll just wait."

He didn't hear me anyway. The vacuum came on again, hoopa-hoopa, and he shoved it off across the old path, wavering toward the door. Dust churned out of the back and hung in the air. Should I tell him the bag needed changing? It was probably information he wouldn't be much interested in.

As I stood in the middle of the lobby, suddenly ill at ease and no princess at all, a face finally appeared at the ticket window. Determined, I shifted my grip on my purse strap, and walked over. I was still early, but not crazy early. Buy the ticket, Kay, and then go buy a hamburger. Hang around and buy a newspaper too. Then you can slip in to this Billy Calloway concert with the crowd and be perfectly normal. But I didn't feel perfectly normal; I felt like half a person, and the wrong half too. So I didn't smoke, toke, do drugs, drink . . .

any of those things. So I was a square. I had two kids and fifty-three freshmen. I liked country-western music. I owned my own car, which was parked legally. I was legitimate.

"You want something?" At least I wasn't invisible.

"Any tickets for tonight?"

"Sure. We're three-quarters sold out, but we've got some in all the sections. Where you want to sit? Orchestra? Mezzanine?"

Should I be extravagant? Gas for the Trail Duster would probably run over thirty dollars. But then I wasn't staying over, so there'd be no hotel. In a peculiar way, I had been invited.

"How much is orchestra?"

"Top is fifteen dollars. I've got some in the back of the orchestra for ten. In the Civic, the orchestra back is worse than the mezzanine, though, because the slope is so bad." He sounded bored but professional.

"Well, I'll splurge. One orchestra, up front as near as you have. In the center, though, not right by the speakers."

He nodded and began to flip through the packets of tickets in the lower right-hand compartment behind him. I opened my purse and reached for my billfold.

It wasn't there.

Oh, this was crazy. I looked in the side pocket of my purse. My paperback something-to-read-if-I-get-caught-in-a-blizzard book was there, Dickens' *Little Dorrit*, and the sunglasses that I never wore. Car keys, lipstick I hardly ever wore either, a comb, a package of Kleenex. Three twenty-cent stamps. Two pens. The remnants of a leaf Jake had brought home last week, brittle and jagged. It disintegrated in my hand.

"Sorry to take so long." I controlled my voice. "I can't seem to find my money."

"Take your time. Seat won't go away." He began to grub under the counter.

If it were only that easy. I chewed the skin along my index finger and dumped my purse out on the carpet, then spread everything flat, a still life on a red background. I maintained confidence my billfold would appear; I hadn't lost anything big like that in two years. But it didn't. I hadn't put my checkbook in my purse either, because I never carried it unless I planned heavy shopping. My two credit cards were in the lost billfold.

"I must have left my money home." Why did I sound fourteen?

"You can write a check." His voice came up over the edge of the counter, under which he was still hunching.

"I left my checkbook at home too."

His head thrust up, then the rest of him. I hadn't noticed what he looked like at first, but he seemed more vivid now, older, half bald, stubble on his right cheek where he'd missed a spot shaving. His fingernails weren't clean. "Look, lady, you may be nice and all, but nobody gets free tickets to this show." His voice had turned rougher. "I don't know what you expect. People have to keep track of their money."

And mine was home with Lisa. Now I remembered last night and the Coke contribution. I must not have put my billfold back in my purse. Probably it was sitting on the sofa still, or on the coffee table. In Fargo.

"Look, could I possibly mail you a check? I'm going back right after the show. It would be here Monday."

"Shit, lady, I'd be stupid if I believed that. Go beg off a friend." He had put the pack of tickets back.

"I don't have any friends here."

"Tough luck, lady." He disappeared from sight in the back of the ticket booth.

Numb, I bent down and refilled my purse. This wasn't really such a crisis. When people started coming in, maybe I could buy a ticket from . . . but I didn't have any money. I couldn't buy supper. Well, that was no tragedy. But I didn't have gas money either. I had planned on filling up just when I reached the beltway on the way back.

Obviously there was some simple solution and I would think

of it in a minute. But right now, stupid as it was, the roar of
the vacuum cleaner had emptied out my head. I swallowed
and nothing went down. My throat hurt. This was so dumb.
I felt like I'd banged my elbow on something hard, because
my eyes were suddenly full of tears. The red carpet was
smeared along the edges of the wall and across the lobby as
I turned around and started down the hall toward wherever
the bathrooms must be. Around a corner. A brown door with
a figure outlined on it slid into my vision, blurred, but I could
still see the knob. I opened it and moved inside, rubbing my
eyes with the back of my hand.

Something was funny. Somebody tall was standing with
her back to me on the other side of the room. Well, at least
I wasn't the only person wearing jeans in the Civic. Testing
myself, I swallowed, and my throat opened. My eyes were
drying up, and in the clarity I could finally lay hold of, the
tall figure shifted a little, arms akimbo, self-assured and deliberate. My God.

I started back toward the door at a run, but I'd let my
purse slide down and my foot got caught in the shoulder
strap. I didn't trip, but I couldn't get loose without walking
on the purse itself, and it was my favorite one. Desperate, I
balanced one-footed and tried to disentangle myself. The
purse tipped, spilling Dickens and my sunglasses on the tile,
the glasses clattering as they hit.

"Jesus Christ," said Billy, swinging around and zipping up
his fly with record speed. "It ain't even rainin'."

"I'm sorry." That phrase had never sounded dumber. "I'm
really sorry." My eyes were wet again, damn it, and my voice
cracked. I bent down and stuffed my purse full again, snapped
it shut, all the time trying not to look in his direction, trying
not to see him at all, trying to make him evaporate like a
Halloween spirit. It didn't work. I stood up and tried to leave.
The palms of my hands smarted, as if I had been pressing
them against something hard, and when I willed my fingers to

open, there was a row of red nail prints starting at the base of each thumb and running straight across.

I got to the door and then outside, heading down the hall. The door slammed behind me. And slammed again. I put my head down and moved faster.

"Shit, there ain't no need t' run away." Even bouncing off my back, that voice was perfectly clear. I hurried more, shutting my ears. Something touched my shoulder. As I spun around, I slammed into Billy's chest.

"For crissake! One of us is gonna break somethin'." His hands pressed down on my shoulders until I felt even shorter than I already was. "Stand still, goddamnit. Ain't you never seen a man take a leak? It ain't nothin' t' be ashamed of."

But I'm ashamed of being *alive*, I thought, the idea racing into my head even while I tried to get my breath with my face jammed into his shirt pocket. I'm ashamed of *myself*. I opened my mouth to explain and found myself mute as the moon. I had forgotten what a man smelled like, and it was nothing like a six-year-old boy. I just wanted to sink into him forever. Appalled, I tightened my fists again. "I can't breathe," I choked out. If I kept my eyes down, he wouldn't be able to see what a mess I looked.

"Jesus." He stepped back a little, his hands still on me. So far so good; he was tall enough so that he wouldn't be able to angle his line of vision down under my bangs. Maybe we could both go back to the tea party again. It was a real possibility that I could get everything together, that I could gain control, pull this out of the fire, that I could go back to Fargo with a funny story for Jake and Lisa, poised and efficient Kay, the lady who could make everything right. After all, this was just country-western, sentimentality, my aberration. This didn't matter.

Billy's hands slid off my shoulders. He squatted down in front of me about a foot away and looked up into my face. "Shit," he sighed. One hand reached out and touched my

cheek. "Goddamnit, it ain't worth cryin' about, little lady."
A finger slid down to my chin. "Not my pecker, that's for goddamn sure." His shoulders shook a little, then stopped, and
he heaved himself upright. "Hell, we'll go down t' the dressin'
room I got and have a drink, that's what we'll do. Show's all
set up and ready t' roll. Come on now."

13

THE DRESSING ROOM was deep in the theater substruc-
ture, down a dimly lit hall spotted with decals from some
long-ago attempt at decoration. Each door had a fake brass
lamp next to it like a series of old second-rate apartments.
"Nothin' fancy, is it?" said Billy as he shoved the last door
open and pulled me inside. I hadn't been touched so much by
anyone over fourteen in a long time.

"It doesn't look so bad." Back to the tea party. The dressing
room walls were painted institutional green, the floor covered
with shabby linoleum. Instead of being crowded with theater
props and musical equipment as one might have expected, it
was almost empty.

Billy was paying no attention to me. From a shelf that ran
along the wall next to the door, he swept a handful of something and dumped it into the wastebasket. Above the shelf
was a long mirror, the silvering giving out into little black
flecks, dust thick all over the surface. Billy ran his hand over
it in one great diagonal sweep, leaving a pathway through
which the reflection of his face suddenly glinted. He started

to do it again but stopped halfway. "Shit," he said. "Ain't no use. Like a barn in here." He looked over his shoulder at me, focusing just slightly to one side of where I was standing, as Dennis would have. "You alright?"

"Yes, thanks. It wasn't your fault. I did a stupid thing and left my billfold in Fargo, so I couldn't buy a ticket, and that got me upset." My eyes were drying; my hands felt competent again. "Would you like me to help clean up?" That was something I knew how to do.

"Shit, no!" Billy shouted as he lunged toward me so precipitously that I sprang backwards and stumbled against an old platform rocker with an attached footstool that stood without logic in the center of the room. "Sit down, for crissake. You ain't no cleanin' lady. Sit *down*." As I sank into the chair, he dropped a newspaper into my lap. It was folded backwards and crumpled. "*Read* somethin'. What you wanna drink?" He was back at the shelf, then squatting to look through a row of cabinets underneath it.

"Do you have Sprite? Seven-Up?" I didn't have any idea even what category I should choose from.

"Ain't got no icebox in here, that's what a goddamn hole this place is. Can't even keep beer cold." Please, I thought, please don't offer me anything hard, Billy Calloway, because I won't be able to drink it; I won't know how to be polite and casual about it either. I willed my thoughts into his head right through the tangle of curls on the back, right through the cortex and out between the eyes. Right between the eyes.

"You drink tea?" He ducked out from under the shelf and turned in my direction. Dangling from one hand were two forlorn teabags hanging by their strings, their protective envelopes long gone.

"Yes, I do. When I can't get cocoa." And why did I say a senselessly personal thing like that?

"You like cocoa too?" Underneath the mustache dropping down over his upper lip and the sides of his mouth, there was a tiny movement. I had never seen him smile, even on his album covers, except for that one moment on stage in Kensington.

"Well, it's convenient to drink something the family likes too so I don't have to get two pans dirty in the morning. I've liked chocolate ever since I was a child, chocolate brownies, chocolate chip cookies. Cocoa has to be real cocoa, though, not that powdered stuff with the milk already in it." I stopped myself from going on. Maybe the two of us ought to collaborate on a cookbook.

"My mama always made cocoa for us kids when it was winter in West Texas. Said it kept you warm. It did that." He paused and leaned on the shelf; I could see him shuffle through possibilities in his mind. "But there ain't no milk 'round here. Cocoa neither."

"Tea is fine." Good Lord, he looked positively melancholy. "Tea is really fine. Besides, I read somewhere that singers shouldn't drink anything with milk in it before they perform because milk will clog their vocal cords."

"That so?" For a moment he sounded interested. He had unearthed a little aluminum saucepan, dime store variety, and was walking toward a door that must have led to a bathroom. "Shit, don't figger it'd make a helluva lotta diff'rence with the way *I* sing." The water ran, then stopped, and he brought the pan back in careful balance to an ancient hot plate on the shelf under the mirror. Then he was rummaging underneath again, I assumed on a quest for cups. Over his shoulder he said, "You got kids?"

"Jake and Lisa. Six and fourteen." There didn't seem to be anywhere to go from that.

Billy stood up with a cup in each hand. Apparently his fingers wouldn't fit through the handles because he was holding them both with his hands circled completely around the rims. He placed them on the shelf, lining them up along the edge like a fat little china couple. "You married?" he asked.

You do ask your questions in an unusual order, Billy, I thought, but he wouldn't have caught the irony. Was he planning to match me up with somebody in his band? "Yes," I said, leaning back in the chair. That wasn't clear, though. "Not anymore."

"Workin'?" The hot plate under the pan was already glowing orange.

"I teach freshmen in college how to write."

Billy looked uncomfortable but recovered himself. "Shit," he said. "Worse'n bein' on the road."

"It's not so bad. The students usually try hard. It doesn't pay very much, that's true, but enough to help out with the bills. And it's better than staying at home alone."

Suddenly the water began to boil, smacking against the metal. Billy stepped forward and flung out his hand to grab the pan off the burner. With all my protective instincts on super alert, I plunged out of the rocker, leaving it shaking on its platform, and wrenched his fingers away just short of the handle. At this rate I would need a nursing degree. "You'll burn yourself!" I shouted. "And you have a concert to give tonight!" I was afraid to let go of him for fear he'd grab at the handle again.

"Jesus Christ, you scared the shit outta me!" Gruffly, he dropped his arm to his side, mine still attached. Neither of us seemed to know how to disentangle our fingers.

"Don't you have a pot holder?" The water was starting to spurt out of the pan, sizzling on the burner.

"Not likely." Our hands slid apart.

"Well, use a bandanna or something. It'll all boil dry." I went back to my chair.

Billy located a rag of some sort and got the pan off the stove, muttering. He filled the cups and dropped the teabags in, taking a very long time, careful not to spill. His mother must have trained him in kitchen behavior, I thought, as I settled deeper into my throne. Little Billy. No, that was ridiculous; he must always have been huge. Everything he wore was outsize: jeans with a Chinese laundry pleat ironed down the front, wide leather belt with one of those rodeo silver buckles you could buy at a pawnshop even if you'd never ridden a bull or roped a calf. His shirt was faded flannel, black and red plaid like a lumberjack's. The famous vest was missing. As I glanced around to see if it was hanging somewhere, Billy bent down for the cups. His dark hair curled over his collar, almost to his shoulders. One side of his face was bent into the light where I could see it; he must still be shaving a little to make that clean curve where his beard started out of his skin. No gray that I could see. How old *was* he? Thirty-five? Forty? His shoulders were so broad that his shirt pulled tight across them as he hoisted the cups up and began a careful turn. Dark skin, like Lisa's despite her honeyed curls. A big nose. With the light behind him it was hard to see his eyes, and on the record jackets they were always shadowed by his hat. Where was that hat? It had become inextricably painted on my mental picture of him.

"Remember, I ain't got no milk. Might be some sugar someplace." He handed me my tea and looked around for a place to sit. Opposite the door was a folding chair, which he seemed to consider, then turn down. Instead he squatted on the floor next to my rocker.

"I drink it plain, thanks." The tea was already strong; dark surges circled from the teabag whenever I shifted my wrist. There was no saucer. Should I dispose of that teabag somehow? It looked like a little dead mouse in my cup. If it touched my lip, I was going to retch.

Billy looked up. "Somethin' wrong?" His eyes might be gray.

"I'm sorry." What a miserable, tiny, irresoluble situation. "It's the teabag."

"I ain't got no more."

"No, I didn't mean that." He was still looking at me. "I can't drink the tea if the teabag is in it."

"Give it here then." He held out his hand.

"But it's all wet."

"Goddamnit, yes, but it ain't hot anyways, not if I hold on

the string." He caught the teabag string with his fingers, yanked it out of my cup, and dropped it on the floor next to him.

Well, not exactly Oscar Wilde, Billy, but well meant. I took a sip of the tea, Lipton Bitter, but just at the edge of my vision lurked that teabag, oozing in its puddle on the floor. My throat shut down.

"Now what?" He had his legs stretched out in front of him and was leaning one shoulder against the side of my chair.

I was past shame. "I can still see it."

"Goddamnit!" He grabbed up the teabag in his hand, squeezed it until the drips ran down his wrist, and pitched it into the wall across the room. It left a tiny wet spot and disappeared somewhere behind a pile of extension cords and old newspapers.

I took another mouthful of tea. Awful tasting, but comforting somehow. Billy had his head down and was holding his cup in both hands, one boot beating out a gentle rhythm. He had started humming, a deep rumble in his throat. Did he even remember I was beside him? Only if he noticed his hand was still wet from the teabag.

My cup in my lap, one hand holding it steady, I leaned back and listened. After all, I'd never had a private concert from a country-western singer, so this was a kind of honor. When I concentrated, I thought I recognized the song, but not absolutely for sure. Was it from *Lone Man on the Road*? That had been around for a while.

"What song is that, Billy?" I hadn't called him by his name before. Did he even remember mine?

He went on humming. At the end of what must have been the chorus, he lifted his head and said, "That's 'Stranger in Town.' "

"From *Lone Man on the Road*, right?"

"Didn't know anybody but me and the boys even remembered that cut." A real smile this time, his head tilted back. "You got my albums?"

"Everything I could find in Fargo. I didn't put tracers on any of the ones they didn't have or check a discography."

"Some of 'em are prob'ly not up for sale now anyways. I made seventeen all together. How many you got?"

"Fifteen, but they're not all the originals. Two are reissues of ones you made in the late sixties."

"You kin start a fan club." He turned his cup upside down on the floor, then moved it aside, leaving a wet circle in the dust. He made an X through it with his index finger. "I appreciate that you buy 'em. Makes me feel good."

"But you sell thousands. I am one fan of many."

"Yeah, but I never see the people what buys 'em. Jest git the goddamn statements from my accountant every six months." He said "accountant" as if he were sounding it out from the dictionary.

I sat silent, feeling like a teacher and not liking it. Billy had his head down, and for a moment neither of us came up with anything more to say. Nobody hummed either. I scrambled for a new topic of conversation, shuffling my mind like a deck of cards, and came up with his guitar, gleaming blue through the transparent plastic on all his album cover photos. That should carry us through the next five minutes, and anyway, I'd wondered for years why he didn't play a brown one like all respectable cowboys.

"Why do you use a blue guitar, Billy?" That was clear enough.

For a minute he didn't move; then his head came up so suddenly it jolted my chair. "Shit, when I started out, somebody said every guitar picker hadda have a guitar looked diff'rent from the others. Nobody's got a blue guitar, so I figgered that would do it." He was talking so fast that his Texas drawl smeared his words. "Hadda special order the first one, cost me twice as much as it shoulda. Now it don't matter what I play, but people git an idea, they don't let it go. Easier t' keep on the way I was than try t' do it diff'rent."

A long silence. The flood of words was over. Since we'd

come down the basement hallway, there hadn't been a noise from anywhere, not even preparatory sounds from the auditorium above. The place was built like a castle for sure, soundproofed by granite. Wasn't he lonely in all this quiet?

"Why isn't your band down here with you?" I asked.

"They keep away before the show once we git the equipment up. I live with them bastards on the road, ain't no need I should live with 'em every hour we settle someplace. When the boys start up, Tweeter'll come down t' make sure I ain't drownded in the john or somethin' and bring me upstairs." He looked at his watch, an old Elgin on an expansion bracelet. "That'll be in 'bout ten minutes, I figger."

I didn't feel like interviewing any more. Gently, I put my teacup on the floor.

"Wanna see the guitar I take 'round with me? It's an ol' Gibson J-200, top of the line." He had crossed the room and was yanking open a closet door, temporarily fastened to its frame with cheap metal hinges. "See here?" He brought it over to me. "Purty, ain't it? Knocked around, but still looks good. I don't use it no more on stage, 'cause it takes such a beatin', but I used it on *Lone Man on the Road*. We laid down that track in jest one night, 'bout nine till breakfasttime. Wrote most of them songs myself. When we got goin', I felt like I was dowsin' with this, jest reachin' down and knowin' right away where the water was. This guitar was *talkin'* then. All I was doin' was turnin' it loose. The boys, they didn't know what in hell was goin' on, jest followin' me wherever I let it go. Old D.G., my steel man, he jest kept chokin', had t' keep turnin' his head away so his mike wouldn't pick it up. When I first listened t' them tapes, 'bout dawn, I went out and ate a steak. Couldn't believe we done it so good."

Billy sank down again, his back against the side of my chair. The top of his head brushed my elbow on the rocker arm. He held the old Gibson across his knees, running his thumb along its edges as if he were outlining it. The blue had faded to a glazed violet in spots, but whoever had put the special order finish on it had done a good job. It wasn't peeling.

"You git attached." He ran his fingers over the strings. "A good guitar, you git attached. Won't never leave you 'less you're dumb enough t' leave it somewheres yourself. Ain't never done that."

Oh Billy. Life is full of things that leave you, and you don't have to be careless for it to happen. But I didn't say that out loud. Instead I tightened my arm muscles just a little so I could lift my hand without it wobbling, then slid it over his head and let my palm down far enough so his curls brushed it. I'd thought they'd be crispy, maybe because they were so dark, but they were so soft I had to tighten my arm some more to keep my hand from sinking right down into them.

"Billy! Showtime coming up!" The door to the hall shook a little.

"Shit!" Billy jumped to his feet. "Put that away, will you?" He handed me the guitar. "Come on in, Tweeter. Got my vest?"

The door shook again, tentatively, then opened. I recognized the skinny figure in buckskin fringes from Kensington. Tweeter. One childhood name I'd have shed as fast as I could.

"I am not able to get those spots out, Billy, but nobody will see them anyway." He handed Billy the vest. "You're going on in that shirt?"

"Jesus Christ, forgot all about it." Billy started unbuttoning. Without self-consciousness, Tweeter stepped over and helped him. I don't think he even saw me.

"Take off that T-shirt too, Billy. It's a good crowd out there. Let the ladies see a little hair."

"Feel like a goddamn *stud*," said Billy as he grabbed the bottom of his T-shirt and peeled it over his head, then dropped it on the floor. "Where's my clean shirt, Tweeter? Can't find nothin' in this goddamn place."

"Right here on the hanger." Tweeter pulled the closet door

open and brought out a clothes hanger with the shirt on it. Pale blue tonight, pressed crisp. Billy looked at it with great skepticism.

"You know I always sweat right through that one. Be purple once I done two songs."

"Best we can do, Billy. A little sweat doesn't hurt. Come on. The band has a good start on us; D.G. is doing that piece he wrote right this very minute. Steve will have the drum bit next. Your hat is on the piano. You ought to be up in the wings right now." He held out the shirt for Billy, who plunged his arms into it. His chest was covered with curly brown hair a little lighter than his beard. As Tweeter helped him snap up the shirt front, I could see the contrasting color through the fabric.

I pulled myself out of the rocker, still holding the blue guitar. "Put her on stage, Tweeter," said Billy, settling the leather vest on his shoulders.

"Put who?" Tweeter still hadn't acknowledged me.

"Put that lady. Give her a seat back of D.G. She kin see OK from there."

"But they're already going, Billy." He glanced at me, appalled.

"Shit, nobody's goin' t' be watchin' what goes on back by the steel. Won't be the first time we had a visitor on stage. Seems t' me you had a few jest this last trip."

"Guess you're right, Billy, but we knew they were coming."

"Goddamnit, Tweeter, it's *my band*. Put down that guitar!" he yelled at me, and then as I laid it as carefully as I could on the rocker, he grabbed my hand. The three of us, Tweeter shaking his head dismally in the rear, raced out the door.

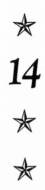

14

THE NOISE was astounding. Even backstage, away from the amplifiers and speakers, the sound banged off the walls. Through the flats angled in the wings, I caught flashes of the band, going like death on "Heartaches by the Number." Someone was running a strobe light on the choruses, reflecting it off the walls in tandem with the music, while out in front the audience was yelling, sounding whoops when something nice happened like D.G.'s little runs on the steel. Billy had disappeared. So had Tweeter, but then he reappeared next to me, his lips moving without sound. Finally he took my head between his hands and pulled it over to his mouth, angling my ear so close I could feel his lips move.

"Get on there. The chair is behind the steel guitar. See?" He pointed out into the din.

"Won't they notice me?" I reached out for his head, but he was an old hand at this and read my lips.

"It doesn't matter. There's always a lot of moving around. Get out there or you'll miss it."

I hesitated. It seemed the most out-of-place thing to do.

"Get *out* there," Tweeter insisted. "Billy will kill me if you don't." He gave me a gentle shove.

He was right, of course, about nobody noticing. Once I stepped onstage, threading through the cords knotted everywhere on the floor, avoiding the beer cans, the instrument cases, the rickety chairs, the clutter of picks and cloths, the amplifiers, the microphones stuck up at every angle, once I found my way past the steel, where D.G. gave me a little wink even while his hands were flying, it didn't seem out of place at all. It was like riding a cloud of sound, fluff and storm together. Had I been deaf, it would have all come up through the chair anyway, because even the floor was shaking under my sneakers. The cowboys in the audience whooped whenever they could find a space.

I didn't see Billy come in because he had been standing offstage on the other side, but I heard the audience. First a rustle, then voices I couldn't distinguish, then "Billy!"—some woman yelling, raucous. A great storm of clapping broke out, then formed into a rhythm. Billy and his blue guitar were partly hidden behind his rhythm guitar man, but when I craned around D.G., I could see all the chunks of him that mattered. Tweeter, drifting out from somewhere like an undernourished ghost, handed him the black felt hat from the piano, and Billy swept it up, held it high like a banner, then dropped it on his head. The clapping got louder. His mike was set up on a higher volume so even I could tell when he started to strum, following the band, getting his bearings. The floor was throbbing.

"Alright." Just like in Kensington. "You like what I got? I got it, alright. Comin' along?" His voice was husky, grating a little over the vowels. "*Now* the show begins, right? Gonna let me take you somewheres, right? Halloween ride, on my broom. Only chance you'll git." Under the spots crisscrossing from the lighting booth in the back of the auditorium, I could see a couple dancing in the aisle.

114

Halloween ride, Billy? I had completely forgotten. Jake would be out with Brian, Flash Gordoning the Fifth Street neighborhood. Lisa would be playing mother, handing out candy from the stainless steel mixing bowl, then racing off to her game, for which she would once again not pay a penny. But she could certainly afford Cokes afterwards. She had my whole billfold.

Billy had already started. First "On the Levee," a real oldie, almost a folk song, with a mournful line on the violin. Fiddle. Someone was backing up with a harmonica too. Then "Gentle on My Mind," modern country but melancholy. Billy's voice was still husky, like he was playing a part in a play, the lonely drifter who always left behind what he loved best. Even his guitar picking had an extra twang. I was getting used to the amplification and could sort out what sounds different players were contributing, a fascinating collage. Jazz must be like this, but more so. People picked up from others, threw the line back, laughed, had a sip of beer, tried something special, slid into strumming while somebody else took over the lead, and kept an eye on Billy so they would never, never trespass on whatever he was doing. I had had no idea how much power he possessed. This was *his* band.

"Alright. Wear myself out here. Nobody'd want that, would ya?" Billy pulled off his hat and hung it on the corner of the chair off to his left. His hair was so wet it gleamed under the overhead spots, pressed tight to his head where the hat had compressed it. He was right; his shirt was purple, stuck tight to him everywhere but along his lower arms where he'd rolled the sleeves up. Tweeter slid up behind him again with a can of something. Beer. Billy took a long swig while the audience howled, then handed it back to Tweeter with a grin. That was a real grin. Tweeter threaded his way back through the group and knelt down by me. He held the can under my nose. No smell at all.

"He drinks water when he's working. *I* have to fill that can up." He was grinning too as he scrambled offstage, almost on his hands and knees.

Up front, Billy was hunched over his guitar as if he were holding a baby. Then he straightened up suddenly and held the guitar, hung on its strap around his neck, straight out at the audience. "Think ya kin pick it? Wanna try? Come on!" I could hear his rushed breathing through the microphone.

"Bring it on home, Billy!"

"Alright. Alright." And the songs came in a surge, from his newest album, from *Cowboy Lovin'*, and then one of the numbers from *Lone Man on the Road*, the ballad called "The Drifter." Did he look back at me when he started that, or was he checking on D.G.? The audience was screaming now, almost like a rock concert if they really were like that, and Lisa said they were. Doing a little dance around his mike, hitting his guitar with the flat of his hand whenever he finished a line, Billy pulled it all together with "Low-down Lady." The whole band was singing behind him except for D.G., who laughed as he bent over his steel guitar. "He's hot tonight," he mouthed at me. "Billy is hot tonight."

Then the concert was over, the last guitar note played, the floor no longer vibrating like some stretched-tight membrane. I was afraid to get out of my chair for fear my legs had melted. "You all right?" Tweeter asked as he hurried past, looking over the heads of the band at the audience, still noisy but heading toward the doors in the back of the auditorium. Billy was gone.

"I'm all right." My voice sounded strange, but that must have been because I couldn't hear it properly. My ears were numb from the music.

"Don't get stepped on." The stage was busier than it had been before, a jungle of cables, cords, mikes, amplifiers, everything moving or being moved. Cases opened, instruments went in, the steel guitar's legs were being folded up. Tweeter signaled toward the lighting booth to adjust the house lights, or so I assumed. Gradually the auditorium got even brighter.

As alien a figure as I must have appeared, no one paid any attention to me at all.

I stood up. It was possible to do that. My purse was next to me, though I hadn't remembered carrying it in that dash from the dressing room. All I needed now was money for gas, and Tweeter would have that; he would trust me to pay him back. I started over to where he was winding an extension cord that ran across the front of the stage and snaked into the wings. He was hunched over on his hands and knees. Somebody was coming up behind him. Billy.

"You bring it on home, Tweeter. Bus out in back?"

"It sure is." Tweeter pulled himself up, hands on his narrow hips, buckskin fringes swaying back and forth.

"Alright. How long t' load that truck?"

"Maybe another hour, Billy. We couldn't get it right to the doors because of those steps. The boys will hoist the stuff on over."

"Didn't like the sound of that goddamn amp tonight."

"I will check it out. It shouldn't be going out on us so soon."

"Alright." Billy wiped his forehead on his arm. "They bring you the money? I took what I needed from the till. Hell, more'n I needed."

"You earned it, Billy."

"I reckon." He focused on me as if he were measuring me for a piece of furniture. "You live where?"

"In Fargo. About five hours away, but it's all straight super-highway. Even getting out of the city is no problem." It was nice of him to be concerned.

"How big's your car?"

"It's a Plymouth Trail Duster, one of those four-wheel-drive ones. It seats five and has a space in back like a station wagon." Was he wondering what kind of mileage it got so he could figure out how much money to give me for gas? But we hadn't talked about gas. Something seemed to be going on that I couldn't quite nudge into place. Suddenly my body realized that I hadn't had a normal quiet moment for almost twelve hours, and my knees started to vibrate toward each other. If I passed out, would I end up in the truck, bedded down among the amplifiers?

"Tweeter." Tweeter heaved the cord in its great circle over onto a chair. "You bring the boys back, alright? We ain't goin' out again for a week or ten days, I figger."

"Not until the eleventh, Billy. A week of one-nighters in the Panhandle." He did not look happy.

"Don't need me then, goddamnit. Got enough t' pay 'em all?"

"The accountant does that, Billy. I don't hand out the cash anymore. You know that."

"Shit, you're right. Don't make no sense though." He cleared his throat and rubbed his arm across his forehead again, then ran his eyes around the stage, dipping them a little as they passed by me but going right on. Maybe he was tired too. Where his vest hiked up across his back, his shirt was creased as if somebody had been beating him.

"Billy, you know it's better if you come on back with us." Tweeter looked distinctly nervous.

"Hell, I ain't never seen Fargo. Where is it? South Dakota? Never been in them Dakotas but for that goddamn fair."

"They're really very pretty if you don't mind the flatness," I said inanely. Something was washing the sense out of my head. "You're welcome to stop by any time you come. We live on Fifth Street, North Fifth, which is right where you'd think it would be if you were counting. The highway enters at . . ."

Billy stepped toward me, his hand out, fingers in a gentle curve. "Baby, you look tired," he said. "Tweeter, find me my jacket. Lemme git my guitar and my gear, then we kin git goin'. Where's your car parked?"

I felt like Alice in Wonderland, down the rabbit hole. All my appendages were prickling. "About a block away," I said, as if this were a normal conversation. "But I can get to it just fine by myself. St. Paul is a very safe city. I would appreciate your lending me a little money, though. I'll have to get gas before I get out of the Cities." I stopped. Billy was digging snarls out of his beard. Tweeter had started backstage after the jacket. Neither one was listening.

Then Billy reached down and picked up my left hand. He squinted at it, pulling it up higher where he could see it better. "Still wear your ring, don'tcha," he said, nudging it with his thumb while his fingers tightened around mine. "Guess a lotta 'em do that. Whatthehell." As if I were Jake's age, he guided me offstage.

15

IT WAS LIKE being in the womb of somebody who was jogging, a steady, rhythmic motion in darkness. No real sound. I was stretched out somewhere in the black, my knees pulled up, my feet against a flat wall. The air on my face was cold but the rest of me felt warm. Cozy was the word. Something with an animal smell was on top of me. Still half asleep, not anchored yet in time, I thought of cattle, horses, something stripped from the range, maybe a saddle but not that heavy. When I turned my head, an irregular but soft texture brushed against my chin. Lanolin. Sheep.

I opened my eyes, though I hadn't known they were shut. Blackness. Then a silver rectangle to one side, split by more blackness on the edges. Flashing silhouettes of tall figures. Trees. But why on silver? I turned my head again and shifted under the sheepskin. Up in the corner, pressed against the silver but partly cut off by the frame, was a circle of brightness. The moon. The Halloween moon. Was a witch crossing it? I couldn't see one.

"Awake?" Who said that? I tried to sit up but couldn't get a grip on anything. One of my hands was asleep.

"Jesus, relax. You'll kick the goddamn door open." Billy. Bracing myself against the side of the car, I managed to pull myself upright, the sheepskin sliding to the floor. Without my cover the air was cold all over me; the Trail Duster had never heated the backseat properly. I got my feet anchored on the floor, then leaned toward the front. Billy was driving with both hands on the wheel, shoulders back so his leather jacket bulged out over the top of the front seat.

"How far have we gone?" English teacher kidnapped by cowboy singer, who has change of heart and brings her home. Did he plan to move in? I hoped he would like Lisa's guinea pigs, permanent residents of the upstairs guest bedroom. Should I ask him?

"Don't know this country. Last sign said Osakis. Goddamn funny name."

"That means about two more hours. What time is it?" I had only blurred memories of leaving the auditorium, but we certainly hadn't stayed around there long.

"Take a look." He shifted in his seat and laid his left hand over the back, palm up. Under his jacket cuff was the edge of an expansion watchband, the watch part hidden against the upholstery. "Turn it 'round," he said. "Dial glows in the dark."

My hand was waking up, so I reached out and pulled back his jacket sleeve, fumbling underneath for the watch. There were two tendons running down his wrist just like there are in everyone's, with a vein passing across them. I could see them in the moonlight. As I took the expansion band in my fingers and started to pull it around, it stretched, and I had to get a better grip. My hand slipped onto his skin, and I felt a repetitive beat, quiet in between, like rhythm guitar, steady, underlining everything. His pulse. The sound traveled up my arm like an electric charge I couldn't get detached from. Frightened, I willed my fingers to move back to the watchband, but Billy had already encircled them with his own. It seemed a perfectly natural thing to have done.

"Goddamn big moon tonight, ain't there?" he said, driving one-handed.

"There certainly is." We sounded like defective lyrics even by country-western standards.

"Hand's cold." His fingers tightened.

The heater has never worked right in this car." Willie Nelson couldn't have made a song of that either.

Billy laughed, a chuckle that at first I thought was a cough until I saw his cheek curve in the moonlight. He bent his head back on the seat and rubbed his beard against my cheek, a little teasing up-and-down nudge like a hairy washcloth. "Baby, you are one funny little lady," he said, "but as long as you buy my records, I figger we kin be friends."

"I don't have all seventeen, remember."

"Shit, nobody does, not even me. Want some music?" He took his other hand off the wheel, the car moving straight down the silver Minnesota highway, and flicked the radio on, then sent the pointer down the dial through the nighttime chatter. "This late, should be able t' git Nashville." He jiggled the pointer a little. "Alright, there it is. Arnie's show. Ain't no damn good, but every trucker between here and the Rockies is listenin'." The music was blurred by static as we passed along a convoy of electric poles, then faded away.

"Try a little further down the dial. We're getting near Fergus Falls, and they have a country-western station." I bent over his shoulder and pointed with my free hand, then turned the knob myself. Crystal Gayle's voice, throaty as Garbo's, pushed through the car.

"Goddamn, she sure kin sing. Better'n ol' Loretta even."

"She's younger."

"Don't make no diff'rence in country. Older, younger, what you got, you got." Crystal finished in a flutelike diminuendo and Johnny Cash came on. Billy hummed along, playing around the notes, then started to sing himself. Their voices had the same range, blending together in an on-the-road duet. Velvet in the night.

"Billy, was that a sheepskin?" It was bunched up on the floor under my sneakers.

"Sure was. Sure is. Carry it 'round with me for good luck. Besides, no picker kin be sure he ain't goin' t' be sleepin' by some road again, and that ground is hard. Couldn't find no blanket in here, and you was out of it 'fore we hit the beltway. You looked like one of them baby dolls with your eyes shut like that. When I got gas, I jest moved you in back and covered you up. Could tell that goddamn heater weren't goin' t' work right."

"Billy?"

"That's my name. Wanna practice it one more time?"

"Is your band really going back by themselves?"

"Hell, yes. I sent 'em back south, playin' cards and buyin' out every booze store on the way. Like Tweeter said, we got nothin' on for ten days, and Elmer kin read maps. I don't drive them rigs, baby, I jest own 'em. Tweeter knows how t' handle everythin' better'n I do anyways."

In the guitar-rich air, I leaned forward and put my chin on Billy's jacket collar. It was like holding onto a big bear who would protect me against anything. He had both hands on the wheel again, eyes ahead, nodding a little with the beat as an old Marty Robbins recording came on, one of the El Pasos. Traveling through the bright Halloween night was like sailing on the fantasy ocean that all midwesterners see in their dreams. Melodies of the deep, teak wheel, bounding main, scrimshaw and blubber, wives on the widow's walk, scudding clouds over the harbor where the ships don't come in. Who was sailing through the skies tonight? Rumpety-rump went the Trail Duster, motor humming along with Billy, and it was George Jones now, the country singer's singer, growing old but still loving her, same old gurgle in the voice, same rich growl above the string section that even classic country-western bands had allowed into the recording studios. The moon's silver was so bright now that the yard lights of all the Minnesota farms were disappearing into the glow like minilights soaking into a blazing Christmas tree. We passed a hillside cemetery where the ghosts would be walking, held only by custom inside the iron curve of EMMANUEL over the entrance. The ghosts would walk tonight if they ever did. I shifted further back in my seat.

"Whatcha doin', baby?" Billy edged his elbow onto the seat back and looked at me.

"Drive smooth, OK?" I balanced on the sheepskin and moved one foot through the central gap between the two front seats. "I'm coming up with you."

"OK, baby. Lemme git my gear outta here." He bent over and slung a dark shape to the floor. "Kin you make it?"

"No problem." I slid through, then settled down. Up front the windshield was a slab of silver. It was like the highway had streetlights blazing all along it.

Billy patted my knee. "Baby, you believe in ghosts?" He had been thinking Halloween thoughts too.

"I'm not allowed to believe in ghosts and teach college English, I regret to say. It's in my contract somewhere." I stretched out my feet against the humming bottom of the car. "But I don't know. Shakespeare did. Funny things happen."

"*I* believe in 'em." He put his hand back on my knee. "Figger we mess up enough in this life, we oughtta git one more shot at it."

"Do you think they ever come back to watch the people who are still alive?" Even when I stretched my hand, I couldn't match my fingers to his.

"Whatthehell. If they got nothin' better t' do. *I* ain't gonna watch nobody, that's for sure. Jest git my guitar and go at it one more time."

I wasn't going to argue with him. Instead I reached out and felt the studs on his jacket running along the pockets and in a line by the zipper. "You look like a motorcycle rider in this, Billy," I said.

"Hell, that's my good jacket. Wool inside too, see?" He

turned over a corner for me to feel. "Had this a long time. Ain't never goin' t' wear out. Gonna leave it t' my kids."

"Do you have any?" Why hadn't I asked before?

"S'pose I got a few floatin' 'round Texas. Mebbe more'n that."

"Any wives?" What in the world would it be like to be married to him?

"Not as of this minute." The phrase was startlingly formal. "Had a few in the past." His voice had dropped. "Weren't much of a man t' 'em, I reckon, leastways not in the long run. I ain't so bad at night, but daytimes they figgered they could do better."

"Maybe you're a night person." Somehow that didn't seem to be what he meant, but he didn't argue. The moon glinted off his throat under his beard as he pushed down on the accelerator.

"Wimmen're alright, though. Got a lot t' put up with." The Trail Duster shuddered and throbbed ahead.

Oh, it was silly, but he reminded me of a student—Dennis, Wayne, Judy, any one of the freshmen who browsed and mourned through my English sections. Against the silver his profile was a Victorian silhouette. On an impulse—the ghost with his guitar, the moonlight, the lost Texas children—I hunched up on my knees and kissed his cheek, the same kind of a kiss I'd given Jake and Lisa ten thousand times. Billy kept looking straight ahead, but he slowed the car down.

"What's the matter?" We had been making really good time.

"You wanna stop?" The two right wheels were already off the road on the shoulder, then the gravel, crunching it underneath.

"Sure, why not? We deserve a look at the moon on Halloween night."

Billy looked at me peculiarly. "I guess we do," he said. "I guess we do, baby." He braked down and slid the Trail Duster to a gradual halt, smooth as a race driver. We sat for a moment; then he reached over and opened my door for me. After that he unlatched his own. "Any ghosts, goddamn it, we'll beat the hell outta 'em," he said. We jumped down together.

Billy had parked the car almost off the gravel, and beyond it to the right was a strip of rough grass, brittle with frost under our feet. It had turned colder since we'd left the Cities, though it probably hadn't reached freezing yet, and only by looking hard could I see the edges of cloud around our breath. Beyond the grass the bank sloped down to a ditch, something dark at the bottom. Probably a layer of muck with a little water on top, Minnesota style. It was too chilly for there to be any smell. Beyond the ditch the bank rose again, scattered with a few rocks farmers had discarded when clearing their fields. At the top of the bank on the other side of the ditch was a barbed-wire fence, silver like everything else in the moonlight. Dark fields plowed up for winter lay beyond.

We walked along the edge of the gravel for a little, holding hands absentmindedly like kids at a school picnic. A small wind came up, rubbing the grass blades against each other, then combing them over into a line. If any ghosts were walking, we didn't see them, even though it was Halloween.

"Ain't you cold?"

"Not yet. Soon. We're almost in North Dakota, Billy. Another hour. You'll feel the temperature drop when you cross the border." So he slept with Lisa's guinea pigs. They wouldn't mind.

"Goddamn moon is like some song I ain't wrote yet. Gonna be fightin' it out with the sun in 'bout two more hours."

"I wouldn't worry about the winner." Without any more words, we turned around and started back toward the car. Billy reached out and took my other hand too.

"Gettin' colder, ain't you." It wasn't a question.

"But your hands are warm. How come?"

"Pickers got strong blood in their hands. All that exercise." He laughed.

"What would you do if you didn't play a guitar, Billy? Did you ever want to do anything else?"

"Hell, no. I been pickin' since I was nine. Singin' too. Wrote my first song when I was thirteen and my voice was changin'. Couldn't hit half the notes on them Hank Williams songs, so I did my own. Hell of it is, I never did git his voice. Turned out like some old bullfrog." He stopped and lowered himself onto the bank. "C'mon, baby. I been on my feet more tonight than you been."

I sat down beside him, about a foot away, then moved closer when I realized how chilly the grass was. Billy was playing with my ring, but when he felt me against him, he shifted and swung his arm around my back. The moon must have been talking to me, however, because before his hand came down on my shoulder or my side or wherever, I did something really ridiculous. I tickled him as hard as I could, jabbing my fingers into his ribs.

"Shit! You quit that!" Billy grabbed at my hand, but I had had lots of experience tickling, and I slid under his defenses with ease, jabbing him again, this time right in the belly. He had probably never tickled a woman back before; they must not do that in West Texas. I knew I'd lose in the long run because he could lie down on top of me and flatten me into submission, but right now I was possessed of the devil. I grabbed him just above his belt while he rolled over on the bank trying to get away. We were both laughing now, and why not? It was Halloween madness. The witches and the ghosts, broomsticks and sheets, must have been laughing too.

"Goddamnit, you little devil. Leave me be!" Now he had both my wrists. Half beaten, I rolled on my back, crunching the grass underneath. The cold was coming up through my blouse; my jacket was wadded around my shoulders. Through my own giggles, my teeth were starting to chatter.

"Aren't you any good, you picker? Can't you even keep me warm?" Even though his hands were still clamped around my wrists, I managed to cling to his open shirt collar through

the unzipped front of his jacket. Go down fighting, bullet in
the shoulder, show Tex how a real cowboy does it. I dug my
knees into Billy, trying to push his legs to one side, but I was
too short and got him in the groin.

"Jesus Christ!" He pushed me off him, struggling to get
loose, then made a clumsy half-leap, holding back his own
weight, and landed on top of me. Our heads banged together.
Both of us said "Ouch" at the same time but neither of us
pulled away. My mouth was in his beard, full of hair and
frost, then on his.

For a moment I didn't know what was going on, as if I'd
planned on seeing one movie but walked into a different one.
Then I knew, all right; my body woke up like the morning
of the Fourth of July. I wasn't a souvenir collector for Jake
and Lisa anymore; I was *me*, hanging onto a man who was
big and warm and who was laughing and saying "Hey there,
hey there" as I pressed myself into him as hard as I could.
When he got his arms around me and started kissing me
back, I didn't care if we'd end up a feature in next Sunday's
Eagle, graphics and all. After all, I was grown up. I couldn't
even get pregnant. I was *entitled*.

It was too cold to take all our clothes off and pretty conspicuous too with the occasional trucker on his way with sup-
plies to the prairie hinterland. Billy got his jeans unzipped
first, then noticed my teeth were chattering and hobbled back
to the Trail Duster for the sheepskin while I lay on the bank
breathing like a distance runner and laughing until I cried.
Once I was on my woolly platter like the Sunday roast, Billy
tackled my jeans, but the zipper stuck halfway down and I
had to shove his hands away so I could wiggle it loose myself.
"It costs six dollars to get a new zipper put in," I found myself
saying, while his mouth rubbed in a little superhighway down
the front of my blouse. Even with the sheepskin, an inch-deep
damp was insinuating itself along my back, creeping up
into my secret places. Still, I wasn't cursing the frost tonight.

There weren't very many love words. "Goddamnit, baby,

you are the littlest woman I have ever seen," Billy exclaimed once when we had both slipped halfway down the bank toward the muck, the sheepskin like a furry sled. "But you sure feel good t' this ol' boy." I was freezing and kept trying to tuck all of myself close enough to him so I could absorb some of his warmth, while he kept trying not to put all his weight on me in case I'd be hurt. "You could *sue* me," he said once, then chuckled as he slid his hands inside my blouse and rolled us both over on our sides. My nipples were like froggy nubbins chilling on my breasts; I couldn't tell my own wetness from the dampness of the crushed grass around us. But then Billy finally stopped worrying about how small I was and came down on me like a great warm blanket. Both of us hanging on, he slid into me, then herded my legs under his for warmth. Riding over the prairie, Billy's climactic humming like the resurrection of summer's mosquitoes at the end of their night's revels, we came together, and then, grabbing at quack grass and rooting in the Minnesota dirt, we slid completely into the ditch and wallowed on the edge of the muck. A beer can floated by my ear, and Billy pitched it up the bank where it clanged against the fence, then dropped into the field beyond. "Still got my arm, baby," he said.

16

THE FIRST SIGN of Fargo when you're driving toward it in the darkness is a long glow in the sky, a strip of silver Day-Glo swathed across the horizon almost off the edge of the world. For a long time it lies there, not changing even as the car gets closer and closer, not individualizing or lifting itself higher into the blackness, just a silver line cutting through the middle of the windshield. Then, when you make the big curve just before the two-miles-ahead warning for the Fargo exits (three of them, almost like a real city), the lights swim apart into identifiable clusters—the Fargo National Bank, the senior citizens' housing unit, the cluster around St. Luke's Hospital, brightest during the night. At dawn, when the gray is coloring over the black sky, it's like entering a prairie Oz.

Without that dawn magic, it's a clumsy town, built to satisfy the needs of pioneers catching their breath between Minneapolis/St. Paul and the Great Northwest. Nothing is fancier than it has to be. All the houses put up since 1950 have six basic designs, varied by the color of the siding or the placement of a garage, and all the ceilings are low, to keep the heat down where the people are. Fargo's citizens seem to have a penchant for that sand-finish paint that covers up seams between sections of sheetrock, and they are also fond of glitter, their only pretension. Most of the living room ceilings I'd seen in Fargo sparkled in the dim light of evening with a gentle fake beauty.

We drove in over the University Avenue bridge, the Red River of the North hidden under overhanging bushes, sludge along the banks, a faint layer of morning mist. At the corner with the graffiti, the only graffiti anywhere in this decent, repressed community, I AM A MAD DOG BITING MYSELF FOR SYMPATHY had been scrubbed down to a shadow. In the last year, though, the mad dog always came back when the good Norwegians were asleep and painted it in again.

My house was twelve blocks north of the graffiti wall, four blocks north of where the old city with its tight core of frame houses with shabby porches came to an end. After that the yards got larger; the houses had pruned shrubbery on either side of their front steps, and the steps were made of brick. The block before ours started with a disconcerting flurry of lilac bushes, which some city planner had spread along the street in a woodsy barricade, but then it became one hundred percent Fargo again, each house (there were three of the basic six models on the block) set neatly on its seventy-five-foot frontage.

In the early morning light the lilacs were charcoal sketches. No other cars were moving on Fifth Street, but that was nothing new. I guided the Trail Duster past the Coleman and Anderson houses, both prairie bi-levels with curtains drawn against the dawn as well as the night. No Sunday papers on the steps yet. Clutching down for control, I slid across the intersection in neutral. For the first time since we bought it, the Trail Duster's heater had kicked in properly, and the car was like a little smelting furnace. I had to keep wiping the condensation from our breath off my half of the windshield with the heel of my hand.

We were home. "Here we are, Billy," I said over my shoulder to where Billy was leaning in the corner of the rear seat, head bent over his blue guitar, fingers touching out notes, changing them, touching out new ones. He had unearthed his black hat and was wearing it pulled down over his eyes, but except for that, his underpants, and socks, he had no clothes on at all. The guitar in his lap hardly counted. Once the car had heated up after we got back to it, he had shed them all into a heap on the floor, muttering, "Shit, I'm soakin'."

"Here we are," I said again. In the backseat he was harder to believe than on the sheepskin, when I hadn't been able to believe anything else. And what about me? Still with one arm turned back toward him, I angled my head and checked my face in the rearview mirror—same brown fluff on top, same blue eyes with dark morning smears underneath them, same egg-sucking grin. Oh dear. The grin was new and dangerous; I turned it off. Willfully, it came right back, but I stopped it before it got to the outside of my face. This was Fargo. This was a serious town.

"If the paper boy sees you like that, Billy, we'll have a neighborhood scandal and I will lose what little credibility I have. At least put on your jeans." I poked him gently in the knee to show how earnest I was being, only to find my arm limp as Jake's spaghetti when I tried to retrieve it. Before it melted away, I heaved it back next to me.

Billy raised his head, wrinkling his nose and shoving his hat back. "This place sure don't look like *Texas*," he grumbled as he set the blue guitar beside him. The grumble modified into a twinkle, his eyes squinting from the window to the sheepskin wadded on the floor next to his jeans. He reached down and captured them while I crept the car across the front of our house, watching him through the mirror. When he held the jeans up, he looked disgruntled. "Can't wear this stuff, baby. It's still wet." Accompanied by a quick all-strings strum with his left hand, he opened the window with his right and pitched the jeans out onto the black-topped street. I plunged across the seat, still holding onto the steering wheel, and grabbed back his shirt before it flew out too.

"Billy, you lunatic! What do you think you're doing?" He knew perfectly well what he was doing from the look on his face, and he was a lot less scared of my wrath than Jake would have been. "Litter makes North Dakotans nervous. You'll cause a Fifth Street scandal." The shirt was hanging like drapery on the neck of the blue guitar while Billy scratched himself, oozing mischief. If he chose to walk up to the house buck naked, or almost, all I could do was drive away. I couldn't stop him.

But Billy wasn't pushing anything. He put his hat on the seat next to him, shoving the guitar over; then he picked up the hat again and dropped it on my head before I could jerk away. "Hell, my duffel's on the floor down there, baby. Jest give it a toss over and I'll turn myself out decent. Don't mind dressin' for Fargo, North Dakota, but I sure as hell ain't goin' t' make myself wet all over again."

I heaved the bag back to him. His smile was beatific.

Clutching down and gliding on the last bit of power, I pulled the Trail Duster into the driveway, stopping silently up near the house. Billy, zipping up his other jeans but still naked from the waist up and bootless as well, climbed out of the car and down to earth. "Jesus Christ, this is the Great White North," he said. "Colder 'n a witch's tit." I hadn't heard that expression in years. Limping on the sharp gravel that lined our driveway, he cut across the edge of the lawn and into the gutter, where he retrieved his wet jeans, which were dampening more by the minute. "Want these folded, baby?" he asked as he turned back to me, the good little Texas boy blossoming out all over the cowboy, recording star, champion picker, man.

17

Now it was truly morning. I turned off the headlights, dropped the ignition key into my purse where it would stay secure, then slid myself loose with a squelch from the seat of the Trail Duster. I had forgotten how wet I was, swamp wet. Lisa and Jake would still be asleep, no school or cartoons either. On Saturdays Jake staggered out at dawn, hair in a rampage, and dragged all his stuffed animals to the living room where the TV was. Together, buried against each other in their own peaceable kingdom, they watched the New Mutants, Kimba, the Flintstones, the Smurfs, Jake as goggle-eyed as Blue Giraffe.

Hefting my purse by its shoulder strap, I headed straight around the shrubs to the porch. Jake was sitting on it, asleep.

"Are you OK?" My voice cracked out of key as I dropped down on my knees beside him. "Honey, are you OK?" This was hardly summer, hardly camping-out weather. "It's not even time for the paper boy, Jake. What in God's name are you doing here?"

No sound. His head, which had been propped against the aluminum screen door, slipped to one side and landed on the milk box. Both his hands were clutching his penis or something thereabouts, and his feet, in their mutilated slippers, stretched out on the brick toward me. For pajamas he was wearing one of Lisa's painting class flannel shirt discards. All his freckles were smeared with some undefined dirt, but he was clearly alive, soft and pliable as a teddy bear, no rigor mortis.

"Jake, come on, wake up!" I put my hands under his armpits and hauled him up to where I could plant his rear on the milk box. My legs shook all the way down. When had he gotten so heavy?

At first I thought he was still asleep, but as I held him erect, checking his breathing through the bedraggled shirt, his crunchy waking-up voice started like a forty-five record playing at thirty-three rpm. "I ate and ate, Mom, but it didn't get *done.*" Long pause, his lids still shut, the lumped eyeballs moving back and forth beneath them. "The music stopped, Mom. It's all gone." His eyes opened, and with what started as a yawn but then extended itself into a deliberate gape, he opened his mouth too and pulled back his upper lip. "See, it's gone," he said. Pause. "But the tooth fairy didn't come."

I wrenched at the screen door (where had I put the storm panels last spring, and would we be freezing all winter?), which swung open so wide that it banged against the house. The main door was still shut; my key was on the car key chain in my purse. I upended it over the step, everything in it clattering into a miniature junkyard on the doormat. I picked up the keys, which had landed on top of *Little Dorrit.*

"Baby, this is open already." Billy was suddenly between me and Jake on the steps, his hand on the knob as he pushed the front door open into the hall. Then he reached down and gathered Jake up, supporting him in his right elbow with Jake's dirty face resting in his neck. "Jesus, we'll all freeze t' death out here." With that he launched himself by me, filling the doorway so fully he had to bend his head as he went in. A good thing I was momentarily the one with the black hat.

Then his free arm reached back and swept me over the threshold too, Jake's interested face peering back at me with his eyes like plums. We tottered together on the linoleum, my face rasping against the button on Billy's shirt pocket and then sliding across the cloth as I pulled myself free. At least he'd put on a shirt. Meanwhile Jake regarded me speculatively, one hand buried in Billy's beard.

"Alright." Billy plopped Jake down in the corner of the sofa, then wandered off on a diagonal, his stocking feet digging into the carpet. Through the dining room window the first lines of sun were making the dust rise in stripes that angled toward the ceiling and then broke into fragments of light. Billy stopped and looked outside. "Never had no sandbox when I was a kid," he commented. Then he disappeared into the kitchen.

I felt as if I were wrapped in some kind of long narrow cloth and couldn't get unwound. It must be exhaustion. Marshaling my energies, I went over to Jake, sitting motionless on the sofa with his slippers on his lap, and lowered myself discreetly next to him, not infringing on his space but making sure he knew I hadn't disappeared either. Make it simple, Kay.

"OK, Jake. Tell me what happened. Why weren't you sleeping in your bed?" A two-year-old could have figured that out.

"I slept at Brian's, Mom. You remember. My tooth came out and Brian hid it until his mother made him give it back to me." He looked me over mildly. "Why are you all wet, Mom? You're making spots."

"I had to walk through a ditch, Jake. I'll change in a minute. Come on, tell me why you were sleeping on the porch."

Jake was holding his big toes, one in each hand, looking peacefully at the wall in front of him and exploring the empty place in his mouth with his tongue. "I fell out of bed at Brian's and my pillow was all gone. So I came here to finish my dreams."

"Fine. Fine. But why didn't you come *in* the house? The

door wasn't locked. Why didn't you ring at least until Lisa came down and let you in?"

"Lisa's not here."

"Of course she's here. She just went out with her friends for the evening. Now she's up there sleeping in till noon."

"Nope."

"Come on, Jake, what do you mean 'nope'?"

"She's not here, Mom. I looked. And it was dark. On the porch.the moon was out. Will she be mad 'cause I wore her shirt?"

But I had already leaped up from the sofa and hurried past Jake to the stairway, suddenly cold and damp beyond my clammy jeans. In the kitchen there were little purring noises from what had to be the toaster, and a series of metallic clatters. I ran up the stairs bent way over, my fingers touching the steps two ahead of my feet, an old trick from the days when I'd been so afraid of heights that I couldn't stand upright on the stairways in Wisconsin. Lisa's door was shut but not tightly; the warp where the frame was attached to the wall had kept the latch from catching. I pushed it open and swung into the room right at the foot of her bed. No one was in it.

Gasping, I sat down hard right by the footboard. Lisa made her bed only sporadically and it was all in a tangle now, top sheet wrinkled, yellow blanket and fake patchwork quilt sliding off the edge onto the floor. I reached out to pull them back, then found myself punching the mattress instead, as if my fist could knead out the fear rising inside me. It wasn't hard enough to do any good, so I hammered once on her nightstand, jolting the toy chickens she collected and knocking down the junior high pictures of blond girls in pink sweaters. Jeff's picture fell too, but I snatched it upright again. Down the hall the guinea pigs began their stupid chatter, expecting lettuce and caresses.

From downstairs I heard Jake's voice. "Can I draw a truck?" he asked. "Mom doesn't like trucks very much."

All right, Kay. I forced my hands into my lap. Be reasonable. Could she be in the shower? But there was no sound of water in the pipes, and the bathroom door downstairs had been open. In Jake's room? I tore down the hall, breathing so hard the air whined as I drew it in, and raced inside. She wasn't there. Across his carpet Jake had wound a line of comics and superheroes, classified into piles according to his fantasies. I gripped my hands behind my back to keep me from destroying them all. Had Lisa been there, I would have hit her, or Jake too. And I had never even spanked them.

I didn't cry, though. What had happened had happened. I'd been a fool, caught up in the Halloween moon. More than a fool. *Wrong.* I deserved this. Now I had to talk to Jake again, call Rebecca even if I woke her up, ask when Lisa had left. Find Jake's shoes and throw those slippers away. Find *her.*

"I like big trucks best," came Jake's voice from downstairs. "I am fond of very big trucks with stripes."

Hating myself, I started toward the stairway. Think of the positive things, Kay. One task for each step, and if Margaret appears at the door being helpful within the next half hour, tell her that everything is under control. That's all it takes . . . control. Don't let anybody take that away from you. Stay in charge. I'll say that until it comes true. I'll say it systolic and diastolic, in-breath and out-breath. I'm a good mother, I take care of my children. I feed them and they love me.

"Jesus, baby, I had no idea you was there! Damn near dropped this stuff." As I turned the corner at the bottom of the stairs, Billy jerked out of my path, my one enameled tray in his hands with three cups of cocoa and a pile of toast on it. He walked into the living room as if he owned even the furniture while Jake followed him, enraptured. Looking around, he put the tray on the coffee table, then sat down, lifted Jake onto his lap, and started breaking the toast into squares with both hands. "You like it dry, kid?" he asked. "You kin dunk it in the cocoa if you wanna. There's jelly too, or whatever this stuff is. Here, take a bite. Shit, you don't need t' finish it. One gallon takes you further than an empty tank." Jake leaned back against Billy's chest and began to eat.

I watched them. They looked like some greeting card picture. My throat hurt; my hands were knotted so tight that my fingers had glued themselves together. Then I lunged across the room and grabbed Jake out of Billy's lap, sending the cocoa onto the sofa in a brown arc. Jake started to cough frantically, gagging on the toast caught halfway down his throat.

"Shit, he didn't do nothin' wrong!" Billy snatched a napkin from the tray—how had he known where I kept the napkins when he couldn't even find a decent teabag?—and made a great sweep at the sofa arm. Did he have to clean up after me too?

Furious beyond words, I raised my arm and found myself brushing the brim of his black hat, still on my head. I threw it on the table. Then I made a fist and hit him as hard as I could right in the mouth.

With a scream Jake spat his toast on the rug and scuttled for the stairway, as far away from me as he could get. Cocoa, toast, napkins slid across the coffee table in an overlapping line, then catapulted off the edge onto the rug. "Jesus Christ," said Billy quietly, his fingers running along his lips. He spat blood into his hand, then a piece of tooth. "Jesus H. Christ." Without looking at me, he pulled himself to his feet, the lamp by the sofa arm wavering back and forth as his arm touched it, and walked out the door. In the front hall he passed Lisa coming in.

For a moment the house was absolutely silent. My hand hurt and I almost couldn't breathe; my chest moved up and down, but I couldn't feel anything coming in or out. When I looked at Lisa and tried to say something, my mouth tightened on itself so suddenly that I bit my tongue.

"Mom? Where *were* you?" There were blue smears under her eyes and her sneakers were sopping wet. When she turned toward me, she raised her hands at the same time as if she were pushing me off. What did she mean, where was *I*?

"Lisa, you scared me to death." I was having trouble enunciating. "Jake said you weren't home all night." At the mention of his name, a high keening rose from Jake's room. "He was sleeping on the front porch when we got here, because he was scared to be inside alone." Suddenly I was shouting at her, shouting like I never did. "Lisa, for God's sake, what kind of a way was that to act? You were supposed to be back here after the game and Cokes. You *know* that." It couldn't be my voice cracking the crystal. "You're only fourteen; you can't even drive. How am I supposed to have any respect for you?" All the while I was screaming at her, she was looking back at me, focused just above my eyes . . . because, my God, yes, she was taller than I was, finally taller. Under her dingy curls, missing their morning shower, her eyes tossed back the light from the living room window. Then the light splintered and she was crying.

"Mom, he hurt me. Why did he hurt me?" She had her blouse collar open and I could see the edge of her bra, the one with the tattered pink lace. Another wash and I had planned to throw it out. I couldn't concentrate; I couldn't hang on to what she was saying. "Right down here, and it still hurts me," she whispered, touching her breast.

Not knowing whether to avert my eyes or run to her, I hesitated, the backs of my jeans clinging to the edge of the sofa cushion. All right, Kay. Handle this. Had she been raped? Was she pregnant? How could I help her in this stiff Norwegian city where no one ever did anything wrong? Oh, who cared! What mattered was that she was scared to death, angry and pitiful both, leaning against the banister in the front hall, her face half covered by her hair. Then I was in front of her holding her hands, all stretched over with unused skin, no crinkles or veins. As if she were an honored guest, I guided her to the director's chair next to the sofa and pulled her into

140

my lap. Her little rear, hard as a punching bag, still fit against me when I hugged her.

"Mom, we went to the game, and then after the Cokes we went to Cindy's house. Her brother Mike had the car. I told Cindy I shouldn't be real late, not like two in the morning or anything."

"Where was Jake all this time?" I ran my fingers through her hair, separating the strands into sections.

"I knew he was sleeping over at Brian's, Mom. I fixed supper for him before he went out trick-or-treating, and I handed the stuff out here like we planned. When I went to the game, I didn't lock the house because I thought he might come back for something. Like his slippers."

Against my breasts I could feel her backbone quiver. I hugged her more and willed her to keep talking, telegraphing my words into her head. Lisa. Don't stop. You scared me to death, but we can make it all right. I can't imagine what happened to you between that stupid game and this frosty dawn, but I'm listening to what you're saying. Trust me.

"So what did you do then, honey?"

"Nothing much. We just sat around playing cards until Rebecca started her crazy Spin-the-Bottle game. If the Pringle can pointed to you, you got to do something secret to anyone you picked. The rest had to guess." She tossed her hair back, right into my face. "I knew it was sort of late, but we were having a neat time, and when the can pointed to Mike, he wanted me to be his partner."

She stopped. I waited, then pushed us both up and over to the sofa. When she slid off me and into her own corner, I gathered up the cups, threw out the toast, ran warm water on paper toweling, and mopped up the stains on the cushions. We'd live with the spots on the carpet. Jake came out of his room and sat on the stairs for a while, watching, then came all the way down to fill his favorite blue bowl with Alpha Bits and watch us some more from the kitchen table. For once in his short, untactful life, he didn't interrupt, though nobody was saying anything anyway. After a few minutes, he took the bowl back upstairs with him.

Through the big window, the sun was thawing the living room. Lisa pulled her legs up and sat cross-legged, holding the fat red pillow on her lap. "If it was your turn, you went off together and decided what to do. What he'd do. Eddie took Rebecca's ring and had her hold it under her tongue. Nobody guessed that, so they had to tell." She was silent. "Mom, do I have to talk about this?" Her eyes were full of wet light.

I didn't intrude on her space, but I picked up the ladybug pillow and put it in my own lap so we'd match. "No, honey, you don't have to talk about anything." From far away my tongue gave a little twinge; I'd forgotten I'd bitten it. "I'm sorry. You don't have to, and I can't make you, but I guess I need to know. This is kind of important." She looked past me, straight out the window. "Did he . . . attack you?" I asked. I couldn't phrase the question right. But how could Mike, who still drank my summer lemonade with both hands around the glass, ever attack anyone?

Lisa's line of sight, from sofa to window, was so unwavering that I could have rolled a marble down it. Outside, the Sunday morning cars were beginning to move on the street, two or three people in each, sometimes more, heading down toward the churches on Broadway. The paper boy, who had flooded the sandbox with Jake and Brian until last summer, when he started giving advice over the fence, suddenly passed the window, followed by the *Eagle*'s thud on the porch.

As if her visual roadway had been demolished, Lisa flung herself flat on the sofa. She wadded the loose pillows together in a heap, the two Indian ones with their silver sequins, her fat red one with a hole in the corner, and put her face into them, her voice a suffocated mumble from their depths. "We went upstairs to Cindy's bedroom and just sat on the bed. I didn't have any ideas. Then he said maybe he could put something in my bra, and he put his arm around me. Then he *nuzzled* me. I was scared the other kids would hear or Cindy's parents would come in, Mom, so I didn't yell. I thought maybe he was teasing, but then he unbuttoned my blouse and he kept grabbing my hands and laughing. When he pushed me down on the bed, I kicked, but he just put his head down and . . ." She was crying again. "He *bit* me! Right by my br . . ." She couldn't get the word out. Dippers of tears spilled down her cheeks.

I had no appropriate response except the desire to kill Mike. Stop it, Kay. That won't help. "And then what, honey?" I asked, figuring it was better to get it all laid out on the coffee table to calm us both.

"I got my foot loose and kicked him again, right in the balls!" She spoke the words with pride. "Then I ran into Cindy's bathroom and locked the door. The window was open a little, so I shoved it open more and got out on the airing porch. There was a little railing, but it was easy to climb over, and I just let myself slide down right into the bushes. I didn't even get scratched."

And whatever worries that boy had when you were gone, he richly deserved, I thought. "What time was it then, honey?" I asked, trying to decide what part of her to pat and ending up with my hand on the back of her leg.

She looked up from the pillows. A sequined imprint ran all the way down her right cheek, disappearing into the dingy curls under her ear. She glared at me and plowed down into the sofa again.

"Was it late?" It seemed important.

"I don't know what time it was, Mom! I just went walking."

"Until this *morning*?"

Silence. She burrowed her feet between the cushion and the arm of the sofa, leaving me the edge to balance on.

"Come on, Lisa. What were you doing all the rest of the night? I don't want to imagine disasters." Silence. "You'll feel better if you tell me."

"Who cares how *I* feel? All you care about is what *you* feel! I could drop dead like Daddy did, and after you made the arrangements, all you'd do is say 'Now, how do *I* feel about this?' " Her imitation was devastating; I felt like I was at the edge of a high place. Was that really how I acted? Oh, have mercy on yourself, Kay, you know she doesn't know what she's saying. But she knew perfectly well what she was saying.

I knew I should pet her and untangle the curls, but I felt like slapping her. She had no idea what it was like to be left. She had no idea at all.

My thoughts stopped. With a peculiar sense of being watched, I turned toward the window. Billy was looking in from the edge of the yard, his guitar lined up horizontally across his front, hands gently curved around each end. Had I been able to clip him out with three inches of dull autumn green as a margin, he would have been an album cover. Boots on now, he was standing right in the perennial border with a span of withering asters in the leaves beneath him. Deliberately, he stepped onto the grass and disappeared toward the front door.

Lisa sat up. She stared out the window with her shoulders tight as a rubber band. Then she bit her lip and turned toward me.

"Who is *that*?"

"Lisa, honey, who could it be but Billy Calloway?"

"Mom!" She sounded like Jake when someone went after his bedroom slippers. "In our *yard*?"

"Didn't you see him when you came in?" I asked lamely. "He walked right by you."

"Mom, this is Fargo!" She grabbed a crumpled napkin I'd forgotten and rubbed it under her eyes. "What is he doing here?" She was halfway across the living room when Billy came in the front door, depositing two handfuls of purse contents on the hall shelf. He kept his head turned away from me.

Scene Seven. Take One. Camera. Young girl sees cowboy

singer nearing her living room, falters, braces herself, smiles, goes forward (like sunshine through a rainbow). Mother feels pangs of embarrassment, bites lip, smiles too, thinks "What the hell," gets up and approaches singer. Front hall suddenly crowded. Small boy comes to top of stairs, sees singer, starts down, falls precipitously, hitting every step. Sudden appalled silence, broken by burst of laughter from mother, who is incapable of more reasonable response.

"Christ, this place is a zoo," sighed Billy as he unslung his guitar, picked up Jake, too stunned to make a sound, and put his other arm around Lisa, who huddled against him like she was coming home and then pulled away in a seizure of fourteen-year-old embarrassment. "OK, hombre?" Jake was starting his pretend cry, but only halfheartedly; his bottom and head were both tough as rocks. "Young lady, I had better introduce myself goddamn quick before you throw me out. Had enough of that today already. Billy Calloway. Came home with your mama for a little rest, which has sure as hell not started yet. I was thinkin' it was time for breakfast. If your mama will pass over them car keys, the three of us might look up a Pancake House."

"But I have my slippers on," said Jake, who was very fond of pancakes.

"Won't make no diff'rence if I carry you in, which is what I was thinkin' t' do. Got them keys?" He still kept his head tilted away when he approached me, but he held his hand out, flat and firm, until I extracted the keys from my pocket and put them on his palm. Then he took his hat off the coffee table and set it on his head. As the three of them went out the door, I could see the Band-Aid on his lower lip, half hidden under his beard.

For a moment I couldn't believe they'd gone, as if they'd had a hundred Sunday morning breakfasts together. Iron-footed, I went to the big window and looked out. Billy had backed the Trail Duster out of the driveway and had it idling in the middle of the street, blinkers on. I moved behind the curtain and watched him open the driver's door, jump down, and saunter to the perennial bed, half buried in October leaves. He had left the car door open; inside I saw Jake's soft profile, scooped out of bread dough, facing straight ahead in the death seat. He was beating both hands on the dash. With a little dance step, Billy swung around toward him, arms out, both thumbs erect, then moved his arms back to give a few hot licks on an imaginary guitar. He squatted down in the leaves, his long back arching, head bent. Then he stood up and walked back to the car, right hand out. In it was the last aster, small as a button, a blue eye I could hardly see from the house. Reaching over the back of the front seat, he handed it to Lisa, pulled himself up, and put the car into gear. As they rounded the corner and started toward Main Street, I saw her bend forward, light head near but not too near his dark one, and begin to talk. Her arms were raised and she was tucking the aster into her dirty hair.

18

I HADN'T WANTED to go with them, of course. First of all, I wasn't hungry, would never be hungry again, though I couldn't remember supper or lunch the day before. The thought of cocoa was nauseating. Lisa had made me terrified and furious both; she had no right to break rules and then to suffer. I had the market on suffering. Jake would be whimsical and cuddly with anyone who could pick him up and nourish him, an indestructible kid. Oh hell. Hitting Billy was like hitting somebody's mother. The ditch and sheepskin didn't count. At least I should have given him an ice cube right away so his mouth wouldn't swell. I would have done that for Jake.

My head wouldn't come clear. I forced it back on the track by swinging my eyes around the living room disaster, then gave myself fifteen minutes to straighten the sofa pillows, spit on and wipe up one last cocoa spot, swab off the dusty end table with my sleeve, close the top of the record player, pile the magazines, move the director's chair back to where its dent holes patterned the carpet, and dribble my purse contents back into my purse. Housewife Kay could put the world to order, couldn't she? She could put things back to rights as if they had never happened.

Lots of luck. My tongue started to hurt again, then my throat. What next, wash the kitchen floor? My knees were wobbling.

A knock at the door. I prayed it was the wind, but that was ridiculous. There wasn't a branch close enough to blow against the house anywhere in the front yard. I waited a minute, holding on to the hall shelf, thumbs tucked under, my stomach muscles pulled so tight that if I'd been in labor, I would have fractured the baby's skull when it hit the floor. I could not, absolutely not, deal with the paper boy (but he had already been there), the milk man (but he didn't deliver on Sundays), Jake, Lisa, Billy, any of the ghosts I had buried deep and weighted down. It was not fair. I wanted to stagger off to bed, curl up, and disappear.

"Kay?" Another knock. "Kay, are you there?" The latch wiggled, a discreet indication that whoever was there was planning on being persistent. "Kay, it's Margaret. May I come in?"

Of course she knew I was there. Where else would I be? Thank heavens Billy had picked up his jeans or she'd be bringing them in to me. But where had he put them? Oh God, that guitar. It was leaning against the banister. I bent over, my belly cracking, and gathered it up into my arms.

"Kay!" Margaret pushed the door open. "Oh, I didn't know you played. Are you busy?" She stepped onto the linoleum, then over to the carpet. "It's getting like winter out there," she commented as she shut the door behind her.

Over the years we'd lived on Fifth Street, Margaret had been very good about keeping track of me. She did my wash when my washing machine broke down (she had a ten-year-old Maytag as tough as she was), brought me tuna fish casseroles when the cloud descended on our house, took Jake on picnics with Brian and her husband. Taller than I was, of course, Margaret had a smooth Norwegian face, tight fair skin like a stretched canvas. No wonder she dressed in A-line skirts. I would have liked to attach myself to her, one of those hairy pseudo-babies growing in some unsuspecting mothers. I would have liked to burrow inside her and be safe forever.

I put down the blue guitar, leaning it up against the director's chair in the living room. When I turned around, Margaret was looking at me with a faint vertical crease between her eyebrows. She checked the room out of the corners of her eyes but came up with nothing. I would be her only source of information.

"Kay, I'm afraid Jake left some time early this morning. Brian just got up and said he was gone. Did he get home safe?"

"Oh sure." Why did my voice sound so normal? "He's out at the Pancake House now with Lisa."

"That's good." I stepped to one side to deflect her gaze and banged against the guitar strings with my knee. The sound was like Billy's voice. Suddenly the vomit rose in my throat and I swallowed, pushing the bitterness as far down as I could. My eyes were full of tears, like some cheap paperback Lisa would read, three for a dollar with the front covers torn off. That's what I felt like, no front cover at all. My mouth tasted awful and my tongue hurt. My hand hurt too—why was that?

Margaret glanced out the window at her own house, then back at me with a quick intermediate sweep into the kitchen. "You know, this morning just after I got up, I heard the doorbell. The paper boy never rings on Sunday, so I thought it might be Brian playing a game. When I went down and opened it, there was this"—she paused delicately—"this *man* there. He was so *big*. I was going to call Jim, but he just stepped back and said, 'I won't trouble you for long, ma'am, but I certainly would appreciate a Band-Aid.' Then I saw that his mouth was bleeding. He didn't even try to come in. I got him a Band-Aid and some paper toweling, and he fixed himself up. Then he said 'Thank you, ma'am' and walked up the street. He was wearing boots. Do you think he was one of the cowboys from Bonanzaville? I thought they only hired retired cowboys. Besides, we're way on the other side of town from Bonanzaville, but Jim said he might have had a fight in one of the bars downtown. Though we're pretty far from downtown too." Margaret's voice trailed off, and when I didn't respond, she bent down to pick up a cluster of lint from the carpet. Why hadn't she brought her vacuum cleaner? She straightened up with the lint in her hand, held daintily between finger and thumb, but there was no place to put it. The draft from around the door fluttered it like a tiny memory as she transferred it to her other hand, then began to roll it into a woolly ball.

I took mercy on her. "Throw it outside," I said. Then, maliciously, "There's some more by the coffee table."

"Do you think we should call the police?" She was still holding the lint.

"Well, he's gone now. He didn't mean any harm." The insides of my front teeth tasted like beet greens, that tartary dark flavor. "Margaret, I'm sorry, but I was driving all night and I can't think straight anymore. If I don't get to bed, I'm going to fall asleep on the rug." And the lint will be softer than eiderdown, Margaret, I added to myself, and I will float away to dreamland on it, pillowed by my own delicious neglect.

"If you do see him, Kay, remember Jim is home all day. He'd come right over if you called." She pulled the door open, then let the lint ball slide out of her hand onto the front steps. "Have a nice day." She walked carefully down the drive, her hands straight at her sides but not touching her hips. Would anybody but Margaret look both ways with a dead end a block away and not the sound of a car on the late fall air? She crossed safely and went up her front walk, between three matched pairs of privet and two white cement urns all covered with trussed canvas for the coming winter. When had I trussed a shrub? Her door closed behind her. I closed mine.

Shower. Jeans and blouse, dry now but squared with creases

like a woven pattern, into the bamboo hamper. Underpants and bra, not even fastened anymore, after them. My socks were black on the bottom, hopeless for restoration. Hot water burning down my back, parting my hair, pouring over both ears like drain spouts. My knees were wobbling again . . . come on, Kay, stay on your feet. No one has ever drowned in her own shower. The soap. Two cakes, Sunday's riches. Only one big towel left . . . have to do a wash tomorrow. Good, it's Monday anyway. Keep the week on schedule. Pretend nothing has happened. I patched wet footprints into the bedroom, then guided my body under the comforter where I buried myself in darkness, saying "I'm sorry, I'm sorry" over and over until it beat in my ears like blood.

19

I was riding. But on what? My hands were tied behind my back, but I was moving up and down as I rode, staying erect, not falling off, not even worried about falling off. There was a sunset. Or a dawn. Jake and Lisa were riding next to me, and someone I couldn't see was throwing great fuzzy balls at them until they were covered by a gray cloud. I could hear Jake's laugh even when the cloud hid his face. Then they were gone and I kept on riding. My mouth was dry, but there was rain coming down somewhere in the distance. When I turned my head, I could hear it coming closer. Good. We needed the moisture. But if it was so loud, why wasn't I getting wet?

The rain stopped. My hands came free, but I couldn't feel them. They lay on my face like fleshy blocks until I flung my arms aside and they went with them. I turned on my pillow and looked at the door. Billy was standing in it, dripping and steaming, bright pink except for the furry carpet down his front. He began to rub his hair dry.

"Towel's wet," he said.

"It's the only one left."

"Don't matter. What they say?—drip dry? Might as well

drip dry." He crossed to the bed, bringing a little wave of heat with him. "Move over, baby. Save some covers." He pulled the bedding aside and slid in on the bottom sheet, then threw the comforter up in a great arc and hunkered down underneath as it fell back over him. "Jesus Christ, my feet are stickin' off the end," he moaned. "No peace for the wicked." With a deep sigh he slung his legs out diagonally toward the opposite corner, shoving mine back into my own space. "Keep me warm, baby. I am altogether wore out."

It had been a long time since I had lain in that bed with a man. Well, a little over two years wasn't a lifetime—I knew that. But I'd thought about it until my mind went blank, especially in the first bitter weeks when I couldn't even bring myself to change the sheets, smothering myself to sleep at night with the last of Jeff's smell caught in the wrinkles and in the crumpled pillowcases. At first I had rocked myself on every surface, opening my skin to what was left of his underarms, his crotch, his hands which were never quite free of that turpentine smell because he showered in the morning and not at night, but after that I'd gone to sleep lying stiff as a mummy in my own exhibit case. All the smells were going away. I had finally burned the sheets in the fireplace one day when Lisa had taken Jake to the playground. Smoke ghosts played on the roof. A fire in September? Margaret had said, but not wanting to hurt me, she had said it quietly. A fire in September? That's right, Margaret, a fire in September. And in October too, and November. My charred skin will burst like a pork sausage in the broiler while I feed the kids, teach my classes, deal with the bank, make my bed with the new sheets I bought from Sears. I'm using them now, Margaret. Did you know that they have little garden plots on them with trees around and a hut in the background, all pastel and perfect? I calculate there are six garden plots across and eight down. Jake doesn't know that makes forty-eight yet, but Lisa does. The pillowcases (they're extra-long, Margaret) have two garden plots across and one down. Billy's head is right between

153

the two across now, tilted a little toward me, his beard just touching the left-hand hut. His eyes are shut; his eyebrows meet in a line across the bridge of his nose. He's taken off the Band-Aid, but his lower lip is swollen on one side and there's a cut in the corner of his mouth. I feel like kissing it. For once I'd like to make somebody well again.

I thought Billy was asleep, but he wasn't. When I kissed his mouth as softly as I could, he opened his eyes and smiled. "That's still kinda sore, baby," he said, "but most any other place'd be jest fine." Then he shifted on the pillow and reached out for my hands. "Give 'em here now, alright?" He pulled me a little closer to him and put my arms alongside his head with my hands touching his cheeks. I could feel the rough skin on his fingertips before he let go. "Jest touch me a little," he said quietly. "I like that. Puts me right t' sleep. Or wakes me up. Don't matter." His eyes were half shut, but he was looking at me. "Where you want mine?"

"On my breasts." I had never said that to anyone in my life.

"Alright." His fingertips moved up my arms and along that ridge of muscle under the shoulder, then down my sides where my ribs curved around, barely touching. "No rush. I'll git there. Takes time. Kids are at a double-bill movie, case you'd like t' know. Won't be done for three more hours. Bought 'em enough popcorn and chocolate-covered raisins t' make 'em both sick. Happy as clams."

Curved into Billy's side, I moved my hands along the line where his sideburns edged his skin. His wet hair curled on the pillow, and I pressed a handful of it together, then squeezed it out. A dribble of water ran down his cheek. "Wringin' me dry, ain't you?" He smiled.

"When did you start letting your hair grow?" I walked my fingers over his forehead, smoothing the two wrinkles. They blended in for a moment, then came back. I tried again.

"Been growin' it for a long time. Used t' let it hang in my

154

neck even when I had all the grease up front. Looked good under the hat, Tweeter said."

"Losing any?" His pillow was soaking.

"Lord, I hope not. Figger that's all I owe my Maker— couple good songs and a full head of hair."

"Nice philosophy." His fingers tightened and I caught my breath.

"Like that?"

"*Yes.*" I ran my fingers over his eyelids. "May I kiss the other side of your mouth?"

"Kin you reach?"

"If you turn your head a little more." I caught my breath again. "Billy, that really feels good."

"Shhh. Teachers talk too much. Course it feels good. What you're doin' feels good too." He turned his head toward me. "Be gentle now."

When I kissed him, he tasted first like cigarettes, as if his skin had soaked up so much honky-tonk smoke over the years that even two bars of soap wouldn't get it out. I liked it. Underneath was something like sage, maybe thyme. A warm cave. My face was wet from his beard.

"Did I really break your tooth?" I ran my finger lightly over the edges of his mouth, trying to see.

"Tooth's jest plastic anyways, baby. Broke it a long time ago when some drunk knocked me through a window in Austin. I'll git it glued when I git back. Don't worry."

"I didn't mean to hurt you."

"Yes you did. Woulda broke all my teeth if you'd had the chance. Mean little lady, you are. But you kiss nice. Nice tits too, with them pointy nipples. Come on up on me. Wanna see what else you got that's nice."

"You've got too much hair, Billy. I'd get buried." I ran my thumbs along the lines on each side of his mouth, testing how deep they were. They were deeper than I had thought.

"Try it this way, then. Rock my hammock." He turned all

the way on his side, like a big wall across the bed, and eased himself up against me.

"What?"

"Rock my hammock. It ain't hard t' do. Gimme your hand again."

"I thought you wanted it up there."

"Feels good there, feels better down here. Mmmm. Back 'n' forth. Give them little fellers a swing too. I like that, yes I do. You got a good hand, you know that? Got me all woke up here. Mmmmmm. Ride me down easy, baby. Ride me on down."

"Do it to me." I had never said that to anyone either.

"Only got two hands. How about this?" Pause. "Baby, you are *ready*. Go for it. That is *right*. Play that gig, baby. Listen t' the music. Nothin' like them cowboy songs, is there? Dobro and steel. Best music there is, baby. Listen t' ol' Billy, he's the man who knows. Feel them drums, baby? Feel them drums?"

20

THE BEDROOM had turned half dark when I felt the mattress shift. Billy was getting up. "Sleep tight, baby," he said, balling the comforter around me like a Christmas package. "Keep warm. Be right back." Next, later, I heard Jake's voice, backed by a tinny syncopation from the kitchen. The stereo went on—Side B of *Cowboy Lovin'*. A roar from Billy, a flare of giggles from Lisa. Stereo off. Jake put on his Sesame Street record. Stereo off again. A scream from Jake, followed by "Goddamnit, you two, how am I supposed t' *cook?*" Giggles from both Jake and Lisa. Stereo on again, this time an old Calloway album, greaser days. Billy was singing along. The phone rang, then someone picked it up. The singing trebled in volume and the phone crashed back on the receiver. Billy hooted. It sounded as if someone was dancing. Will you dance with me, you three? Will you ask me for the next dance? Will you waltz across Texas with Jake, Lisa, the freshman students, two guinea pigs, and me? Billy, will you waltz across Texas with me?

21

Night. Or absolute darkness anyway. A toilet flushing somewhere. Music still on the stereo, but old country this time, Hank Williams, not Junior, faded and monochromatic even in this gussied-up stereo version. I hadn't listened to that in a long time. It was nice. I should get up, though. I hadn't spent so much time sleeping in years.

Disengaging myself, I slid out of bed, shivered, then walked to the closet. Billy wouldn't have done the wash by now, would he? But something should still be clean if I could just get along without another towel. I put on the blue bathrobe I hardly ever wore because it was too long. Cozy, though. The wool rasped against my nipples as I pulled the front together. Go back in, you little devils. My God, I was still wet. Where was the Kleenex?

Somewhere in the distance, Hank Williams' solo became a duet, resolved into a solo again, then ended. Music in the night, Kay. How long since you've heard music in the night, you who go to bed at ten, drink tea and read the Victorians until your neck gets stiff, fight through your dreams until five, then lie awake and listen for the first mourning dove? A very long time.

Billy was in the kitchen, spilling over in one of the Pennsylvania Dutch chairs pushed back from the table. The dishwasher was running and the counter tops wiped. Bent over his guitar, his back was to the door so he didn't hear me as I came across the living room, not even tiptoeing. He tried a chord, then another, shook his head and went back to the first one, playing it over and over until the new sounds joined a gentle wave of aftertones just like them. His left hand moved along the frets while his right teased out a tiny high melody against the chorded line. From where I stood, I saw the edge of his jaw shift; he must be smiling. Another chord, strummed out and stretched to breaking, another spate of melody. So softly that I had to bend forward to hear the words, Billy began to sing.

> *"Found me a little lady, likes me fine.*
> *Needs a man in her bed, I'm lonely in mine.*
> *Hear that music, baby . . ."*

His voice rasped, and he coughed. He started again, leaning his head down so the notes came out just inches from his ear.

> *"Hear that music, baby, touch me where it feels good.*
> *I think you would.*

"Whee," said Billy, with a little whistle. "She *would.*" He crossed his legs and hoisted the guitar to a new position.

> *"Body needs a woman, can't make it alone.*
> *Head's gotta picture, road for a man t' roam.*
> *Take what I got, babe, holdin' each other tight . . .*

"Don't like that," said Billy to himself. He tried a different chord. "Don't like that neither. Shit." He stopped for a minute and rubbed the back of his neck. "Alright." The third chord pleased him, and he stamped one boot on the linoleum.

"You need a last line." I moved up behind him and began to massage his neck, digging my thumbs down on both sides of his spinal column. His curls kept getting in the way, but I finally channeled my hands down to his skin while he pushed his head back against me.

"Got it already. Keep that up, OK? Feels good. Listen and tell me what you think.

"Body needs a woman, can't make it alone.
Head's gotta picture, road for a man t' roam.
Take what I got, babe, holdin' each other tight.
Make your own picture, 'cause I'm headin' on out
tonight."

The guitar faded out with three slow minor chords, distant and terribly sad. "Ain't bad," said Billy.

"Did you just write that?"

"Been runnin' it 'round since we was comin' back from the Cities. This prairie sure as hell puts the mind on music, nothin' much else t' think about, it's so goddamn flat. Least we had them little hills some places in West Texas. Boy could think 'bout what was behind the next one."

"That sounds like a song too." I bent over to kiss his forehead but miscalculated and got the curls instead.

"Wanna write it with me?"

"I'd better get something to eat first or I'll collapse." Suddenly my stomach came alive, and I followed its bidding to the refrigerator, where I ferreted out a package of extravagant pastrami and some mustard. The bread was just this side of mold in the breadbox, but I found two untouched pieces in the middle of the loaf. "What time *is* it?"

"One thirty in the mornin'. Witchin' hour."

"I haven't been up this late since graduate school. Want some milk?"

"Don't drink much plain milk." Billy looked at the carton as if something alive were about to come out of it.

160

"Sprite? Orange juice? Jake left a little cider too."

"Got any beer?"

I hadn't expected that, but it was perfectly logical. "No. I wasn't planning on a visit from a beer drinker. Besides, it'd probably knock you right out, considering how sleep-deprived you are." Too many syllables. But what was wrong with that? He wasn't *stupid*.

Billy was rubbing a spot off the finish of the blue guitar with a paper napkin, and he looked so busily domestic that I wasn't ready for the edge in his voice. "Don't tell me what I kin drink, baby." He wet the napkin with his tongue and rubbed some more. "A man drinks what he *drinks*." Then he looked up and tossed his hair off his forehead with one hand. "I'll pick some up tomorrow." His mouth twitched, then tilted at the corners as he broke a piece off my sandwich and swallowed it down without chewing.

"It is tomorrow. Or is that sentence impossible?"

"Wouldn't know, baby, you're the one went t' college. Don't matter." As if in reconciliation, he swept his arm toward me, narrowly avoiding the remains of the sandwich. "Wanna try 'n' play this?" He whanged his hand across the guitar strings.

"Maybe you can just explain it to me, Billy," I said, as I slipped the tail end of the pastrami inside my mouth and leaned toward him. "Truthfully, I could never even learn the piano when I was a kid." It would have been fun, though, I thought, if we had a month or two to work on it.

"Hell, I ain't no *explainer*. Been doin' this since the Alamo, but I ain't no good *explainin'*. Seems like a picker jest knows what he's doin'." He was rubbing the napkin over the finish again.

I leaned over further and touched his watch, then the skin next to it. "When did you first hit it big, Billy?" I asked, running my mind along a string of radio stations, ratty dance halls, old cars full of guitars and worn-out pickers on their way to the next show. Was it really like all those books said?

"Oh, 'bout '64 or '65, I reckon, playin' them clubs in West Texas. When the band started gittin' booked for three, four weeks at a time in one place, we was on the way. First real good break was Jimbo's Lounge in Amarillo, big crowds every night, couldn't hardly fit in that old roadhouse. My first wife was playin' piano with us then and layin' it out for me backstage between sets." He laughed. "Was a wonder I could walk. Last night there, the boys gave me the biggest goddamn metal spike you ever saw, painted silver. Took Tweeter and D.G. both t' drag it on stage, two of 'em 'bout dyin'. Thought the place was gonna come apart. I was laughin' so hard I fell off that goddamn stage on somebody's table, broke four glasses and 'bout cut myself t' death. Jill sure didn't think it was all that goddamn funny."

Right on, Jill, I thought, and was struck with an irrelevant vision of the two of them, her face a white oval, thumping at each other behind some backstage soundboard. At first it was funny, then it wasn't funny at all. Not one bit. "I suppose there's lots of sex on the country-western circuit," I commented, trying to be objective at least in my choice of words. He was spread out over the back of his chair, winking one eye at the overhead light, then the other.

"Baby, what you got t' understand is that it ain't the *sex*. Screwin' you kin git anywheres, all kinds. Some of it jest blows you out, cools you down. Some of it you feel for a while. Mebbe once in a long time it comes out a song. And *that's* what it's for. You start pickin', and you remember how it was, and how she eased you real good, and how you felt like you was really doin' somethin'. All them others, once they was done, they was done. This one you're goin' t' pass on."

It didn't make sense. But maybe it was just another grading system; I certainly knew about those. "How many wives have you had, Billy?" I asked from somewhere. Did he keep book on how they rated?

162

"What?" He was taking off his guitar.

"How many wives have you had?"

He looked puzzled. "What you gittin' at, baby?"

"Sex, wives, songs—I thought there might be a connec-tion." *My* voice had the edge now. "All I know about you is what I read on your album covers. Maybe I just want to know a little more. Anything wrong with that?"

He rubbed his forehead. "Lemme think. Three. No, four, countin' the one before Jill."

"You said *she* was your first wife."

"Well, did you mean law wives, or wimmen who was actin' like they was my wife?"

"Oh, who knows what I meant, for God's sake?" I replanted myself on my chair seat. "How did you ever get time to be famous if you were spending every free hour you had chasing women?"

Billy laughed, then lunged out of his chair and grabbed my shoulders, pulling me back on top of him as he slid down into his seat again. He rubbed his chin in my hair while he reached for the blue guitar. "Baby, the only wimmen that matters is twofold. First is the one a man is with. Also first is the one he wrote the song about. As of this moment, one forty-five by my daddy's old watch, you are both them wim-men. Now set here on me and lemme show you how t' pick."

22

"Mom, I can't find my shoes."

"Ask Lisa, honey, she'll probably know."

"Lisa can't find her shoes either. But I ate two bowls of Alpha Bits." Behind the door, his voice began to drift away.

I opened my eyes. No mourning doves; the tree was quiet. For once I felt warm, and the prospect of finding two pairs of shoes was not intimidating. What time was it, for heaven's sake? I pulled myself up on my elbow and looked at the bedside clock. Seven thirty. That wasn't too bad, and I hadn't even set the alarm.

I sank back on my pillow. So it was possible to sink back on one's pillow like all those negligeed heroines, to loll in the riches of the dawn. The mirror on my little French vanity, Louis XVI imitation but still older than even my mother would have been, caught a glitter from the window and tossed it back to me. The sun must be coming through. Mathilde, relax. But my breasts weren't big enough for a French novel. Oh yes they were, yes they were.

"Billy, I'm getting up. The kids have lost all their shoes.

What do you want for breakfast?" I zipped into my slacks and Panama pullover, dotted on perfume. I hadn't used it for so long the stopper was stuck in the bottle with gunk, and I had to dig it out with my fingernails. "Billy, do you want Canadian bacon? I have some left. Do you want to eat after the kids go to school? I think I'll put a load in the washer now—are your dirty clothes in the bathroom?"

Silence.

He couldn't have evaporated, I knew, though a strip of tension ran down my back as I turned toward the bed. But he was there, lying on his back diagonally so all of him would fit, head under the pillow, his chording hand thrown across the comforter, fingers curled. Jake's fingers had curled like that; they still did when he was sleeping deeply and his dreams were sweet. I sat down next to Billy on the bed and put on my socks, then my shoes. He didn't move. I slid my index finger into his hand, rubbing it gently along the insides of his fingers, then between them, then down across the top of his palm where the lines started. Across in a little excursion, then back again to make an X. Down to his wrist. He was still wearing the old Elgin, jammed halfway up to his elbow. Trying not to jiggle the bed too much, I slid myself down next to him, moved his fingers open a little, and kissed his palm where the life line began. I left a little damp spot where I'd sealed it with my tongue.

"Don't break 'em."

"What?"

"Don't break 'em. DON'T BREAK 'EM!"

"Break what?" I had never been more gentle. His hand still lay on the comforter, half shut and unmoving, but the tendons in his wrist were twitching and his other hand was grabbing frantically at the pillow over his head.

"Christ, that hurts. Mmmm. *Hurts.*"

"Billy, you must be dreaming. Everything's all right." I reached out to touch him, but he turned aside, flung his pillow to the floor, his eyes still tight shut, and began to roll his head back and forth hard on the sheet. Even Jake never had nightmares like that.

"Can't pick no more. Shit. Shee-e-t. Jesus, that hurts." Sweat was spotting his forehead and collecting in his eye sockets. Without knowing what I was supposed to do, I leaned over and wiped his face with my hand, lifting his wet hair away from his eyes. His free hand caught at mine and pulled it away; for a minute I thought he was going to hit me, but he kept holding on.

"Mom, I found *one* shoe. I made you cocoa with brown sugar because I spilled the white. Can I come in?" Jake rattled the knob, then sat down on the hall floor, leaning against the door from the other side. The crack underneath darkened.

"Wait a sec, honey." My voice cracked. I braced myself to try to get my hand free, but Billy had already let it go. His eyes were open.

"Are you OK?" I whispered. He sat up in bed next to me, looking at his hand, not blinking. I leaned over and massaged his shoulders, rubbing through his T-shirt. It had a rip under the collar.

"Shit." He flexed his fingers, closed them into a fist, opened them again. "I was dreamin'." He lay back on the sheet.

"More like a nightmare!" All at once I was shaking. "Go back to sleep. I'll take care of the kids." He had sweated through his T-shirt too, and I was afraid he'd catch cold, so I pulled the top sheet back over him and folded the comforter halfway up his chest. With a sigh he flopped over on his belly, hands hidden underneath. I displaced Jake from the door and went out to give the troops instructions. Lisa was running down the front steps, but she came back up on the porch, frost settling on her damp hair, to give me a kiss.

23

MONDAY'S CHILD is fair of face/ Tuesday's child is full of grace/ Wednesday's child is full of woe/ Thursday's child has far to go/ Saturday's child works hard for a living, while Friday's and Sunday's children are too incredibly lucky to be allowed to exist. This Monday I almost felt that I might allow them to, however. I did the wash, picked up the house again, swept up the sugar, watered plants, finished correcting the "Culture Heroes" essay I had unfortunately assigned, trimmed my bangs, explained to Margaret that the Mysterious Stranger was really my visiting brother-in-law who hadn't been able to find my house and had been having some other problems besides, and finally drove out to the shopping center to buy Billy two packages of new T-shirts, extra-large. For lunch I finished the pastrami, then went out again to get groceries. I swept through the Shop-Rite aisles with such fluid generosity that my bill was $87.32, and I had only $69 in my billfold. Normally that would have meant anger and humiliation; today I just told them to hold the bags for half an hour, drove home, and went to get some money from Billy. He was still asleep, breathing slow and deep, comforter heaped on the floor, and he wouldn't wake up even when I tickled him. I found his wallet in his jeans (which were under the bed), took a twenty, drove back to the store, floating higher above the pavement than even the Trail Duster normally carried me, and brought back all the groceries. Lisa came home from school in time to help me unpack, and then Jake stopped by for his bedroom slippers before going to play with Brian. We sat at the kitchen table eating Fig Newtons from Shop-Rite together, all three of us damp and newly born. Billy was still asleep.

"Won't he cook our supper?" For the first time I could remember, Jake seemed reluctant to leave for the after-school ritual at Brian's.

"He said he'd make tacos if we had the shells," Lisa added. "I told him Jake only ate the shells and the lettuce, but Billy said that was the cheap way anyhow, and he'd make Jake's separate."

"I eat the cheese too!"

"I wasn't making fun of you, Jake." Lisa's voice had a motherly tone. "You can eat your tacos any way you want. Billy said he'd let you use his knife to chop the onion too."

"Mom, wake him up!" A Fig Newton in each hand, Jake thumped on the table. One of the cookies crumbled under the impact, and he bent over to lick up the crumbs with his tongue. "He's my *friend*."

"Kids, look. It's four fifteen, right? We eat at six. Jake, if you play with Brian a while, there'll still be time to chop, and by then Billy will be up anyway. Lisa, you can finish your history paper" (how had I managed to remember that it was due tomorrow?) "and then I can check it over after supper. Is that OK? Are your lives arranged to your liking?" I pushed my chair back, got up, slid around between them, and hugged them both. Jake gave me a crumby kiss in return; Lisa held herself tightly erect, then thawed an arm and slid it around my waist. Both of them got up at the same time. "See you,

Mom," they said in unison as they left the room. Their discretion was embarrassing.

I wiped off the table slowly, making damp half circles with the sponge, then erasing them with half circles in the other direction. As I swabbed, the furnace turned on, and a moment later the dry smell of newly warmed dust came up the kitchen heat vent. The rattly hum brought a message from the heart of the house—warm you, warm you, a percussion spangle, then warm you again. Exactly the way I felt.

I dried off the table and went to look at Billy. The late afternoon light had been mostly blocked by the big tree, but at the corner where Jake had hollowed out his clubhouse, a few rays filtered through. Standing in the doorway, I saw the room illuminated like one of those Rembrandt paintings, all browns and blacks, with one light source that picked out the edges of whatever it flowed by. Until my eyes adjusted, I wasn't sure if he was awake or not, but as I ran my fingers along the frame of the doorway, a great upheaval tore through the bed and Billy's voice came out of the middle of it. "No matter how long you look, baby, I ain't goin' t' go away," he growled. With his beard he looked like an old Dutch figure, some burgher, scales and watchpiece. No. The Netherlands didn't provide cowboy hats, and he was wearing the garden plot pillowcase too, tied around his shoulders like an oversized bandanna. As I smiled, he draped the sheet demurely over his legs and lap.

"Did you just wake up? The kids are off doing their business, dreaming of your tacos. Only you could love Jake for not eating the filling."

"Hell, you got a bargain in that kid. You buy the stuff I need t' make 'em?"

"Yes indeed. Matter of fact, I spent twenty dollars of yours along with a good chunk of mine. I'll pay you back when I go to the bank." I knelt on the bed and started to untie the pillowcase, his beard bristling against the insides of my arms. "Do you want the change?" I asked.

"You kin put it in my pocket." He folded back the sheet around his waist and waved it to one side like a Spanish dancer.

"Come on, you nut. Get up and comb your beard. If you do a good enough job, you can take me dancing tonight, waltz across Fargo with an English teacher." I began to shove at him from the side.

"Knock me over, you'll never git me up."

"I'll call the kids. Three against one."

"Goin' back t' sleep. Dreams is better 'n you." Like a hairy mountain, he began to slide inexorably back under the sheet.

"Not your dreams." I leaned over and put my arms around him, even though from this angle they hardly reached. "Remember this morning when I was getting up? You were having a nightmare—I was afraid you were going to hit me."

"Never hit no wimmen. Don't remember no nightmare." He was pulling the sheet over his head. "Git off me, you little lady. Drivin' me crazy." His left hand reached out to anchor the sheet, and I took it in mine.

"This hand, remember? I kissed it and you started saying that it hurt. No, first you said something about breaking. You were sweating like mad." I touched the tips of his fingers. "What were you dreaming, Billy? Do you remember?"

For a moment Billy let his hand stay in mine while the sheet slipped down to a line of folds across his chest. Then he took his other hand and removed mine, setting it aside like a china cup. He interlaced his fingers, making one of those cathedral ceilings kids fool each other with, then checked from both sides. Big strong fingers, all right.

"Long time ago." He stopped. "Shit, that *was* a long time ago. I was screwin' with the wife of the guy who owned the club we was playin' in Dallas. Goddamn stupid thing t' do, but Jill run out on me and this lady was quite a looker for somebody old as she was. Worth the fuckin'." He stopped again. "Shit," he said, "I shouldn'ta said 'fuck.' " Under his beard some pink color was rising.

"Norman Mailer says 'fuck.' So does John Updike. I can handle it. What kind of repressed western chivalry are you suffering from?"

"Some words a man don't use in front of no lady."

"Sexist."

Billy looked hurt. "That's jest the way it is," he said. The story dangled. I picked up his hand again and put it in my lap, running my index finger over his watchband. Had it really been his daddy's watch?

"Anyhow, we was havin' a relationship, and her old man found out. We had a fight and he broke my fingers." Billy bit his lower lip, then winced. He pulled his hand out of mine again.

"Were you dreaming about that?"

"S'pose so."

"Did it stop you from playing the guitar?" Stupid question.

"Couldn't pick till they was outta the cast. Then it was alright."

"Did it hurt?" Oh shut up, Kay! What have you ever broken?

Billy had both hands under the sheet. "Don't remember no more," he said. "Reckon it did for a while." Then he threw the sheet to one side and rolled across the bed. "I'm gittin' up, OK? Got a big fryin' pan?"

Dear Billy,

*I cannot believe that you are standing in my
kitchen, Jake's hand buried in yours like a
peach pit, while the two of you massacre onions
on the cutting board. Lisa is perched next
to you with a box of Kleenex on the ready to
wipe up your tears, laughing so hard at both
of you that she is crying herself. Your knife
has* BILLY *imbedded in ivory on the handle,
as well as a sinister blade that I would never
let Jake near if you weren't helping him.
The onions glisten like pearls.*

*When I opened the taco shell box, not a single
one was broken. Every other time I've done it,
the bottom has been littered with fragments
like potato chips. Did you will them whole
all the way from Texas?*

Kay

24

"OK, YOU TWO. Got your homework done?"

"I had to cut out a picture of a sink. This was the only one in Mom's *New Yorker*." Snuggled up under Billy's arm on the sofa, Jake pulled a crumpled square of glossy paper out of his corduroys and waved it around for a wide audience. The sink was one of those gold and platinum penthouse models, probably with the owner's initials in diamonds on it somewhere. A woman of indeterminate age was leaning on it.

"Sure as hell wouldn't know how t' shave at that goddamn thing." Billy helped Jake fold the square with only one crease and put it back in his pocket. "What about you, little lady?" Lisa was across the room reading a magazine, looking at Billy whenever she could manage without his knowing she was doing it.

"Mom looked over my history paper with me. It's OK." She giggled. "You don't shave anyway." Excited by her daring, she turned a handful of pages at once.

"Might start again one of these days. No law against it. Figger if I kin cook, I kin shave, right?"

"You're a good cook, Billy." Jake had his sink out again and was admiring it.

"Say that one more time, hombre. I like t' hear them words."

"You're a *good cook*!" Jake thumped Billy in the stomach for emphasis, and they both rolled off the sofa onto the carpet. Stuck together, Jake squealing, they crawled and wiggled toward the stairway, Lisa not even pretending to read anymore as she kept her eyes on them.

Almost wishing I was on the floor too, I got up from the director's chair and took up the role of referee. "Time for bed, Jake. Lisa, maybe you'd better go up too. You have early chorus tomorrow." Billy and Jake had reached the bottom of the stairs and were lying flat out on the hall linoleum, Billy's boots stretching over the edge into the kitchen. Both of them had their eyes shut and were holding their faces immobile. Their hands were crossed on their chests.

"Mom, it's only nine! Nine thirty. I want to stay up and listen to records."

Well, why not? I was a soft touch. But Billy answered her for me. "How's about I sing you two a bedtime song? Better 'n them goddamn records, the real thing." He hoisted himself to his feet and waltzed over to Lisa, who was trying to hide herself in her magazine again but had gotten it upside down by mistake. "C'mon, beautiful." He had her by both hands and lifted her to her feet, swinging her across the living room in some kind of Texas two-step. "Be right back, baby," he said as the two of them swept past me. He hoisted his guitar from the front hall, then herded both kids upstairs. Next came a burst of incoherent chatter. Silence, followed by water running. More chatter. Jake's questioning voice rose, with Billy responding "Shit, they look clean t' me." A murmur and several small crashes. "What song you want?" asked Billy.

" 'Ninety-nine Bottles of Beer on the Wall,' " asserted Jake. It was the longest song he knew.

" 'My Woman, My Woman, My Wife,' " stated Lisa loudly. Good Lord, I had no idea she'd ever heard of that sentimental gush.

"Jesus. I ain't no Marty Robbins." Billy sounded disconcerted. "Lemme decide. C'mon! It's me what's gotta sing." Sounds of scuffling. "Now you two git in them damn beds. I'll set myself right here where you kin both hear." An emphatic thump directly over my head. Silence again. He must be tuning the blue guitar. "Alright. Shut up, you two. Big star doin' a show here. Listen now." Drifting down the stairway came the insidious notes of "Sunday Morning Coming Down," Kristofferson's classic loner's meditation. How in the world had he ever arrived at that?

While he sang, I knew I should pick up, do something. There wasn't much to do, though; Billy was probably the only man on earth who cleaned up after himself in the kitchen. My papers were corrected too. As his last notes died away, I gave myself permission to do the same and curled into the sofa arm. I might even get some sleep tonight. We might.

"Good night, Billy. Rachel Bear says good night. Blue Walrus says good night. Frog says—"

"Jake, stop it!" Lisa shouted. A pause. "That was nice, Billy," she said just loud enough so I could hear it.

" 'Night, you two. Sleep tight." His boots tattooed the hall, and I hardly had time to get my own feet back on the carpet before he was in the living room. He laughed sheepishly as he walked over to me.

"That *was* nice, Billy. Not a very happy song, though."

"Jest the way it is sometimes. Ol' Kristofferson, he's been through the mill." He had my hand. "C'mon, baby. Let's go drivin'."

"What?"

"Wanna drive, see the world. See some *cattle*."

"Billy, I have to teach tomorrow."

"Shit, it ain't late."

"Besides, there aren't any cattle."

"Ain't this s'posed t' be the west?"

"Yes, but not your west. Sunflowers and soybeans, tractors and three-wheelers." He had me in the front hall and was putting on his hat. "What will the kids think?"

With a sound that needed no amplification, Billy bellowed up the stairs. "Goin' for a drive, me 'n' your mom. Back soon!" I expected yowls, but both voices shouted back "OK!" without any objections at all. We were out the door in ten more seconds, clutching our jackets, and backing out of the driveway before I could catch my breath for another word.

"OK, baby. I drive, you direct. Where to?"

"You didn't mean that about cattle, did you?" We were drifting aimlessly down Fifth Street, swooping by parked cars in wide parabolas.

"Sure did. Gotta show you a cow."

"I haven't any choice?"

"Nope. We're ridin' out on the prairie, and you're hangin' on t' me so you don't fall. Ridin' like wildfire, baby. Ol' Paint, he's still gotta helluva lotta life in him. Point me where t' go."

"We could try Bonanzaville and see if they have any cows to go with those old buildings." I was getting caught up in the fantasy. "No, I know a better place. The university barns. Turn right here and go straight. The Animal Science kids have herds out there. But we'll get arrested. Nobody goes out there at night."

"Time somebody did." Billy churned around the corner. "Why you got that seat belt on, baby? I gotta stretch way over if I wanna give you a little hug."

"Why don't you have yours on? You could get killed."

"Didn't have yours on comin' back from them Cities." His eyes were full of mischief.

"I was crazy that night." Certainly I was too old to blush.

"Shit, so was I. Wonder we didn't both drown in that goddamn ditch."

"We'd have to have tried awfully hard in those two inches of muck." I heard a giggle. Who was that? Me!

Already we were on the west edge of Fargo, my long and narrow town pressed against the side of the winding Red River. The university buildings were still all lit up. Past the library, past the English building tight to the ground at the end of the long driveway. In front of the gym, boys in sweat pants were demonstrating karate with straight-armed lunges. "Hell, they wouldn't last long in no bar," stated Billy as they disappeared behind us.

"Did you punch people when you were little, Billy?" I didn't dare ask him if he had played cowboys.

Billy looked at me with his forehead wrinkled. "Well, sure. Kids always fight. Me and my brother 'bout killed each other every chance we got. When we was little fellers, we used t' go to it till we was both bawlin'. Never would quit. 'Bout drove my mama crazy."

"Which one of you was bigger?"

"Jesus, what you wanna know that for? He was a year younger, but we was the same size pretty much all along. I outgrew him 'bout the time I quit high school and started my band."

"Are you friends now?" Up ahead I could see the first university barn, white-painted, set back from the road like a medieval estate.

Billy was very quiet. "Don't see him much. Night he graduated, we had a big fight. We both been drinkin', but I got started sooner 'cause I didn't hafta march down no aisle. I cut him up pretty bad, put him in the hospital. He don't want no part of me since then."

I sat quietly too for a moment, then turned to ask Billy what his brother's name was. A car sped by going in the other direction, and in the flash of its light, his face was grim. I didn't say anything.

We were almost parallel with the barn now, and as we approached, I directed Billy up the driveway. There was a big parking circle right up against the corral that was built along one side, bordered by clumps of tall grass the mower hadn't been able to catch. Billy parked up as near the fence as he could get, then turned off the lights. We sat for a moment. "Where's them cattle?" he asked.

"Let's hope in the pasture. I don't feel up to breaking into a university barn." Billy was out of the car already, leaning his arms on top of the fence and craning his neck around. I hurried to catch up to him, and when I finally did, we stood together peering into the darkness for cattle. I knew the university boys raised goats, too, and sheep. Hopefully I had the right corral.

"Don't see nothin', goddamnit. Gotta be some cattle 'round here someplace. *Smells* like it." I was straining my eyes as far as I could into the depths of the pasture, trying to sort out something bovine. When I looked around, Billy was halfway over the fence.

"Billy! You're trespassing!" He had one leg slung along the top already.

"Goddamn right." He dropped to the ground on the other side and disappeared into the night. "Whoo-ee!" His voice would have awakened absolutely anybody. "Whoo-ee! Git yourselves movin', dogies. Whoo-ee!"

When I couldn't see him anymore, though the rough echo of his baritone still swept back occasionally, I resigned myself to waiting on the other side of the fence, my cheek and hands against the wood. I had a momentary temptation to join him, but even if I could get myself to the top of the fence, I would never have the courage to drop down into the pasture. Someday I was going to own a house without an upstairs. I rubbed my fingers gently along the wood, then my cheek. Smooth.

From the distance a blurred shape loomed against the darkness. *Two* shapes. A great shuffle of feet scuffed through the grass, along with some miscellaneous whoofings and heavy breathing. A large Holstein cow, udder flapping pendulously just above the pasture grass, was hurrying toward the fence, looking like some Norwegian matron racing through the aisles of the Shop-Rite, late for a PTA meeting. Behind her Billy was running, waving his hat to urge her on. She made amazing speed for anyone so large and milk-laden, the one eye that I could see rolling with indignation at her having been unwillingly transformed into a Texas longhorn. Just past me, Billy cornered her at the edge of the corral, whooping and hollering as he leaped in front of her. Her bony rear was wedged into the corner of the fence, ropy tail flapping against the logs. A desperate *moo* drowned out even Billy's herding obscenities.

"Billy! Stop it! She'll have a heart attack! Or you will!"

"Hey, baby, this is livin'! Lemme see if I kin git her down, jest like in them roundups." He flung himself at Bossy's head, trying to get a grip on her skull. Without horns, she was impossible to grasp, and he ended up flopped over her backbone, swearing and twisting at her ears. Suddenly she seemed to discover her natural weapons after a lifetime of university domesticity, and she began to kick frantically. With Billy draped over her neck while he held the top of her head in a determined embrace, she extracted herself from the corner and began to gallop, bellowing, toward the other end of the pasture. Billy's "Whoo-ee" drifted off into the dark.

Ride 'em, cowboy! In the cool night air I began to laugh. Who would believe this? Certainly not that poor cow; her cud would be curdled in every one of her many stomachs, and she would attribute it to some bad grass. Dear God, this was no time for puns. I laughed harder, and Billy wasn't even there to share the joke. Oh yes he was. A little ways down from me, he came up to the fence, shaking his head, and clambered over. When he ambled up to where I was standing, he smelled total barnyard.

"You are absolutely crazy, you know that?"

Grinning, he put his arms around me, and for a moment I relaxed in his embrace until I realized he was rubbing something unpleasant on the back of my neck. "Stop it! What are you doing, you nut?"

"Jest sharin' the wealth, baby. Goddamn cow knocked me off right in the muck. Got it all over my shirt too. What I git for playin' cowboy." He took his hat off and shook his shaggy head. "Should be glad she didn't walk me down like a carpet, I s'pose." He ran his thumbs down my cheeks. "There. Now you look like one of them Indians. A *little* Indian. C'mon, let's go git somethin' t' eat."

"Looking like this?"

"Whatthehell, I didn't mean no place fancy." He gave my rear a gentle swat as I climbed into the Trail Duster. "Little honest dirt hadn't ought t' make that much diff'rence in ol' Fargo anyhow." Great waves of cow filled the car as we pulled out of the lot and back onto the highway.

"With you beside me, I can handle anything." It was too dark for me to check my dirty face in the rearview mirror. I started to fasten my seat belt and then didn't bother. What the hell.

Billy had started to hum a little as the first buildings of Fargo's minimal suburbs appeared along the side of the road. "Ain't had my arms 'round a cow, leastways that kind, since I was twenty-one. On my birthday. Bet Tweeter I could git this ol' steer down in less'n three minutes. Did it too, but that goddamn steer landed on top of me and broke my ankle. I was flyin' so high I didn't know what was wrong till 'bout four in the mornin' when I couldn't git my boot off. Tweeter still gives me hell 'bout that."

"It's a wonder you've lived as long as you have." I opened the window to dilute the cow.

"Gotta keep goin', you know. Once you quit, ain't nothin' left." He was humming again, an old favorite of mine called "But That's Alright." Then he reached over and ran his hand through my hair. "You always got them funny little curls?"

"They aren't curls, they're cowlicks. And yes, they're always there." His hand was around my back, fingers beating out the rhythm of his song on my shoulder. I slid over nearer him and hummed along.

"This place OK?" I hadn't noticed, but we were near the university again, almost to Roger's, the traditional student sandwich shop with its fake wood shingles and its advertised specials stuck in the front window. The R on the fluorescent sign had been out ever since I could remember, but no one had any trouble identifying the place. We pulled alongside.

"Sure." I hadn't been there in more than two years, but Roger's hadn't undergone any revolutions. Billy swung into the lot, parked, and got us both down, ushering me to the asphalt with an Elizabethan flourish. Under the remaining neon letters, I could see that he was pretty much of a mess, smears on his shirt and jeans, dirty hands, and a great black splotch running down his right cheek. He carried it off well.

Once we were inside, we found a booth enough out of the way not to shock any potential customers. Roger's had been pretty nice once, but years of student invasion had worn the orange carpet down to a river of brown in the middle, with little speckles of cigarette burns. The booths were like old church pews except for the exaggerated height of their backs and the split vinyl padding, tobacco brown, on the seats. Even the menus were brown around the edges, as if the light had gotten through the plastic coatings.

"How can we be hungry after those tacos?" It was a rhetorical question. For whatever reason, I was perfectly capable of eating again.

"Don't know 'bout you, baby, but I been workin'. Drivin' them cattle. Hard life out there on that goddamn range." Billy had the menu at arm's length, looking over the sandwich selection. Good heavens, was he getting farsighted in his middle years too?

"Do you want cocoa?"

"Rather drink yours tomorrow, baby. Beer. One of them double burgers. Order for me, OK? I'm goin' t' the john." When he unfolded at the edge of the booth, his head reached above the coat hooks on the wall. Mutt and Jeff, that was us.

The waitress, when she came up, was a very young student, assignments and football games written all over her soft face. "Readytoorder?" she chanted, her mind far away, and a good thing too, with my striped cheeks and general disreputable appearance. I told her what Billy wanted, got egg salad and tea for myself, and watched her check off the appropriate squares on her little pad. She had a peach-colored blusher smoothed so carefully along her cheekbones that even my attentive scrutiny didn't discover where her natural skin started. Did she spend that much time on her philosophy homework? Hardly. She moved off toward the kitchen with a saunter so feminine that her polyester skirt did a little walk all on its own.

I put the menu back behind the napkin holder, straightened the salt and pepper shakers, and checked the ketchup to make sure the bottle wasn't clogged. It wasn't. Did Billy's brother have a beard too? Every time a little piece of his background floated up out of West Texas, I set it aside like a puzzle piece surfacing after years under the bed. Three years ago, what in my past would have located me in Roger's-without-the-R tonight, eating egg salad while Billy Calloway washed off cow manure in the men's bathroom? I was the one who should be taking the philosophy course, that was for sure. Sliding a pen out of my purse, I drew a smiley face on Billy's napkin, then set it back on the other side of the booth next to his silverware. He shouldn't be too farsighted to see that.

Back by the entrance I heard a voice, familiar. It got louder, punctuated by the waitress's attempts at breaking in. "Jesus Christ!" I heard Billy say. "You musta seen her. You was here all the time!" Who in the world could he be looking for in Fargo? The restaurant was practically empty anyway.

I started sliding over on the cushion, forcing out little tufts of stuffing as my rear moved over the crack. At the edge, I stuck one leg out into the aisle and looked around. Billy was waving his arms at the waitress, who looked stunned as she pressed herself back against the cash register. "Goddamnit, she ain't here!" shouted Billy.

I stood up, holding on to the table. "I'm over here," I said, modulating my voice halfway between polite conversation and

182

a scream. "Who are you looking for, for heaven's sake?"

Billy dropped his arms and shot across the room to the booth. Like a snowplow, he swept me back along the cushion and plopped in beside me. His voice was rough. "Jesus, I thought you run out on me."

"Why would I run out? Besides, you have the car keys." He looked so desolate that I put one hand on his cheek. "Billy, what's the matter? I'm right here. They'll bring our food any minute."

"Don't feel like eatin'." He rubbed his eyes with his hand, not much cleaner even after a trip to the bathroom. "Where was you? I couldn't see you nowheres."

"I was right here all the time." Was he nearsighted too?

"Stood by that door and looked over at every goddamn booth. Wasn't a brown head like yours stickin' up any place." He rubbed his forehead. "Thought you'd got mad, didn't want t' wait for me no more." He drained his glass of water, then slammed it back on the table.

"Billy, when I sit in one of these booths, I'm so short that my head doesn't show over the top. Couldn't you remember where I was?"

He hesitated, then shook his head slowly. "Guess I jest figgered you up and took off without me."

"Why should I do that? You're the world's champion milk cow wrestler. Besides, I need you to pay the check. I don't have any money."

"Better not need me." He crumpled up his napkin without looking at the smiley face. "I ain't much for bein' needed." He jumped to his feet. "C'mon, let's git outta here. Ain't hungry no more." He pulled me out of the booth with such suddenness that I had to do a little dance step to keep my balance. We swept by the cashier with Billy dropping a twenty next to the register. Before I could say another word, we were in the Trail Duster, and before I could formulate any kind of theory about what was going on in his head, we were turning into Fifth Street and then into our driveway. Billy had been absolutely silent the whole drive, but when he leaned over to open my door he stopped for a moment before getting down and touched the back of my hand with one finger. "Sorry, baby," he said, and stalked up to the house.

By the time I got inside, Billy had *Lone Man on the Road* on the record player. He sat in the corner of the sofa listening, leaned over with his head down so far that his hair covered everything but his profile, while I hung up my jacket, put my purse on the hall shelf, and bustled around like a good little housewife. I went upstairs to look at the kids, who were both beatifically asleep. Jake had all his stuffed animals arranged around his head like a halo, while Lisa was buried in her quilt. It still wasn't midnight, though it seemed later, as if the night hours followed a different timetable. Downstairs I could hear Billy cross the room to turn off the record player.

Well, Kay, time for bed. Billy was back in the corner of the sofa when I came down, looking at the floor with his chin propped in his hands, elbows on his knees. I walked by him, hesitated, thought about touching him, and decided not to. In the bedroom I turned down one side of the comforter and got undressed. I was just going through the bureau drawer for a clean nightgown when the door opened with a crack like a gunshot. Billy charged in, buck naked. I was too at that point, and there wasn't even a towel available for me to drape around myself, so I snatched the first garment my hand hit in the drawer, an ancient beige thing from my trousseau, and pressed it up against me.

"C'mon, baby." Billy had me surrounded by his arm. "Let's shower."

"What?" I tried to pull away, but it was hopeless. I couldn't even keep the lace monstrosity hanging straight.

"Let's shower t'gether. Save water. Git rid of that cow all at once."

"Oh Billy!" I hadn't even bathed with my kids when they were little. "I can't do that. You go first, and I'll come later. Or I can shower tomorrow morning." He had me so close

against him that I was standing on his foot. He didn't appear to notice.

"Got no choice, baby. I'm one helluva lot bigger 'n you." We waltzed off to the bathroom, steam-wreathed, the lace slipping to the floor at the threshold. Billy hadn't pulled the shower curtain, so the water was spurting all over the linoleum. Trying to keep my balance, I grabbed a towel from the rack and held it in front of me, backing myself against the wall to protect my rear. Billy yanked at the towel with a positively wicked gleam in his eyes. "C'mon, c'mon," he chuckled. "We ain't too old t' have a little fun. Bet you ain't never had a twosome shower." The bathroom was so thick with steam that it had dissolved the line of muck on his cheek, and it was running down into his tangled beard. I thought of screaming for help, but no one would hear me except the kids. What an appalling thought! They would be psychologically scarred for life. Or could Billy sing that away too? The towel came loose from my left hand and I threw it at Billy's head. He caught it in his teeth and shook it. Meanwhile he had his hands around my waist, and as I struggled to stay on my feet, he hoisted me over the edge of the tub and leaped in after. I didn't even have time to shut my mouth before the water poured down my face and made me cough. Somewhere above me in the deluge Billy was laughing.

"You are awful!" I would have been angry if I hadn't been concentrating on keeping from drowning. I thumped at his chest, trying to keep my eyes shut, but I doubted if he even knew I was hitting him. I felt a washcloth running over my neck and down my back. "Can't let my gal go t' bed dirty," came his voice, and then a line of some mournful cowboy ballad, bellowed out so loudly that it won the competition with the water. I gave up.

Billy was so tall that I wasn't much help washing him, but between the two of us and the cascading water we eliminated all obvious traces of the pasture. He commandeered a bottle of Lisa's shampoo from the edge of the tub and washed my hair with it, holding one big hand over my eyes so it wouldn't sting, then squatted down so I could do his. Hair I had had experience with, but beards were a mystery, so I ended up getting shampoo in his mouth, and he sputtered and spat for a minute before I got his face properly rinsed off. Then we just stood under the spray and held each other as tight as we could for a long time, Billy demonstrating that he could fold his arms around me so far that his hands came back around to his own chest. By then the hot water was running out, so we climbed out of the tub, and Billy shut off the shower while I spread all the available towels except one big one over Lake Lombard on the bathroom floor. We dried each other off, one more-or-less equivalent part at a time, taking turns so that if the towel got used up early we'd be left equally damp. After that we went to bed, kissing and touching each other so gently that when we finally made love it was like hearing it in a song on a faraway country-western station, sweet steel guitar and all.

Afterwards, when I was lying almost asleep, tucked into Billy's side like one of Jake's stuffed animals, he jerked half upright, then spilled back on the pillow. "Hell!" he said.

"What's the matter?" I put my arms around his neck and nuzzled his chest.

"I forgot. Goddamnit. You wanted t' go dancin' tonight."

I rubbed my hand under the curls on the back of his head. "Oh, Billy. That doesn't matter." I nuzzled him again.

"You ain't mad?"

"No, of course not."

"We kin do it tomorrow then. Don't let me forget. But 'cept for jumpin' 'round like I do on that goddamn stage, I can't dance worth shit."

25

Somehow, though, we didn't go dancing Tuesday night either. When I woke up late that morning, so tangled in the sheet that for a moment I couldn't figure how to get myself free, I had to race through preparations for school, complicated because I couldn't find my copy of the textbook to review the good old Hemingway story I was supposed to be teaching in an hour. Billy slept through everything. I hurried to class so I could improvise the Hemingway to my reluctant freshmen, but as I spoke, a velvet curtain in my head kept wrenching up, and on the back wall would be projected a towering shadow, a silhouetted hat brim moving along to the rhythm of "Lovesick Blues." Sometimes the shadow of a large cow trotted along too.

That afternoon when I stepped into the front hall, the first thing I heard was quiet music, something with a guitar, but not Billy's blue one. I started for the kitchen, desperate for a cup of tea, but as I passed the living room entrance, a flash of color caught me and I stopped. The old sofa nothing could make me like was completely covered in scarves, old pillows from the linen closet, even some of the kids' baby blankets stored in the attic for years. Like a great patchwork ship it sailed puffily through the reaches of the living room with Jake and Lisa holding hands on the main deck. Lisa had a scarf around her head like a peasant girl, and Jake was wearing a painter's beret that I'd hidden in the attic years ago. Across the room, pressed against the window, Billy was kneeling with my camera, taking their pictures over and over again.

"What in the world are you doing?" I felt like an interloper.

"Shhh." The kids spoke together.

"Billy, what are you doing, for heaven's sake?"

"Jest takin' their pictures. Looks great, don't it?" He snapped one more, then glanced up at me.

"Where'd you find my camera?"

"Right in that drawer in the kitchen where you keep everythin' and its brother." He stood up. "Got any more film?"

"I didn't know I even had that left." No one else had ever used that camera.

"Well, you did. Goddamn good thing, too."

"Billy . . ." But what could I say? He hadn't burned the house down or raped anyone.

"He thinks we're good enough for Hollywood, Mom." Lisa had untied her scarf and gotten up. "He's going to send us copies."

"Copy-doodle-doo," squealed Jake as he scampered off upstairs, Lisa after him. I could hear the two of them thumping down the hall, and as my eyes followed their footsteps along the living room ceiling, the edges of my vision caught an extra piece of color on the coffee table. My private photograph album. I bit my lip in anger.

From where he leaned against the wall next to the picture window, Billy was watching. "What's the matter, baby?" he asked.

"Where did you find this?" I moved over to the sofa, sat down, and picked the album up. It was silly to look for fingerprints on the cover.

"Right in that there bookcase. Crazy pictures you got in there. Don't make no sense, most of 'em."

"They make sense to me."

"Need somebody t' tell me what's goin' on." He was coming over to sit by me, but I put the album down on one side and shoved a pillow against me on the other. Billy sat down anyway, on top of the pillow, tottered for a moment, then settled in. "You don't look so happy, baby," he said.

"Sometimes I get tired teaching." How could I explain the truth? Billy lived in a world of endless photo albums with his picture on every page. His songs were common property. Everybody knew everything about him.

"Wanna go out 'n' eat?" He was trying to stuff my hand into his jeans pocket.

"Why did you mess up the sofa like this?" Some of the things on it I couldn't even remember. If I had put them away, they should stay put.

"Ain't no *mess*." When I pushed at his hands, he thought I was being affectionate, smiled quickly, and lifted my arms around his neck. "C'mon, gimme a hug. Two hugs 'n' I'll buy, you and the kids too." He rubbed noses with me. "This house is like the one my folks had, all them things stuck away everywheres. Should bring 'em out sometimes, look 'em over. Kids figgered it was great."

Then Lisa came downstairs furious about her English assignment, and we wrestled with subordinate conjunctions for a while. Billy drifted off, humming. A little later we all found ourselves in the front hall with our jackets on, and we drove slowly out to the Highway Host, where we ate the ribs with hot barbecue sauce. Nobody dripped, so after that we went to Bischof's for banana splits as a reward. Billy ate his down to the banana, which he captured whole to upend in his mouth and glug down all at once. He got ice cream all over his beard, and Jake thought that was so funny he laughed until he choked. All of us thumped him in turn, Billy finally taking him outside and turning him upside down.

Back at the house, after the kids had settled in and I once again had forgotten all about dancing, Billy and I sat on the sofa together and listened to his albums, Numbers Eight, Nine, and Eleven, taking turns putting them on and then flipping them, paying attention to each little squeak. At first I didn't feel very cuddly, but Billy ended up getting my hand, counting my fingers as if he were learning his numbers, then playing with my ring. I finally slid over enough for him to slip one arm around me. We shifted positions a few times as we changed records, and when he finally went to sleep around eleven or so, he was propped up halfway against the arm of the sofa, his legs stretched out over my lap and our left hands linked. By some careful calisthenics I got my legs loose, but he was gripping my hand so tightly that I couldn't slide it free, and I ended up kneeling on the floor next to the sofa, our fingers still intertwined. I really didn't want to pry his fingers apart, but while I was pondering what to do and "Born to Ramble" was finishing up, he smiled in his sleep and let me go.

After that I thought I'd have no trouble sleeping, but it didn't work that way. First I read a little, just my same Victorian poetry with the gold leaf on the edges of the pages. Then I got up and made some tea, drinking it at the kitchen table. On the way back to bed I stopped to check on Billy, who had slid further down on the sofa. His eyes were moving under his lids, snatching back and forth at the pictures in his dreams. I pulled loose the afghan from the sofa arm and unfolded it over him, though it didn't reach to cover his boots.

Back to bed, but it was cold. I had burned out on Victorians. Come on, Kay, it's after midnight and the kids will be up early for school. Like a child, I wanted to crawl in next to Billy on the sofa, but there would never have been room for both of us no matter how much I might have scrunched up. He wouldn't wake up and come to bed either; he slept like the dead. The dead. Nobody slept like the dead. The great sleep was their prerogative. Then why did they keep coming back? I turned over onto Billy's pillow. Stay gone. *Gone.* Gone Girl . . . no, that was Billy's song, not mine. Album Eight. Go away. I couldn't stop it happening. Don't haunt me. Don't touch me in my dreams.

Dear Billy,

*I covered you up with the afghan before I left
you for good, because even with the furnace
on, it gets chilly in the living room at night,
especially at the beginning of winter when the
house is adjusting to the cold. You look funny
when you sleep, Billy. A little of that Texas
boy saunters back across your face, mischief
and danger, but your mouth is so soft under
your beard when you aren't being a tough cowboy
in the waking world that what I see isn't a
tree-climbing water pistol stealer from the
local five-and-dime, but a skinny dreamer under
a cottonwood when the sky burns blue like the
inside of a Japanese bowl, your eyes molding
the clouds into a tune and then into words to
furnish it. What color are your eyes, Billy?
When you're asleep, I can't see them, and when
you're awake, you've always got the lids down
so far and your brows slanted so that I just
get glimpses. Or else I'm not thinking about
your eyes at all. If I were to see, would you
have to let me in? Is that the rule in the
hill country of West Texas?*

Kay

26

T H E   H O U S E was quiet—why should that wake me up? Billy? No, in the silence I could hear him breathing, heavy on the sofa, steady. A creak. One of the kids sick? But they always screamed for me *before* the agonized trip to the bathroom. Footsteps. Someone was up. A robber? Good luck . . . I've still got Jeff's gun. But no one knows, do they? I never threw it away.

The darkness around my door cracked, letting in the lines of yellow from the streetlight in front of the house.

"Mom?"

"Lisa, what?"

"I'm awake."

"Come on in, honey. Want to get under the covers?" I started to slide over to make room, but there was plenty of room already.

"Yup." The door closed and the room was dark again. "What time is it, Mom?"

I looked at the clock, huddled behind the Victorians. "It's almost morning. Darkest before the dawn. Quarter to five."

"Gee, I thought it was about midnight. Is this my pillow?"

"Sure is. Would you like *Peter Rabbit* or *The Little Prince?*"

"Mom!" She laughed in spite of herself. "They were both great books, weren't they?"

"I think I'll read *The Little Prince* again myself when I've buried all the Victorians deep, deeper, deepest."

"Mom?"

"I'm here."

"How long is Billy staying?"

"I have no idea." Delicate ground, delicate ground. Good thing this is his night on the sofa. "He's no worse than Aunt Louise."

"I like him. He makes me laugh, but he listens too. Why does he have that *beard?*"

"I guess he thinks it makes him look the way a cowboy singer should, all shaggy and masculine. Underneath he probably has no chin at all."

"Yes he does. He showed me a scar he got when he fell off a fence back in Texas. He said it was the nearest he had ever come to cutting his throat. Goddamn near, he said."

"I'm sure that's what he said."

"Mom." Even though I could barely see her, I could tell by her shifting on the pillow and the awakened scent of shampoo exactly what she was doing. She was braiding her hair.

"I'm here."

"You haven't really talked to me since Sunday morning."

"That's because Billy's been here, I guess. I've certainly thought about you." I gave her a discreet squeeze at the tender spot where her hip began.

"I never told you where I went. I really was just walking around all night. I even walked down along the river and back."

"There was no way I could make you tell me then, Lisa. At least not without making us both miserable."

"Were you worried about me?"

"Of course."

"Were you worried I got raped?"

"*Yes.*"

"I didn't. Still a virgin." A choked sound. She was laughing. "Funniest thing I've heard in months, daughter."

"Will it go on Johnny Carson?"

"Not unless Billy sings it. Maybe we can hire him to write a new song."

"I don't think he needs the money." She put her hands on her belly with a little soft plop. "Mom, why is Billy here?"

"God knows. No, that's not fair. I got to know him a little when I went to get his autograph after the Kensington show. Then he sent me that clipping about his concert in St. Paul, and I just felt like going out to hear him sing. Afterwards we were talking, and he had some free time. He'd never spent any time in North Dakota, and he decided to drive back with me. Show people pick up and do things like that."

"Mom." There was a long, long pause. The dark on her side of the bed changed shape as she turned toward me, leaning on her elbow. It must be getting closer to dawn because her pigtails, sticking out like handles on each side of her head, were edged with gray. "He sleeps in this bed, doesn't he?"

"Yes, he does, honey. Tonight he just happened to fall asleep on the sofa, so I covered him up and left him be."

Oh Lisa. This is it, isn't it? And I have to be honest, don't I? No lying or false morals or excuses or anything like that. Even you couldn't have expected me to hold out forever. Daddy has been gone a long time, and it doesn't always work out that someone asks you for a date, takes you to the movies, buys you candy, and pops the question while you're dancing cheek to cheek at the Biltmore to some off-key Norwegian accordion. Though I am going to the other extreme, aren't I? Is this going to be something you can't forgive me? Well, we'll battle it out together.

"Mom?" She giggled. "Mom, guess what? You're not a virgin!"

27

"W HATTHEHELL, I jest might visit that school of yours today," said Billy the next morning, holding his cocoa with one hand and watching Jake wedge three stuffed animals (Rachel Bear, Frog, and the Littlest Mammal) into his backpack before heading off to first grade. "Time I learned 'bout the world of schoolin'. Think they'll let a picker in? Songs is pretty near as good as them books." He helped Jake zip the pack closed, then swung him up on his knee. "Ever seen your mama's school, hombre?"

"It's full of students," said Jake, unzipping his backpack again. I knew what he wanted; on Wednesdays the Littlest Mammal had cocoa. A wave of puzzlement vibrated over Billy's face as the Littlest Mammal dipped into his cup. "Shit, kid, that's a waste of good brew."

"You've got more." Jake restuffed the Littlest Mammal, leaving brown spots along Billy's jeans, and slid down to the floor. For a moment the two of them looked at each other, and Billy lifted one hand toward Jake very gently, then dropped it back on his knee. " 'Bye now," said Jake, already halfway to the door. I watched him talking passionately to himself as he cut across the lawn and started down the sidewalk, his pack bulging.

"Jesus, what a kid." A smile began on Billy's face, but he yanked his lips back into a straight line before his mustache even quivered.

"I like him. I like Lisa too. We do all right together." I checked the kitchen clock—still before nine, with three hours until office duty. Wednesdays were tenser than teaching days because I couldn't predict who would drop in. I drank the last of my orange juice, avoiding the fragments of pulp. Surely automation in the frozen food business ought to be able to control pulp.

"Ain't it hard t' take care of both them kids and work too?" Billy's question came out of the Texas distance; I hadn't expected it.

"Why are you asking? Just because I'm small doesn't mean I can't do two things at once."

"Jesus, baby. I do two things at once every goddamn time I sing 'n' pick. Ain't nothin' so special 'bout that." He dipped one finger in his cocoa and sucked it.

"Besides, they manage themselves pretty well now that Jake is in school. I like their company," I added, suppressing the impulse to dip my finger in my cocoa too.

"You like that teachin' you do? Can't figger out how anybody could go on that long in front of a bunch of people without no *music*."

"The last thing they need is music." But I thought about saving that idea for a slow day—maybe a few country-western lyrics and an impromptu theme about the masculine frontier image. "The hardest part is dealing with the papers the students write, all those different mistakes but the same eighteen-year-old feelings. I'm more helpless than their parents."

"Jesus." That almost sounded like sympathy, except for the "You gotta read all them goddamn things?" that followed it.

"Of course I read them all, and correct them too. It's like walking on a bridge and knowing I'm going to fall off one side or the other. Either I'm too gentle and they love me without learning a thing, or I'm too harsh and they cry in my office. If you come in today, you can watch one or two of them cry. I can guarantee it."

Billy edged himself out of his chair and started to wedge another slice of bread into the toaster. "Goddamn stuff's bent," he said, as it caught in the slot and wouldn't go down. He wiggled the offending corner until it fell off, leaving a crack through the rest of the slice. As he tried again to put it into the toaster slot, it disintegrated in his hand.

"Shit!"

"There's more in the bread box."

"Wanted this one." Again the suppressed smile.

"You're a funny man, did you know that?"

"Course I know it. Gotta be funny in my business." He looked down at me and winked. "Ain't you known no funny men?"

"Not a one. Every man in my little life has been deadly serious. I'd forgotten how to raise the corners of my mouth in a smile until you came along. And you can't even make toast."

"Made a plateful that Sunday we come back from the Cities." He sat down again, sliding his legs under the table, a round maple antique we had picked up at a farm auction. He raised his knees too high, cracking them against the underside of the top. Both of us grabbed for our slopping cocoa cups at the same time while Billy moaned, "Everything in this goddamn house is too *small*."

"It's *my* house, you picker. It's designed to fit someone like me." Both of us were looking at our cups, smiling but a little wary. Size and fit mattered.

"How much you git paid for that teaching?" Another Texas question out of space.

"None of your business." Billy looked up, his forehead

wrinkled. Maybe that was too harsh. "Not very much, but enough."

"Hell, I ain't meddlin'. Nobody gives a shit 'bout money if you got enough. Kids eat a lot."

"Only if you're cooking. Or maybe at Christmas when we frost cookies and listen to the wind howl." I couldn't tell if that was funny or not.

Billy tilted his chair back and looked up at the ceiling as if he were measuring its height. "This place cost a lot t' heat?"

"That's a real North Dakota question, Billy. You're catching on. Nobody would ask that in West Texas." My voice had a sudden bite to it, and I even surprised myself. I'd had that same question asked me at least twenty times before, and there was nothing unreasonable about it.

Billy had his chair back on the level and was looking at the table, curls sliding over his forehead. "Thought maybe you could use some money, baby. I got plenty on me. Picked up a few thou after that last show. Sure as hell won't need that much t' git back t' Texas with."

"Is that an offer?"

"I reckon. Name what you need. I figger it ain't easy gittin' through them winters when you been left by a man."

Oh, I knew I wasn't allowed to hit him again, but since I couldn't stop my hand before it reached him, I struggled to uncurl my fingers and ended up jabbing his cheek. He raised his head, startled, his hand already pulling his wallet out of his jeans.

"Jesus, baby, that was some love tap." Then he focused on my face. "What 'n hell's the matter?"

My hands were clenched so hard around my cup that it was rattling against the table, and only by gripping all the muscles in my thighs could I keep my knees from shaking. These last four days had never happened, because I could never have allowed my life to be taken over like that. Who did he believe he was, that big cowboy, stepping into my world and thinking that he could pay me off as nicely as his Butte whore, help the little lady support her enterprise, because without a man, a big man, she just couldn't bring it off? *If* he thought. For two years I had done everything that had to be done, and there were no complaints. Our lives were running just fine.

The cup cracked and crushed together in my fingers. Billy jumped. Glaring him right in the eyes, talking as slowly as I could, enunciating every word so clearly that the Vietnamese immigrant in my morning class would have nodded and smiled, I said, "Ever since my husband died two years ago, I have run this house perfectly well, and my life too. You came here four days ago. Do you think I really need your money?" Then I got out of my chair, went to the bathroom, shut the door, and threw up.

It took a long time for the heaving to stop and for me to catch my breath, longer than it would have taken for Jake or Lisa, swept by flu or anxiety, longer than it would take Billy to wipe up my spilled cocoa, longer than I had ever spent in a bathroom before, because mine was the life of the mind, wasn't it, conducted a long way from toilets and flushing water and Ajax and threads of vomit down the side of my face? I sat on the bathroom floor with my head on the tub next to Lisa's old hair conditioner bottle and cried until my throat hurt so much I had to hold my neck with both hands. The light from the window fractured and split around me, and every tile I hadn't scrubbed swam up, bowed, and disappeared. Then I cried some more. There was a little part of me left that could hear myself crying and trying to hold it in, that little part which never stopped being a teacher and making sure that descriptions were understated rather than overblown, but most of me, all the parts that mattered, were just washed away. I couldn't stop crying. I couldn't stop crying even when I felt my face pressed against Billy's shirt, the one with the pearl snaps down the front, and he was squatting awkwardly beside the tub, patting my back with first one hand

and then the other, holding me as close as he could without flattening me, rubbing my cheek against his shoulder, saying, "Baby, baby, there weren't no more of them little blue flowers left in the garden, but I sure will go out and buy you some as soon as I kin. I had no way of knowin' he passed away. Lemme jest hold you for a little bit, baby, lemme jest rock you till you don't hurt so bad. But first we gotta git outta here, 'cause I jest plain don't *fit*."

I don't remember how Billy got himself shifted around, but he managed. Suddenly I was up in the air, head still against his shoulder, his arms around me like wrappings holding me together. I wanted to say something, tell him that he really didn't have to do this, but I just didn't have the strength. Besides, it wasn't true. Someone did have to do this, because I wouldn't have been able to; I would have drowned on that brown bathroom linoleum, strangled on vomit and tears. Even as he edged us both through the door and then into the bedroom, I had trouble breathing through the ache in my throat and chest. I fought against choking as he lowered himself onto the edge of the bed, still holding me right up to him as close as he could. My nose was running into my mouth, and my face was so wet that even the air moving by me as he sat us down was a little cold wind against my cheek. I must have looked awful, small and wet and bedraggled. I couldn't do a thing about it.

"Oh, baby. It's alright now. Don't hurt so bad, baby. It's alright." Billy was swaying back and forth on the edge of the bed like a slow-paced metronome, humming a little and rubbing my back in great sweeping strokes all the way down. "You scared me, baby. I ain't never heard no woman cry like that." He yanked up one corner of the comforter and wiped my face with it, or at least the part that wasn't tight against him. "Was it so bad, baby? Weren't there nobody t' help you? You hadn't ought t' have t' hurt like that, no matter what. Nobody should."

Holding onto his voice, I came up part way through the

waves, still choking but able to feel the oxygen again. One of his hands was lifting the hair out from the back of my neck, and I wondered blearily if I was too much of a mess to kiss. But halfway through the thought he grabbed me with both arms and rubbed his face back and forth across the top of my head. Then his lips were on my forehead, moving from one side to the other as if he were talking to my skin.

"Billy." Well, at least I could say that and not have my voice break. I couldn't find a place to put my hands, which were wandering across my lap like cold exiles, so I undid the bottom snap on Billy's shirt and edged them down against him. They just seemed so lonely outside. When he felt the chilly invasion he jumped a little, but he kept right on rocking me. It was easier to breathe again, like being on a giant respirator and not having to try for myself. Billy had started to kiss my cheeks, first one and then the other, right through all the damp. If his mouth was full of salt, he didn't seem to mind.

"Did he go quick, baby?" It was a real question, though he was still kissing me. He had one hand tight over my hands on his chest and was rubbing them back and forth against his skin, pushing as hard as he could.

"Yes." I was going to cry again, but Billy was kissing my eyes and wouldn't let the tears out. "But I knew it would happen." Maybe I wouldn't have to explain anything else.

"Do you miss him a lot, baby?" Billy's voice had a funny crack in it, the *Lone Man on the Road* sound. He pushed himself over on the bed and swung me up next to him on top of the comforter. For a moment he lifted his mouth away so he could shove the pillow under my head. His eyes were a light brown with little flecks of gray. He kissed me on the tip of my nose and then brushed his mouth over mine, barely touching it.

"Yes." My eyes were wet again. "I do. I did." Maybe if I said it just before Billy's mouth touched mine again, I could get it out. "But part of me was glad he died." I still couldn't say it all.

"He musta hurt you, baby, for you t' feel like that. Men, they mess up the best things they got. I done it too. Couldn't help myself one bit." He had started smoothing my hair back, putting all the cowlicks to bed, then kissing my ears in little circles. I put my arms around as much of him as I could reach, like a giant block of balsa wood I could float downstream with forever.

"Baby, want me t' love you? I kin do it real slow and make you feel so good, jest like them songs, only for real. Then you won't need t' cry no more. I don't like you t' cry, baby. It makes me feel like I wasn't worth shit." His head pressed into my neck, his left side overlapping mine, he started to un-button my blouse, his hand stopping for a moment to reach under my arm and pull me closer. Then he began to stroke me up and down, tracing my edges, pushing me up against him. I couldn't help it, I put my own hand on top of his and pressed down so I could feel him harder on me.

"Jest lay there, baby. Lemme do it all. Lemme git them things off of you so I kin kiss you all over. You are so purty, baby, like a little doll. Can't hardly tell you had them two kids. I don't mind your needin' me if I kin give you what you're longin' for. I could jest about play music on you, yes I could." His mouth was moving across my hips and I could hardly hear what he was saying. "Jest lemme do it all, baby. Comin' in you is like goin' home t' Texas, but I don't hafta. Jest if you want me when you're ready. Jest if you want me. I'll make it so good for you anyhow you won't never need t' cry again."

And he did the very best he could.

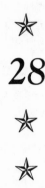

28

"IF YOU DON'T MIND, baby, I'll jest drop you off 'n' pick you up when you're done." Billy was pulling the car into the long drive up to the English building, resolutely holding the middle of the road against any members of the educational community who might be coming at him. "Figger maybe school kin git along without me today." He moved his eyes away from the blacktop ahead for a moment and glanced at me. "You ain't mad?"

The wind was blowing in the first edge of winter, pushing against the trees planted a year ago along the bare driveway. Good thing I'd gotten out my red wool car coat. "Little Red Riding Hood," Lisa had teased me when I wore it for the first time, and she was right. I didn't care; it kept me warm. "No, I'm not mad," I said. "You've probably about had it with crying."

"Got nothin' t' do with it. Thought I might pick up some things. Don't feel like no housewife today." A stricken look crossed his face, and he slapped one hand against his knee. "Shit, baby, I'm sorry. Didn't mean that, goddamnit."

"Billy, that's OK. I'm all right. I really am." In the rearview mirror I could see my eyelashes were still stuck together with damp, but I *was* all right, tired down to the pulp, but functioning. Billy's leather jacket was open; his shirt was still spotted with wet along the shoulder. He saw me looking at it.

"Water don't stain, baby."

"Salt either?"

"Nope." He leaned over as he swung the car into a parking space and rubbed his beard along my cheek.

"You didn't have to park. I could just get out by the main door."

"Too late now, baby. Shit, you got ten minutes 'fore the first one comes in and cries on you. If it rains today, we'll sure as hell git enough water t' float us right down your Red River t' my Red River in Texas."

"My Red goes north, Billy, to Lake Winnipeg. It's a confused glacial lake that melted wrong."

"Never knew much geography." He flicked on the radio. "Want some music?"

I did, but not Tom T. Hall or the Gatlin Brothers. "Why don't you sing me something?" I had a sudden picture of his voice around me like a second red coat.

"Ain't got my guitar. Don't feel much like singin' neither." He poked the gearshift with a petulant finger.

"Are *you* OK?" There was some signal I was picking up but not interpreting right. Out of the mirror I saw a cluster of students approaching. The English Department parking lot wasn't a very private place.

"Shit, I'm fine. It ain't always the right time t' do music, that's all. Can't do it if you don't feel like it."

I didn't push. What would have been the use? Instead I turned to him and said, "I'll be through with office hours at three thirty, Billy. Can you really make it back then? My office is Room 104C, but if you have any trouble finding it, the secretary will show you." If he had the Trail Duster, he'd have to come for me. I didn't want to be stranded.

"That secretary's the one you don't like, ain't she?"

"Yes, but that hasn't destroyed her ability to know where to find me." I dug my gloves out of my pocket and started putting the right one on, working my thumb through the ripped lining wadded halfway up the opening. "I'd better go, Billy. Sometimes they come early."

Billy leaned across me, stretching along the seat to unlock my door and push it loose. A line of cold air went up the side of my face. Then he shifted a little in his seat without looking in my direction, stretched his arms around me, and dropped his head in my lap, rubbing his face against my red coat, Sears' best, like Jake used to for comfort when he'd been hurt. In the back of my throat the tears began to move again, and I pushed my ungloved hand through his hair, smoothing it to one side and then rumpling it a little, pressing down on his skull underneath. Beneath my palm I found a little cluster of white hairs on the back of his head almost hidden by the brown. No more, just those. I wound them around my finger like a ring, then let them go. As if I'd given a signal, though he couldn't have known what I'd been doing, he sat up and kissed me a chaste good-bye.

Outside the wind stopped momentarily, then picked up with a thrust and pushed me up the steps to the main door. Behind me, Billy was heading for the Texas hills by way of the departmental driveway, great spurts of dust churning out from under the rear tires. Classes were about to change, and more groups of students were heading toward the building, motley the way students are just before winter, jeans and ski jackets, heads still bare. One girl was holding her ears and laughing as the wind gusted around her. Several stopped to watch as Billy tore by them, gunning the car into the street without stopping to check for traffic. At that distance, he was just a dark shadow in the driver's seat.

29

"KAY, want to have lunch with us?" Emily and Hazel, the department's Renaissance specialist, were walking by my door. "We're going over to the Union."

"Sorry, not this time. If I don't finish correcting my papers for tomorrow, the teacher's nightmare will occur, and I'll be standing in front of my freshmen with nothing to hand back. Besides, someone might come by. Thanks, though." Hazel was Emily's friend, a good teacher who was a lot more experienced than I. They were both classical music fans; actually Hazel preferred madrigals and those sixteenth-century wind instruments. They were affectionately tolerant of my bizarre tastes.

"You're too thin anyway, Kay. Shall we bring you back something? A malted?"

"All right. Chocolate. Let me get some money." I had put my purse on the floor under my desk where no one was likely to uncover it. If I locked my office when I was somewhere else in the building, needy students couldn't get in, and I'd find sad misspelled notes taped to the door when I got back. That kind of guilt I didn't need.

"Wait until we bring it to you. Still be here in an hour?"

"Oh yes. I'm not leaving until after three."

"See you." They walked off together, buttoning their coats. Did they have the faintest idea about me? But I was a nice person too, wasn't I?—conscientious about the students' papers, effective in the classroom, uncomplaining about all except the most offensive of the administration's actions. I could even handle Lucille if I'd had enough sleep. No guilt trips, Kay. You're all right. That is *right*, baby. Oh dear. I heaved the remaining essays out of my side drawer and started reading.

I used to think, back before I began teaching, that essay correcting would be dull. What I wanted to do was write my own. But once I actually started reading what the kids wrote, I knew that nothing I could write would approach what they were doing. Oh, I could spell better and I was consistent about topic sentences. My vocabulary was considerably larger. The big difference, though, was that the kids had no idea how to hide things with words. They just wrote it all: the car wrecks, the parental divorces, the struggles in the backseats of 1970 Chevrolets. Here on this single-spaced typed sheet was the narrative of how Tom couldn't come back next quarter because his dad's multiple sclerosis had gotten worse and someone had to help take care of his mother and the twins. I knew Tom by sight, a pimply kid not much taller than I was, dusty bronze hair chopped off around his ears. How much could he possibly earn even if someone gave him a job and his complexion cleared up? Ignoring his inability to use any punctuation mark correctly, I gave his paper a big B-plus in the upper right-hand corner.

Somewhere in this diminishing heap there must be a happy essay. Cecilia Lynn's? But she was so *dull*. Only misery was interesting. No wonder they all wrote about their car wrecks. They had me suckered right out, shaking like Jell-O, giving the best marks for the deepest torments. A bona fide amputee would be guaranteed the highest grade in the class.

My phone rang, the first extension button blinking. I picked it up. It was Margaret.

"Kay, are you teaching? I don't want to bother you."

"No, it's fine. I'm just correcting papers. The kids are all right, aren't they?" Margaret was the one named on the children's school forms as Person to Call If Parent Is Unavailable; she was home all the time.

"They're fine, I'm sure. I haven't heard a thing."

Then why did you call me at work, Margaret, when you knew you could see me at home later in the afternoon? "OK, what's up?" I asked, tucking the phone under my chin and starting on the next paper. Polite but efficient, that was me.

"I wondered how you got to school this morning. I looked out the window a little while ago and saw the Trail Duster in your driveway. I thought I'd better check. Did you have car trouble, Kay? I could have given you a ride if you needed one." Margaret's car was like her Maytag, churning steadily.

"The car is fine." And I hope it still is, after the way Billy was driving. "My brother-in-law gave me a ride to work because he needed to run some errands today. He must have come back sooner than he thought he would." The next paper, Claire Manson's, looked better than most but didn't seem to have a final paragraph. Was there another sheet somewhere I hadn't found?

"Will you need a ride home? I could come by on the way from the post office. Jim has some special delivery things I have to mail."

Emily dropped off the malted on my desk, smiled, and waved her finger as she went into her office. I unwrapped the straw with my free hand and took a sip. Thin, college cafeteria style, but drinkable. Claire's paper didn't have another page; it simply broke off as if her pen had been stolen. How was I supposed to grade that?

"No, my brother-in-law will come to get me when I'm done." Better allay her fears. "The car may be gone again when you look, Margaret. Don't worry. I really will get home safe." Oh, why be hard on her? She patrolled the neighborhood with her heart and soul, and she had been a good friend.

"Bye, Kay. If Jake gets home early, I'll take him shopping with us."

"Great. So long, Margaret." I pried the receiver out of my neck, muscles reluctantly letting go, and put it back on its cradle. It immediately rang again, little light blinking.

"Yes, what is it?" It was hopeless, once the interruptions had started, to think of getting anything done.

"Mrs. Lombard, there's a bouquet here for you. Should I have him bring it down to your office?"

"There's a what? Who?" The phone blinked off.

I pushed back my chair, a standard swivel model too big for me, and one of the casters sticking out from the central pivot slid off the plastic carpet under my desk with a little bounce. A bouquet? But it was November. The last flowers I'd been given had been early last spring when Jake found three new dandelions in the neighbor's backyard. Dandelions don't last long in a vase, but these had held up longer than most. When they finally collapsed into sodden strips, Jake had wrapped them in an entire roll of toilet paper and buried them under Brian's forsythia.

Footsteps were coming down the hall, hesitating at the corner, then continuing. If someone was playing a joke, I was going to sic Billy on him. I stood up.

"Mrs. Lombard? Flowers for you." He was a skinny, middle-aged man, too old to be doing this for a living. Then he smiled. "Looks like someone thinks you're pretty special." Heaving a little, he planted the most enormous bouquet I had ever seen right on top of Claire's paper, and left.

Billy. Dear God, I will have to find somebody to sic on *you*. Timidly I pulled aside the green tissue clustered around the altarpiece. The base was a thick ceramic Grecian urn, but I had to bend down to see it because there were flowers hanging over the edge, clustered inside, sticking straight up toward my fluorescent light. "Want 'em *all*," I could hear Billy saying.

A dozen sprays of gladioli, all the off-color mauves and pinks, peaked to a mountain in the middle and descended like organ pipes along the sides. Daisies, two kinds. No, three. But maybe those were some kind of mum, they had so many petals. A knot of roses on each side, the buds jammed so close together they could never conceivably open even if I did dump that packet of energizer into the water. And those must be carnations, even though they were purple. *Purple.* Blue was bad enough. I put my head down on my desk and tugged at my hair with both hands. I suppose he figured that as long as he was coming to pick me up, I wouldn't have to carry it out myself.

Caught between desperation and laughter, I opened my eyes and raised my head. Then I saw the envelope, impaled on a green stick struggling among the decorative fern. I slid it off and ripped it open with my finger. Inside was a florist's card, one of the embossed ones with "In Sympathy" printed in scrollwork across the top. On it was written one line, right out of a Kris Kristofferson song that Billy had recorded along with a lot of other country-western performers a long time ago. "She ain't ashamed to be a woman or afraid to be a friend," it said. The "ain't" had started out as "isn't," then been crossed out and restored to its original form. Billy must have been dictating to someone who knew his verbs. There wasn't any signature.

Oh Billy. I put my arms around the ceramic monstrosity as if it were my dance partner, and some water spilled on Claire's opus. Served her right for not bothering with her last paragraph. I knew all the words to that Kristofferson verse, had known them for a long time . . .

> *Coming close together with a feeling that I've
> never known before in my time,
> She ain't ashamed to be a woman or afraid to
> be a friend.
> I don't know the answer to the easy way she's
> opened every door in my mind.*

*Dreaming was as easy as believing it was never
going to end.
Loving her was easier than anything I'll ever
do again.*

Buried behind the bouquet, I couldn't even see the door
to my office, but through the great floral cluster I could still
hear footsteps in the hall. A set stopped at my door. Absolute
silence, except for the drip of water on Claire's paper. It must
look like the entrance to a funeral parlor, and with that blos-
somy fragrance it must smell like it too. Probably appropriate
for an English teacher's office. Loudly enough to pierce the
flowery barricade, I called, "Who is it?" while trying to keep
as much teacherly dignity as I could in my tone.

Dennis's voice answered, "It's me."

"Fight your way in, Dennis. Have a seat. But pull it around
behind my desk so I can see you. I seem to have been given a
large present."

"It's nice." Dennis appeared around the farthest fringe
of carnations and sat down. He was left no choice except to
look at the bouquet or at me. After an anxious moment, he
concentrated on a pink glad.

"How are you?" I asked. "Everything going OK?" His gaze
was transfixed. "Weather got cold, didn't it?" He must know
that, because he was wearing his hunting cap with the ear
flaps tied under his chin.

Dennis gathered himself together. "Coming to the dance?"
he asked. My mind was a complete blank. He waited graciously for a reply.

"What dance?" I wished I didn't have to commit myself to
my ignorance, but Dennis was unlikely to say another word
unless he got some encouragement. He had shifted in his
chair so that I could see him only by craning through the fern.
I pushed futilely at the bouquet but couldn't budge it, so
I gave up and leaned back. Half of him came into view. "I
haven't danced for a long time. Teachers exercise mostly with

212

their brains." Would Dennis think that was funny? Would he even hear me?

"The one the Rodeo Association is putting on. I told you about it in September. Want to buy a ticket?"

"Well, I guess I could do that. Now where is this dance?"

"It's in the Night Hawk Lounge above the bowling alley. We've got a pretty good group, country-western but a little rock too. Those Linton boys I told you about. So far we sold two hundred tickets, and there'll be a lot of people who just buy at the door."

"When is this great orgy?" Dennis looked at me blankly. "I mean, when is this dance?" "Orgy" must not be in the basic freshman five-hundred-word vocabulary. Oh, that was mean. How could I be malicious behind about two hundred dollars' worth of floral bad taste?

"It's tomorrow night. We start up at eight, but nothing much will happen before nine."

"Why on Thursday? Any dance worth its salt has to be on a weekend, doesn't it?"

"There's no school Friday." Dennis looked at me strangely. "It's Focal Problems Day. Nobody goes to that except people who *have* problems. There aren't any classes."

"Somehow I don't think the administration would see it your way, Dennis, since Focal Problems is meant to be a great advance in educational theory, not just a vacation. But you're right. I forgot what month it was." And what would he think of that?

The scent of flowers was filling my office like sound waves. Even Dennis looked wobbly, but he was still waiting patiently for his money. I had my billfold out and was sifting through it for any reasonable amount (would he be too timid to tell me what tickets actually cost?) when I heard an out-of-character shriek, half pleasure, half pain, from Lucille in the central office area. Oh God, it must be after three. I looked at the little clock on my desk. It was.

"Jesus, baby, this is a helluva lot diff'rent from that shithouse school I went to." Billy was talking to me, but he wasn't even at my door yet, growling out comments on Texas education as he thudded down the hall. It sounded as if he were bouncing off the walls on either side. "Goddamn mansion, this is. Goddamn fuckin' mansion!" He didn't apologize. Dennis had slid out of his chair and flattened himself against the bookcase, body slightly turned so he could see as far down the hall as possible. His left hand accidentally shoved a half-dozen texts out of line, and they tumbled slowly down, each one overlapping the one underneath. I grabbed my purse, yanked my coat down from its hook, and started to shove my arm into the sleeve. The quicker I could get Billy out of the halls of academe, the better. He sounded like a whole band.

"D' ya like them flowers?" He filled my office doorway. "Best in this fuckin' town. See them colors. Good enough t' *eat.*" While Dennis watched as if paralyzed, Billy pulled out a purple carnation and stuffed it into his mouth. I was beyond paralysis. He chewed mightily, then spat the remnants into his hand and emptied them into my wastebasket.

"Billy, I'm ready to go. Where are you parked?" Better treat it all perfectly naturally, better act as if this were just an exotic show business act slightly in the wrong context. I put my hand on his arm, but he didn't even feel me as he spun around to where Dennis stood pinned to the bookcase, a handful of dance tickets sticking out from his hand. I hadn't realized he'd gotten them out of his pocket.

"What in hell are them goddamn things?" The tickets slid out of Dennis's fingers into Billy's hand as if they had been greased. "Sellin' those, you little bastard?" Dennis cringed back against the bookcase even harder. "How much you want for them goddamn things? I got enough t' buy 'em no matter how fuckin' much you want." He tossed his wallet onto my desk. "Gimme the bunch. What're they for?" Billy's eyes were racing as he held the top piece of cardboard up in front of his face, trying to read what was printed on it. "Dance! Hell, what fuckin' group you got? If my boys was here, we'd blow 'em out of this horseshit state. Gotta come 'n' show ya how t' make music!" He was plunging his hands into his pockets, trying to find his wallet, yanking at his jeans until I was afraid he'd rip the seams open. I reached down by the bouquet and handed his wallet to him.

All in one motion Billy flipped out a handful of bills and jerked around toward Dennis. "Screw you, y' little shit, that'll do it," he said, as he wadded the money together like wastepaper and thrust it out to Dennis, who juggled the bills in midair and finally subdued them enough to straighten them out in his hands. "C'mon, baby, no more of this goddamn garbage." With one arm Billy heaved up the entire vase of flowers, cascading water over the top of my desk and across the carpet; with the other hand he grabbed me by the waist and shoved me through the door. We plunged down the hall, past Lucille openmouthed at her desk. Billy paused momentarily to look at her. "Fuckin' cunt!" he announced to everyone within miles, then swept on. Dennis tottered behind us, whimpering, "But, Mrs. Lombard, this is three hundred dollars!"

30

I DON'T KNOW how I managed it, but I got Billy into the passenger side of the Trail Duster, extracted the keys from his pocket, and drove home myself. He kept hammering his boots on the floorboards, sending splashes of water from the flowers over his jacket and jeans, all the while humming some disorganized tune I didn't know. The heater took forever to warm the car; my hands were still numb even when we were going up Main Street. By then the bouquet had begun to disintegrate across the front seat, with great spears of gladioli bending against the dashboard, roses loosened from their knots and strewn like a flowery print across the upholstery. We were coming up Fifth Street by the lilacs when Billy leaned toward me precipitously and grabbed my arm. "Gotta stop, baby, gotta stop, gotta stop."

"Billy, we're almost home." He began to laugh, wiping his face with the back of one hand, pushing at my arm with the other. "Let go, Billy, you're hurting me," I said, while I slowed down as much as I could and tried to shake him loose. Impossible. He started to hum again, thumping on the dashboard with his fist. The tune made no sense at all.

"C'mon, baby, goddamnit, stop the car." He was looking at me now, all right, pushing his fingers hard through the protection of my coat sleeve. His voice had dropped to a growl. No more laughter. I turned the car into the driveway and parked halfway up. Should I get him out and put him to bed or what? Could I actually do anything? It was as if he'd gone completely crazy.

"Please let go of me, Billy. Come on in and I'll make cocoa." What idiocy. He was a grown man; I had to treat him like an adult. Firmly I took hold of his hand and began to pry it off my arm. He jumped in his seat, upsetting the flowers completely, tightened his grip, and struck at me with his other hand. He was thrashing around so wildly he missed me.

"Billy! You tried to hit me!" I couldn't imagine this happening.

For just a moment I thought he was going to hit at me again. He kept his hand in a tight fist and held it up by the side of his face. Then he said, "Oh Jesus," and put his head down on the dashboard. "Oh Jesus, oh Jesus, oh Jesus." His hand slipped off my arm.

I was so stunned I just sat there, not even thinking to get out of danger. Something was wrong, something was really wrong. This wasn't supposed to happen. He was too big for me to handle. But I couldn't leave him sitting there. "Don't you want to come in?" I asked, keeping my voice quiet. "The kids are probably home."

"Lemme be, lemme be. Gotta git control." I touched his jacket sleeve, just barely. "Lemme be, goddamnit, if you know what's good for you! Git outta this car 'fore I hit you!" He pitched over on the seat, hands forced against his own chest, as I grabbed an armful of the orphaned flowers and pushed the door open. He had disappeared below the car window when I looked back from the front porch.

"Mom?" Lisa was sitting on the sofa, among its decorative plumage, cuddled like a kitten. "You're early."

"Not very." What was I going to do with him?

"What are *those?*" She sprang up and raced over to me. "You look like a funeral, Mom. Do you want a vase?"

"Lisa, sit down. I'm going to drop these on the floor and tramp all over them. No, I'm going to sit down next to you first and cry." I slid among the pillows and put my head back. One last rosebud, stem twisted, was caught in the fabric of my coat sleeve. I pulled it out and turned it around in my fingers.

"Is Billy cooking tonight, Mom? Or I could do it. Or we could order in a pizza from Miller's. Jake likes that." She was positively bustling.

"I don't think Billy is cooking." Keep it natural and low key, Kay. But Lisa was half me and could pick things up.

"Where is he?" She cupped my rosebud in the palm of her hand and smoothed it with her thumb.

"He was out in the car."

"But he'll freeze!"

"I don't think he's feeling a thing, Lisa. He came charging into the English Department this afternoon, swearing like a cavalry regiment and frightening everyone to death, then just collapsed in the car when we got home." No use telling her everything.

"Billy *always* swears."

"Not like this, my dear. He scared *me.*"

"Mom." She put her head down and touched the rosebud with her lips like an old Victorian photograph. "He took me shopping this afternoon."

"*What?*"

"He took me shopping right after I got home. We were out of school at two o'clock, and I got a ride home so I was early. Billy drove in while I was getting a snack. I heard him crashing around in the front hall, and when I came out, he put his arm around me and said, 'Wanna buy you a present, baby,' and just pulled me out the door. I didn't even have time to get my coat on, but when he saw I was cold, he gave me his jacket. It weighed a *ton.*"

Oh Billy. This was your shopping day of the century. The Fargo economy has been bolstered until the Christmas rush.

"He didn't even ask me where we should go, but I guess he'd been downtown before. We went right to that jewelry store by our bank, that quiet one with the carpet and those glass cases with the wood frames. As soon as we got inside, he hammered on a case, and three different clerks ran up to us. They all stopped when they looked at Billy, though."

"He's pretty big."

"Yes, but he wouldn't hurt anybody."

"They were probably afraid he was going to knock a hole in the case and just take something." Lisa looked at me with a twitch in the corner of her mouth and little sparkles of light caught in her eyes. The adolescent girl's richest fantasy—a demon lover who would break jewelry cases for her. Or a demon father. Or did it matter which? It was clear she'd adored every minute of it.

"He wanted to buy me earrings, but I told him my ears weren't pierced. Doesn't he know that women get their ears pierced, Mom? Then he saw the lockets, and he liked a big one with a green stone in it. The salesman took it out for him and tried to put it around my neck, but Billy gave him a shove and did it himself. Only he couldn't get it fastened. I think his fingers were too big. He took it anyway and gave the salesman a whole handful of money."

"I can imagine."

"Mom." She was trying to count the petals on the rose. "His hands were shaking too. He kept getting caught in my hair. When we got back in the car, he put his arm around me and said he was sorry for pulling." She shook her head. "It didn't hurt that much. He didn't have to apologize."

"Do you have the locket now?"

"Sure." She reached under her collar. "I put it on myself when we got home. I couldn't do it while Billy was driving because he jerked around the corners so much. Want to see?" She held it out in her hand and moved next to me.

Well, at least it wasn't a two-hundred-dollar bouquet. Billy didn't have exactly the best taste in jewelry either, but there's just so far wrong a man can go with a locket. The gold heart lay in Lisa's palm, thick and heavy, with little engraved lines like leaves running around its edges. There was a green stone too, but it wasn't very large, and it had been shaped so it looked like a teardrop right in the center of the heart. On the right side was a tiny latch, two gold wires twisted together like snakes. Lisa watched me finger it.

"Billy said he'd send me his picture for it. He said he has one from back before he grew his beard." She rubbed the stone with the index finger of her other hand. "Mom?"

"What, honey? It's a lovely locket."

"I know. I like it too. I can wear it on my pink sweater tomorrow." But that wasn't all. "Mom, don't be mad. Billy knows about Mike."

For a moment I couldn't remember who Mike was. But Lisa went right on.

"When Billy put his arm around me, he had his hand down my side and it pushed . . ." The stem of the rose broke in two and she tried to stick the ends back together. "It still hurt, and I said 'Ouch.' He wanted to know what the matter was, and I tried to pretend nothing was wrong. But he just kept *asking*. So I told him I had a bruise. And then he wanted to know what happened." She had dropped the rose among the cushions and was rubbing her thumbs together. "I was *embarrassed*, Mom. But he'd just bought me that locket and he still wouldn't stop asking. So I told him about Halloween night. It took almost all the way home."

"What did he say?"

"He said he was going to kill him."

For the space of a breath the pronouns simply wouldn't unwind in my brain. "He said *what*?"

"He said he was going to *kill* Mike. With a *gun*."

I tried to get up from the sofa, but my knees wouldn't unbend. Mike, with both hands on the lemonade glass. Billy. Lisa and her locket. All swaddled in funeral wreaths with lots of purple carnations. I put my hands over my eyes.

"He said everybody from West Texas is a good shot."

"But Lisa! Billy doesn't even have a gun."

"Yes he does. He found that little one of Daddy's in the attic when he fixed up the sofa. It's not very big, but Billy said that doesn't matter. He stopped at the hardware store to get some bullets for it." And while the wind of Jeff's last year began to beat at me, not prairie wind this time, but bitter gales from those parts of the world that had no geography, I heard Lisa's voice, almost drowned by the storm, saying, "I don't think Mike really did anything *that* bad."

31

We did the right thing. Without scaring Lisa, I mentioned all the appropriate facts about civic responsibility, irrational anger, Billy's vulnerability, Mike's essential innocence, all the big words that I owned so completely. They sounded good to her. We walked together to the front hall, holding hands like we used to when she went down the walk to first grade that September. "Hold me to the corner, Mom," she'd said then, winding her fingers through mine. Now she was a little embarrassed, but not too much. She slipped on her jacket; even through the picture window it looked cold outside, with grayness touching the trees across the street. We opened the front door and shut it behind us, then walked down the steps (they'd need replacing next summer, because the frost was crumbling them already) and down the walk to the driveway. I had never noticed before how square the front of that Trail Duster was, like a big construction block someone had dropped on our property. We walked as quietly as we could around the side to the door, stood on our tiptoes, and looked in.

Billy was gone. Where he had been, Jake was asleep on the

seat, his knapsack on the floor beside him. The Littlest Mammal was sticking out where the zipper hadn't closed all the way, and Jake had his thumb resting on its nearest ear. The rest of Jake, all but his face, was covered with Billy's leather jacket.

"He'll freeze to death!" wailed Lisa as she looked down the street.

"He looks warm enough to me." I had the door open and was yanking at Jake, trying to pick him up. He slid into my arms, his mouth slightly open. One hand was clamped so tightly around Billy's sleeve that the jacket followed him out of the car, spilling down against my leg.

"I mean *Billy*." Lisa was jiggling up and down next to me, one hand on her locket, the other holding her jacket shut. "It's freezing out here. He gave Jake his *jacket*."

"He probably hitched a ride wherever he was going. I wouldn't worry about him." Because, Lord, let us worry only about the things we have some remote hope of salvaging. Not the drifters and the pickers. Not the things beyond our power.

Jake rolled his head on my arm. His knuckles were white around the jacket, but he wouldn't let go. "Big Teddy," he said. "B-i-i-g Teddy." Suddenly he was awake and kicking to get down. I let him slide to the driveway and started to guide him toward the house, hand on his disarranged hair. He was trying to get his arms inside the jacket sleeves, but it was too heavy for him to heave up on his shoulders by himself, so I yanked the collar up around his neck for him. Chugging along ahead of me, he looked like some small windup engine, with even his sneakers covered by the black leather.

"Maybe we should call the police, Mom." Lisa was holding the door open for us.

"Look, honey, there is nothing to call the police for. I don't think Billy could find Mike even if he wanted to."

"I didn't tell him where Mike lived, Mom. I didn't even tell him Mike's last name. Do you think he'd ask someone?"

"*No.* I think he's probably in some Fargo bar, picking out

a few tunes and having a beer." Jake was staggering upstairs, barely maintaining his balance under the black weight. "Let's order a pizza like you said. I think that's a good idea."

"But Billy left his guitar here, Mom. I put it up in my room so it wouldn't get broken."

I had had enough. "Lisa, I can't *do* anything about what Billy did or didn't do! I don't own him. He's got his own things on his mind. He's got enough money to buy another jacket if he's cold. Hold your locket and forget about him for five minutes. He's a forty-year-old *adult*."

Hands tense at her sides, Lisa swung around toward me. "You just don't *care*, Mom. As long as he's nice to you, that's OK. If he's nice to *me*, then you don't like him anymore. He said he'd write a song for me!" Her shoulders forced back, jaw tight, the wet in her eyes not quite spilling over, Lisa marched past me and up the stairs to her room.

Dear Billy,

*Where did you go? We couldn't even finish
a medium-sized pizza, though Jake fed two
pieces to his menagerie. Lisa won't talk
to me unless I ask her a direct question,
and she keeps her hand around that miserable
locket even when she eating. How can I
teach tomorrow? There's a storm starting
in Montana, and it's supposed to get here
sometime early on Friday. I put your new*
Letting Her Go *album on the record player,
and it made me hurt so much I snatched it
off before the first song was done. Now
it has a big scratch, and I paid $8.95 for it.*

Kay

32

WHEN I WOKE Thursday morning, the furnace was on
even though I'd turned the thermostat down. I was huddled on
one side of the bed right where the heat came up through the
floor vent, broiled and miserable, though usually I would have
been grateful for the warmth. My hands felt like little wizened
claws; I couldn't have curved a finger to pull a trigger even
to defend myself. Billy's pillow was jammed into the small
of my back. As the silent alarm blinked compulsively on my
nightstand, I pulled the pillow around in front of me and
hugged it. There wasn't even any smell.

So I got up, dressed, made the bed while trying not to touch
it too much, fed the kids, both of whom were surprised at my
attention, and put the house together. Lisa was distant but
polite, while Jake had his thumb in his mouth between bites
of cereal. Like a good parent, good woman, good teacher, I
sent them off to school, then drove to the university, parked,
and went in. Lucille wouldn't look at me, but everyone else
was circumspect. I paid Emily for the malted, then went to
my office and threw its remains into the garbage. The janitor
had been by in the night and mopped up the water. I taught

my morning class without ever noticing the features of one face, though they all looked up at me like damp white lily pads on some stagnant pond. For lunch I went back to my office, dug the malted out of the wastebasket, and started to drink it. It tasted so awful I threw it back. I straightened my desk, straightened my pictures, straightened the plastic under my swivel chair, tightened the belt on my slacks. I braced up the books Dennis had upset in the bookcase. When the girl from Administration brought the faculty mail, I gathered mine out of the pile before Lucille could distribute it. Back in my office, I pulled my wedding ring off my finger, sealed it in a State University envelope, and put it in my file drawer. The ring had grown tight over the years, and my finger hurt once I got it off. I sucked the red line like Jake would have, but it still hurt. It still hurt no matter how much I sucked it.

At four p.m., all the freshmen bedded down in their consoling muck, the pond quiet, I started home. It was like walking through quicksand to get out the door. Most of the students had left too, especially with the long weekend coming, but one chubby girl who knew me by sight was writing at the table set in the alcove by the hall, her long straight hair dipping down on both sides of her paper. I didn't think she'd noticed me or the way my feet were sloughing through weeds and sodden tangles, not touching the floor. But as I turned by her, she looked up.

"Are you OK, Mrs. Lombard?" Her pen was still touching the paper.

"Yes, I'm fine. Well, not really fine. But I'll be all right tomorrow. Nothing too bad." If I once stopped moving, I would never be able to get out to the car and drive home.

"Maybe you have a Focal Problem. I have about eighteen." She laughed.

"I can top that," I said, and I smiled. She ran over and opened the door for me.

Outside, the edge of snow was already in the air, an anticipatory gray, sharp-shinned, the sky spreading itself solid over the campus. I fumbled at the neck loop of my coat, finally giving up and letting it hang open. Still in its autumn response pattern, the Trail Duster started right up, no frozen grinding of its innards, and took me home. I hadn't cleaned it out since yesterday. Crumpled leaves were plastered across the upholstery, but the Grecian urn had disappeared. Had Billy taken it with him, and for what conceivable purpose? Then, when I jerked to a halt in our driveway, it rolled out from under the passenger seat, thunking against the metal rim of the door, rolling back and settling next to my foot. I shoved it to one side and went into the house, where Lisa and Jake had written me a note in two colors saying they were buying construction paper at Ben Franklin. The word "construction" sounded so hopeful that I was afraid I was going to start crying; they had even spelled it right. Refusing to give in, I slid my feet into the bedroom and went in under the comforter like entering Jonah's whale, swallowed whole.

I wasn't dreaming. That meant I wasn't sleeping either, didn't it? That meant I had to keep my eyes open for fear I might tip over the edge, knocked over by a wave I hadn't seen coming. But I could just lean against the pillow. That was allowed, wasn't it? I wouldn't know unless I tried it, would I? Billy had found some pillows I didn't even know we had. He had found things I had forgotten. He had found things I had put away so deep that they were never supposed to hurt me again. It wasn't fair. But I could take it. I had to take it.

"Hi, Mom. Are you asleep?" Jake was holding onto my stretched-out leg as if it were a log he was transporting. "School was good, Mom. Brian helped me wash my slippers. Lisa said she'd be back late because Rebecca made chili." He patted my hip. "I like the construction paper because it has three blues. Mom, I want to cook spaghetti again, but Billy put away the flowerpot and I can't find it."

"What time is it, Jake?" Blue lights. It was like coming up from the *Nautilus*.

"It's nine oh two and a half. Three-quarters. Nine oh three."

He had just learned how to tell time accurately to the second in first grade. "It's late, Mom. I'm hungry." He paused. "No, I'm not hungry. I ate supper with Brian. Are *you* hungry, Mom?" He bent over and kissed my knee through the comforter.

The phone rang. I sprang up and answered it.

"I'd like to speak to Mrs. Lombard, please." There was a great thudding in the background, many people, screams. A dorm party? I shook my head and moved the noise away from my ear.

"Mrs. Lombard, is that you? This is Dennis. Why aren't you here?"

"Why aren't I where?" It made no sense.

"At the Rodeo Association dance! Your friend bought so many tickets!"

"Dennis, I can't hear you." The sound level in the background was like rocket ships.

"I'm shouting! You should be here to hear him play. I didn't know he was famous."

"Who is famous? The Linton cousins?" It was like I hadn't memorized my part of the script.

"Billy Calloway! I didn't know who your friend *was*. He's a great guitar player. Aren't you coming?" But I had already hung up and, shouting for Jake, was shoving my arms into my red coat.

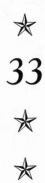

33

THE NIGHT HAWK LOUNGE and the bowling alley
underneath it were on a jag of blacktop road that angled off
from the state highway before it started exploring the farms
north of Fargo. It was a gray frame building with a cracked
portable sign in front propped up on piles of discarded truck
tires. One floodlight shone on the lettering. Near enough to the
university to be a hangout for the kids who had reached drinking age or could convince a bouncer they had, it was also far
enough out of town that the cowboys dropped in too, the two
groups edging around each other at the bar or on the dance
floor, which was worn down to where the nailheads were sticking above the boards. Who patronized the bowling alley I had
no idea.

I parked the Trail Duster as near the building as I could,
but already I was in a far corner of the lot, wedged between
a pickup and an orange Volkswagen with flower decals on
the doors. As I turned off the engine, its dying throbs shook
my knees gently. Then my heart took up the rhythm. When I
bent my neck, I could see the front of my coat going up and
down, steady but fast, fast. I'd forgotten my gloves and my

hands were freezing. No snow yet, but the stars were gone, and the airport searchlight swept like a melancholy broom across the lower sky, reflecting back from the clouds onto the car tops at the other side of the lot.

Billy. Issues to deal with. The gun. Get it back. Where he was last night. Make sure he was warm. I didn't have his jacket either; Jake kept it under his pillow. Request my favorite song. What would that be? All his songs were my favorites. Holding my hand over my heart like a cardiac invalid, I jumped down from the Trail Duster and ran to the door, then up the stairs. Dennis was standing there to welcome me.

"Mrs. Lombard!" He was practically jumping up and down. "I knew you'd come!" Was he looking me in the eye? It was so dark inside, except for the flashes of strobe light, that I couldn't really tell. "This is a proud evening for the Rodeo Association. This is the most luck I've ever had in my life. This is wonderful! I've got a seat saved for you up by the stage." His shyness completely gone, he closed his hand around my upper arm and pulled me out of the doorway, then along the edge of the dance floor, squeezing against the partition. I was sliding behind a wall of bodies like an escaping prisoner. We broke momentarily into the open, and then I was wedged into a folding chair jammed between the EXIT door and a tiny table. Dennis hovered over me, arms out like a barrier. People were whooping and hollering all around him.

"What would you like to drink?" There was so much noise I had to read his lips.

"Sprite. Seven-Up. It doesn't matter, Dennis. You'll be killed if you try to leave, though. Stay here and protect me."

"But you need something to drink."

"We can get it later when this mob quiets down." Two students, hair flying, were dancing a wild midwestern tango behind the next table. Walpurgisnacht. I braced myself against the chair back and turned toward the stage. Until then I hadn't realized that the band wasn't playing. Now I could see them getting ready for the next set, tuning their guitars (but tuning to what?—the PA music was so loud they couldn't possibly hear their own sounds), laughing, punching each other. The drummer was tapping his snares with his fingers, checking out their tension or something. Love taps. On the steel guitar was a shaggy boy I'd seen around campus, head back, a can of beer in his hand. Keyboards. A bass guitar player. Two rhythm guitars, one of them with no shirt. He had "Cowboy Lovin' " painted across his chest; lines of sweat were running through it and puddling the colors in his belt.

And Billy. He was sitting off to one side, head down over his guitar, a shiny flat model that shot off the reflected light like starbursts. Not blue. Somebody must have lent it to him. Big shoulders hunched as if to protect it, he made tiny adjustments with the pegs, checked the strings, took a different pick, plucked a line of notes that nobody could hear. One of the other guitarists hammered his way across the stage with a six-pack of beer hanging in his hand, slipping out a can and holding it out for Billy. The drummer and the steel player watched. Billy didn't take it; he didn't look up. The kid was embarrassed, rocking on his feet with the beer sitting in his hand like a small animal. He tossed it into the air to get a good head on it, but it slipped out of his hand coming down and banged on the floor by Billy's boot. Billy looked up. He shook his head once while the kid retrieved the beer and scrambled back to his station. Billy was at his guitar again.

"He's wonderful, Mrs. Lombard. I'd heard his records but had no idea who he was. We'd just gotten started and there was already quite a crowd when he came in." Dennis hesitated. "I was a little scared at first, but he walked right up to me and said, 'I'm Billy Calloway. Need a lead?' Just like that. Tim gave him his guitar and introduced him, and he just *went*. Half the kids were at the phones calling their friends. This'll be the third set." He leaned toward me across the table, moving his lips with emphasis to make sure I'd hear. "Want me to tell him you've come?"

"I'll wait, Dennis." The sound in the lounge had geared

down. It was time. A yellow spot opened like an eye from a booth above the floor in back, blinked, opened again, felt its way down to the stage, touching the black with fire. The front mike caught it and coded it back. Suddenly Billy was standing behind the mike, adjusting the height, guitar slung loose, shirt open, sweat running down his forehead beneath his hat. He hoisted his guitar and the silver buckle on his belt returned the gleam. Behind him, the band had started a steady four-four, little riffs on the steel, brush on the snares, life beat rhythm, insistent. I felt it through my chair all the way up. Why did my fingers hurt? I looked down; I was pressing so hard against the table that my nails were bending on the Formica. I pulled my hands loose and laid them flat in front of me on my lap.

"Alright." Shouts from the kids. "Alright now. You want the music, don'tcha? *I* know. Want the *beat*. I know what you want." His fingers were picking out something intricate on the guitar, voices chasing each other, heavy strumming in the bass when they almost touched. Under the spot his whole face glistened wet; his shirt was stained dark all the way down, almost the same color as his vest. Drops from his forehead splashed on the surface of the guitar. The kid with the beer, after looking around apprehensively, edged up with a towel. Billy let the band carry the rhythm for a moment while he wiped his face, then dropped the towel on the floor beside him.

"Gonna play you jest one song this set, one helluva song. Alright? Somethin' real, you might say. Wrote it a long time ago, first time I lived it, then goddamn well hadda go live it one more time. Like that, ain't it? Gotta go through it all more 'n once in this world. Song's like a pathway. Hell, that music ain't gonna letcha rest, is it? Shit, any picker knows that. Nothin' you kin hide. Might as well live it 'n' sing it too." He swung around to the band, who were staring at him so intently that they looked wired to the front of the stage. "Back me up, boys. Jest follow me."

I'd never heard Billy's song before, or maybe long ago on

some car radio before I knew who he was. It wasn't on the records I had. Sentimental country-western stuff, sure. Was there any other kind? And if it was so bad, why were they all so quiet?

> *"Like t' do it over if you'd let me.*
> *More I cared, the more I caused you pain.*
> *Messed my mind with crazy ways t' lift me.*
> *Wish I'd held you when sun turned t' rain.*
>
> *"Shoot me down, but first you gotta catch me,*
> *Runnin' wild from all them fears I own.*
> *Lonely dreamin', need someone t' love me,*
> *Empty nights, sure hurts t' be alone.*
>
> *"Never gonna face up that I need you,*
> *I ain't one t' talk when I kin run.*
> *Lady with the gentle touch that warmed me,*
> *Out your window, see that mornin' sun."*

Softly, the guitar sound just on the edge of disappearing, Billy played through the melody again, the steel guitar behind him keeping up the rhythm so gently it was like breathing. No one hooted. Next Billy unslung the guitar and leaned it against the side of the keyboards. He gave a nod, almost formal, to the steel player, then walked off the stage and over to my table. I hadn't realized he knew I was there. Without looking at me directly, he reached inside his vest, took out the gun, and placed it in my lap. Then, head down, with the kids moving aside so quickly that in all that crowded lounge he never touched anyone, he walked out the door.

34

IT WAS STILL before midnight when I picked up Jake, dense with sleep but still smiling blearily, at Margaret's. Already the snow had begun. "Awfully early," said Margaret, shifting Jake's bottom a little higher so I could get a grip on him. "It means winter will go on forever." She had the back of her hair in curlers but was still dressed. "The radio said we'd have a blizzard all day tomorrow. Do you have enough in the house to eat? Jim shopped for us this afternoon, so I could give you anything you want."

"I'll be OK. I don't have to go in tomorrow anyway. Once the kids are off to school, I'll go back to sleep and sleep it right through."

"I don't think there'll *be* any school for the kids tomorrow if the weatherman is right. First storm day of the season, Kay." In the dim light of her two porch lamps, her cheekbones glistened. "We'll have to dig out their snowmobile suits."

"You probably know where Brian's is. That's one ahead of me."

"Oh, you'll find Jake's. The problem is if they grow out of them. A snowmobile suit is a major investment these days."

Margaret, are we really having this conversation? I thought. It's eleven thirty at night and Jake is drooling down my back. I have a revolver in my pocket and outside a blizzard is starting. "Thanks," I said. "You're a good neighbor, Margaret."

She blushed. "Oh, not really. The boys like each other." Even her chin was red. She opened the front door for me and watched as I heaved Jake down the walk and across the street. Her porch lights glowed behind me until I got my door unlocked, then flickered off.

Inside the house was warm, great waves of heat pouring up through the vents. I must have forgotten to turn the furnace down after Dennis called. Dropping my purse and kicking off my boots, I carried Jake to the sofa, now a neglected disarray of scarves, pillows, and blankets, and slid him out of his jacket. Little slits of white showed under his eyelids as he hunched himself into a ball. To heck with pajamas. I squatted down and got my shoulder under his belly, then hoisted him off the sofa and into a modified fireman's carry, my knees shaking briefly but then catching hold. Up the stairs, into his room. Someone had made his bed—could it possibly have been me? I pulled back the quilt and the blanket underneath, its yellow rayon trim frayed and hanging loose from where Jake felt it in the night, and rolled him in. His shoes were untied anyway, so I yanked them off and dropped them on the floor beside his bed. Billy's jacket was sticking out from under the pillow, and Jake slid down until his cheek was on it. The slits closed.

All right so far. But once I got into the hall, all my poise collapsed, and I slid down against the baseboard, my hands braced on the carpeting. At the end of the hall, Lisa's door was tight shut with a piece of paper taped to it; I hadn't even noticed it before. On my hands and knees (no one to see, no one to laugh), I crawled down the hall and felt my way up along the door frame. It was a piece of her stationery, decorated with a daisy in each corner.

Dear Mom, I got back and you were gone but I
knew it was OK. I'm asleep. Don't wake me
up tomorrow because there isn't going to be
any school FOR SURE! I love you.

Lisa

Oh, Lisa. Everything is coming up daisies for you, isn't it?
Snug in your garret, full of Rebecca's chili, an extra day to
get your homework done, snow piling on the edges of your
windowsill, sleeping the sleep of the righteous. My beautiful
daughter, already taller than I am.

I still had my coat on. Downstairs in the hall closet I
scrambled out a scarf and a pair of Jake's mittens, then dug
my feet back into my boots and zipped them up. The doorknob
was already cold when I grabbed it, even through the wool.
I stepped onto the porch, then sat down on the first step,
one foot hunched up under me.

The snow was coming, all right. Against the streetlight,
waves of white passed and passed again. Doesn't snow always
fall from heaven? Of course. But here in North Dakota, in
the night blizzards, it moved from side to side, a horizontal
blanket surging through the air. When the wind came up,
the streetlight rocked frantically on its hanger, and my cheek
burned with the cold. Then the gust stopped and there were
only the flakes, steady, coming down like cottonwood balls
turned to ice. Snow on the front walk that I'd have to shovel
off tomorrow if the blizzard stopped. Snow piling up around
the tires of the Trail Duster. The perennial bed was a checker-
board of brown and white, the snow caught in the crevices
of the leaves and accumulating fast. My red sleeve was spotted,
my slacks, the top of my boot had a white cap. If I sat here
long enough, would I be buried? Would Jake give me a carrot
nose in the morning? Not unless I went inside and found his
snowmobile suit. I put my hand on the butt of the revolver in
my pocket. Had Billy put the bullets in it? After all those years
of cowboy playing, wouldn't you think I would have known

237

how to break open a gun and see? But I didn't.

Down the block, car lights pierced through the snow. Jim coming home to Margaret? Not likely, they'd both be safely asleep already. Mike coming back for a friendly visit with Lisa? His parents would never let him drive in this weather. A stranger, passing through the blizzard on the way to his inheritance? On our dead-end street?

The car stopped in front of our house, motor still running. Snow fell through the headlight beams, tickling along them like little fingers, like silver, like sheets waved in the north wind. The door swung open and a slender figure stepped out, bending against a gust of wind that pulled the door from his fingers and slammed it shut. It was too cold for rape, but I wondered. Anyway, I had the gun.

"Ma'am?" He started up the front walk, shuffling through the little ridges of snow the wind was piling across it. "Ma'am, are you there?" He stopped. "I mean, I know you're there." Soon the snow would bury him and I would never know what he wanted. He came a little closer. "Ma'am, we met once before, in St. Paul. I'm Tweeter Bigelow, in case you recall. The one in the dressing room. Billy's friend." A gust of snow tore at his hair and he covered his ears with both hands. A southern boy. "Ma'am? I am sorry to bother you, but I have got Billy in the car here and I think we ought to put him to bed. I didn't want to just drop him in some motel." He was near enough now that I could see the snow in his eyelashes. "Actually, ma'am, I would not have known how to get him into one, being that he is not walking by himself, and I do not know a soul in this town." I stayed on the step. "Ma'am, are you all right?" he asked.

"Yes." My legs got up and I stayed on top of them. I started down the walk to Tweeter, who edged over to the side so there would be room for both of us. "I don't think there's going to be any school tomorrow," I said.

"Yes, ma'am." He had his head buried in his collar, but he never stopped looking sideways at me. We reached the car and he opened the door, tilting the seat back. As I bent down, the streetlight moved into focus through the rear window, and I saw the outlines of Billy's face in the corner, marked out against the glass. As my eyes adjusted to the dark, I saw that he had no jacket on. Of course. The car was hot like a little oven.

"I didn't want him to freeze," said Tweeter, explaining before I even thought to ask. "Ma'am, I think it would be best if I just edged him out here and you made sure his head didn't hit anywhere. Then once he is out, I can get his shoulders and pull him up the walk." As he talked, I noticed again just how thin he was, even in the Humphrey Bogart topcoat he was now wearing. Were all his buckskin fringes tucked away underneath it?

Together we tugged and maneuvered Billy out of the car, the snow catching in his hair and beard. He never opened his eyes even when I wiped off the first flakes. Tweeter dragged him up the walk, breathing hard, Billy's boots making lines through the white sidewalk and up the steps. I held the door open, and Tweeter heaved him over the threshold with what seemed to be his last strength, then sank down on the floor of the front hall with Billy's head in his lap. The wind was suddenly stronger, and I wrenched at the front door to get it shut. Even then a draft cut around it, negating my September weather stripping. I squatted down beside Tweeter on the floor.

"Should I call a doctor?" Billy didn't seem to be breathing.

"Oh no, ma'am!" Tweeter seemed genuinely shocked. "He isn't *dead* or anything like that. But we probably should get him into bed. If you could tell me where the bed is . . ." he said delicately, tilting his head away from me. I pointed the way across the living room, and Tweeter pulled himself erect, caught Billy under the arms again, and began to heave him in little jerks across the carpet. It was a blessing we had a downstairs bedroom.

Once we actually got past the dresser and up next to the

239

bed itself, Tweeter seemed to gain strength. "I hope this doesn't disturb you too much, ma'am," he said, as he edged Billy up and onto the mattress. I couldn't manipulate the worlds of his politeness and Billy's large unconscious presence together. "I will get his boots off if you don't mind." A long embarrassed pause ensued as he began to tug Billy's right boot back and forth. "You might care to loosen his belt, ma'am, or undo his shirt the rest of the way. Do you have an old blanket by any chance? We can wrap him in that." He went to work on Billy's other boot.

"I'll just cover him up with the comforter, Tweeter. He'll be warm enough then." If I touched Billy's belt or any part of his body, my hands were going to fall off at the wrist.

"Ma'am, I don't like to say this, but he might be . . . might be sick when he wakes up. He wouldn't want to mess up your bedding." Had the wind not dropped for a moment, I wouldn't have been able to hear what Tweeter was saying. He was moving his lips but only a murmur came out.

"Oh, for God's sake, Tweeter. I am the mother of two children. There isn't a mess in the world I haven't cleaned up." I straightened my back, then relaxed it just a little. "But I would appreciate it if you could finish getting him undressed."

While Tweeter unbuckled Billy's belt and slid it loose, I stepped back and leaned against the dresser to watch. Belt done, Tweeter unzipped Billy's jeans and started to edge them down over his shorts. I had always thought cowboys as out of it as Billy slept in their jeans, but Tweeter was going at this like an old-time expert with a different idea. In his trench coat, he looked like a male nurse out of the French Resistance. Gently he pulled the jeans over Billy's feet, shook them out, then folded them and placed them on the dresser next to me, a careful six inches away from my elbow. There was no Chinese laundry pleat in them now.

Like merry-go-round horses, my thoughts kept circling,

going up and down my center of consciousness in a staggered rhythm. Why wasn't I gurgling out a scream as I ran for the door? Why did all this seem so natural? Well, Jake and Lisa would be happy to have him back whether he had any money left or not. From their rooms, force fields with Billy's jacket and guitar as their centers flooded down the stairs and around the bed, little particles zinging like mosquitoes. I wouldn't even mind if he stayed a few days longer; he would certainly be better at shoveling snow than I was. The merry-go-round horses rotated, and I wondered about the song he'd sung at the Night Hawk. Who was the lady with the gentle touch? Had the song been the only way he could be sure of remembering her?

My eyes must have shut momentarily, but after all it was pretty late. When I opened them and looked up, Tweeter was contemplating Billy's torso. He started unsnapping, then opened the shirt and vest back away from Billy's chest. Next he lifted up his left shoulder, shifting him a little on the pillow so he could get some leverage on the cloth. As he lifted, Billy's head slid to one side, and the matted curls hanging on his forehead moved too. There was a purple bruise above his left eyebrow, and when I saw it I felt such a rush of tenderness that I couldn't swallow.

"Tweeter." I hung onto the dresser behind my back with both hands.

"Ma'am?" Tweeter let Billy back down on the pillow.

I extracted one hand and pointed like an idiot. "He's . . . he's hurt." The force field sucked me toward the bed, but I was afraid I would wash into the shag carpet if I took a step.

Efficiently, Tweeter reached out and lifted Billy's hair further to the side. "It looks like somebody gave him a pretty good lick before Billy laid him out." He went back to work on the shirt.

"Shouldn't we do something?"

"There is no need, ma'am. He won't even feel that."

"But he might have a concussion!" I sounded like Lisa.

"That is no concussion." Tweeter was lifting Billy again so he could work his arm out of the sleeve.

"How do *you* know?" Even with the wind I could hear the edge in my voice.

"Ma'am, I have been *with* him when he had a concussion. In fact, more than one. The last time was in Tulsa, and when he woke up then he couldn't remember a thing he had done all that last day. He looked a lot worse then than he does now. So I *know*." Tweeter was standing upright, hands on his hips. There was an edge in his voice too.

"I'm going to get something to put on it."

"He does not *need* anything, ma'am."

Ignoring him, I checked to see if I could walk without melting, and I could. Firmly I set out for the bathroom, not looking around toward Tweeter although I could feel the waves of his disapproval beating into my back. I knew how to take care of people too. I had made a career of it.

Once in the bathroom, though, I wasn't so sure. What did you put on a bruise to make it better? Kisses. Oh no, wrong answer. Some kind of compress. I looked at the medicine cabinet, my intense face cut off at the chin in the mirrored door. Purposefully I opened it and inspected the shelves. All the gauze pads were gone. For a moment I stood in indecision, than ran my eyes over the towel racks. Jake's Wawa Walrus washcloth was folded on top, and I snatched it up, saturated it with cold water, wrung it out, and folded it into a little square as I started back to the bedroom. My hands were so cold the water felt the same temperature as my skin.

Tweeter was bending over Billy as I came in, sliding the other arm out of his shirt. He looked at me as if he had hoped I wasn't coming back and stayed tight up to the bed. It was still his turn on the merry-go-round.

Walking quietly but not stopping, I came up on the other side. Now that just his undershirt covered his chest, I could see that Billy was actually breathing, long slow breaths from

242

his belly with big spaces in between. I couldn't seem to stop watching the cloth across his front go in and out. Suddenly I was struggling to breathe in the same rhythm, but even when I tried to hold out, I couldn't get my pumping lungs slowed down enough. There was a tiny wet spot on Billy's hand from where the washcloth had dripped. Forgetting I couldn't touch him, I reached down and wiped it off.

"All right, ma'am." From his side of the bed, Tweeter looked at me as he lifted back Billy's hair again. It really wasn't a very bad bruise now that I saw it up close, but I laid the washcloth compress over it anyway. Billy's breathing didn't change. "I just didn't want him to hurt tomorrow," I said to Tweeter, though that didn't explain anything at all.

"I don't want him to hurt tomorrow either, ma'am," said Tweeter. "I flew all the way up here so I could . . ." He stopped. "I have known him since we were both . . ." He stopped again. "I'm afraid he'll get cold. We should cover him up."

With one of us on each side, we pulled the sheet over Billy, then the faithful comforter. Because he was a little closer to my side of the bed, I edged the comforter up under his chin, making sure even the edges of his beard were covered. In his cocoon of warmth, Billy stretched himself diagonally, pulling his feet back on the mattress. Then he disengaged one arm and threw it above his head. His face wrinkled. "Shit," he said, still asleep.

"It would be better if we just left him here to rest for a while." Tweeter sounded like something familiar, but what? Oh yes. A schoolteacher. He had begun edging toward the door, his eyes averted but still checking to see if I was coming too. I held out my hands and walked toward him.

"Tweeter, would you like a cup of tea? I have Earl Grey and English Breakfast."

A half smile pushed his cheeks up. "Ma'am," he said, reaching under his coat, "I was just about to offer you a drink too. Only all I have is Jack Daniel's."

35

WE HAD THE FIRST fire of the season, Tweeter and I. He brought in an armful of the dead elm I had stacked along the side of the house while I made the tea. We compromised by having the Jack Daniel's in it. The snow flew by the window in a horizontal path, and even though I pulled the curtain, I left a space wide enough for us to keep track of the storm. Between the two of us we got the fire going, smoldering at first, then roaring up the chimney, pulling out more heat than it put in, of course, but tonight it didn't make any difference.

Tweeter perched on the director's chair. "It was hard finding you, ma'am, if you will pardon my saying so. Billy didn't know the number, just the street. He did say there were flowers in the front yard, so when I saw that lump with the snow blowing on it, I figured this must be the place. Or at least it was worth trying. Then when I saw you on the porch, I was pretty sure."

"Does Billy have a succession of women who sit out in blizzards waiting for him to come home?" The words were out of my mouth before my brain could drop the gate. Tweeter looked shocked, hands woven around his cup, and I retreated. "It's all right, Tweeter," I said. "It's a crazy night. You turned up out of nowhere, and I didn't even think it was strange. I must be hibernating. Or maybe it's your Jack Daniel's. Or the storm." Tweeter was dissolving and reforming in the chair; I had to tighten my eye muscles to hold him in focus. "Do you live around here?"

"No, ma'am. I live in Texas like Billy. About two miles from him, as a matter of fact. He called me this morning, early. I could tell he was on something just by listening to him. He gets all crazy. I flew up to the Cities and rented a car because there weren't any flights to Fargo left that I could get on." Tweeter heaved his shoulders back and held them so long I thought they were hung up on the ridge of the chair. "That is one hell of a drive, ma'am, if you will pardon my saying so. The big rigs and I were about the only ones on the road. Once I got here, I headed for the bars downtown—I didn't know which bar, but people don't forget Billy, and he wasn't hard to find. He was pretty groggy when I turned him up, but at least I could get him outside and into the car. That was about it, though." Tweeter looked hopefully at the bottom of his cup. Pulling myself up in response, I went into the kitchen and made another pot of tea. New leaves too, no cheating. He had already added the Jack Daniel's to his cup when I got back.

"You know, Tweeter, he was playing earlier this evening at a dance the Rodeo Association held. He didn't seem so crazy then." And what was crazy? I would be the last to know.

"What was he like before that, ma'am? Yesterday?"

Yesterday. That was about ten years ago, or fifteen. Still autumn, still cocoa, still Billy kneeling beside me on the bathroom floor. Still being held and washed away without drowning. The flowers. His head on the dashboard. "He was crazy, all right," I said.

"Probably on something, ma'am, like I said—speed, most

likely, or whatever else he could get hold of or had stashed away."

"But why would he do that? Do people even sell drugs in Fargo?"

Tweeter looked at me pityingly. "Any picker knows where to get what he needs. There are dealers everywhere. It's not too cold for them even here." But he looked out the window doubtfully while a fierce gust shook the glass and sent the curtains swaying.

"Is he high now?" All those hours of freshman essays had left me with a few fragments of appropriate vocabulary.

Tweeter paused and rocked his heels in the carpet. "Just drunk, I consider. Of course, he might still be on something too. He wouldn't have called unless he figured on coming down, though." Very gently he turned to me. "I wouldn't worry, ma'am. He'll be all right by morning. Not feeling too good, maybe, but not crazy or anything." The tone of his voice shifted into graduation speech. "You know, he is a just plain wonderful picker and singer. Some of his songs are solid country gold, too. With the Range Riders, he can get booked anywhere."

"He's good in bed too." Some nights you can just say anything, especially when it's snowing.

Sputtering, Tweeter put his palm over the waves sloshing out of his cup. "That's interesting, ma'am," he choked out. Then his mouth quivered in a half smile that didn't seem to know whether to develop or subside. "Tell you the truth, I always sort of thought he must be, considering how the ladies act once they get to know him, but you never can tell. He doesn't talk much about *that*."

"It's probably all part of being a performer." What in the world would I say next?

Tweeter took a long sip of tea and Jack Daniel's, leaning back in his chair. "I don't know, ma'am. Lots of things just plain depend on the man." He had his schoolteachery look again. "You know, most pickers mess around a little, one way

246

or another. Drugs, booze, whatever. As long as they can still play their gigs, nobody thinks much about it. Billy has tapered off a good deal in the last couple years. The worst thing used to be the fights. Still is, sometimes. If I get after him about it, he always says no cowboy singer has to be pretty. If he wants to get his nose broke, he figures he can."

"He told me about when he got his hand hurt. By the club owner in Dallas. That fight didn't sound like much fun." I slid down into the corner of the sofa and pulled the afghan up to my shoulders, then arranged the bottom half down over my legs. All my muscles were unknotting like Jake's spaghetti, despite the chill around the margins of the living room. Even with the fire, the house was being eaten by the blizzard.

Tweeter looked at me as if I were about fourteen. "Well, ma'am," he said, "I wouldn't have called that a fight. Not a *fight*." He crossed his legs with precision and rotated his teacup in his hands. "Billy probably told you, he and that lady were going to it on her couch, middle of the week, middle of the *day*. Her old man was down at the club doing the beer orders. When they're done, she slips off . . ."

Maybe I was falling asleep. This wasn't the way it had been run by me the first time. I pulled my hand across my eyes, tangling my eyebrows with my thumb as it dragged along the ridge of my forehead. "*She* slips off?" I said, trying to find a point of clarification.

Tweeter went right on as if he were explaining a problem in geometry. "Billy likes them on top," he said. "Some men do. Anyway, she slips off and Billy just goes to sleep right there, his left hand flopped over the edge on the floor, one of those shiny wood floors with those little Chinese rugs. He didn't even zip up his jeans. So Charlie comes home—she sees him come too, because she is right by the hall putting on her bathrobe, but she does not say one word to Billy. Too scared, she told me. Charlie comes in, and the first thing he sees is this cowboy picker who has been screwing his wife sound asleep on his couch. He doesn't say a word, just goes across those little rugs and looks down at Billy. He is wearing these big boots with the flat heels. Then he steps right on Billy's fingers, grinds them hard as he can into the floor. Once he's done that, he walks out the door and drives away."

"My God." I plunged out of the afghan to poke at the fire, dwindled to a line of gold along the largest log. What worse thing could happen to a picker? The poker chinked in my hand against the andiron, sending a tiny cloud of soot up into the chimney.

"Billy managed to get to my place somehow, which was not that far away. By then he was hurting so bad he could hardly talk. I drove him to the hospital, let him out by the emergency room. He had been there just two weeks before to get his eyebrow sewed up after he'd gone to it with some drunk after the show. Then I went to park the car and could not find one single slot. Everybody in Dallas was at that hospital. I drove around for about half an hour before some old lady with a van pulled out and I could get in. When I got back to that emergency room entrance, the first thing I saw was Billy. The first thing."

"He hadn't gone in?" The sofa had never seemed particularly narrow before, but I had trouble getting situated on it again. Maybe because my knees were trembling. It was harder to get the afghan tucked smooth this time.

"He was still standing there like a statue, leaned back a little against that granite corner by the door. Only now he was rolling his head back and forth on the stone. I pulled him away, and Christ, there was *blood* on that wall where his head was. He didn't say one word. I got him down to where the chairs were and went to tell the nurse behind the counter. She was one of those nice sawed-off country kids, a little fat but not too bad. It turned out she knew who Billy was, heard him play just the week before. She went right up to where he was standing, ready to leave if he didn't pass out first. Then she did one smart thing."

"What was that?" Under the afghan, I had jammed my

knees together so they wouldn't keep banging back and forth. I was afraid Tweeter would hear them.

"She took him real gentle by the arm, the other arm, and said, 'Mr. Calloway, I need to talk to you, but you're so tall I can't stretch up. Would you please sit down?' Billy went over to those chairs right away. Then she sat down beside him. She didn't touch his hand—any fool could see what was wrong there. She just checked his pulse, asked how old he was, those things. Then she said, 'You know, my brother is a picker too, and he banged his hand up real bad when he ran his car off the road last summer. The doctors here fixed it up fine, and he's got his own band now.' At first I didn't think Billy even heard her, but then he put his good hand up over his face and made a little noise in his throat like he was choking. I had no idea what to do. She gave him a real quick look, then she went and found some Kleenex. By the time she got back, you could see Billy had started to loosen up a little. Pretty soon one of those young doctors came to give him a shot, and they took him away to X-ray."

"And you were there with him all the time?"

"Well, sure." Tweeter matched his own hands together, pointed up, and flexed his fingers back and forth. "It was not a good time for him to be by himself. While they were putting the cast on and he was pretty much out of it, I went back to talk to that little girl. She said she knew how bad it would make a picker feel to get his fingers hurt like that. I asked her what band her brother had, thought I'd go hear them play when we had a free night. She started shuffling all those papers behind the counter and wouldn't tell me. I figured maybe he wasn't so good after all and she didn't want me to know."

"Did you ever consider that she might not have had a brother?" It would have been my first thought.

"Why wouldn't she have a brother when she said she did?"

Oh, Tweeter. I began to pile the pillows up next to me. At five they tottered back down again. Snow was plastered at least three inches up on the outside sill, a strip of white magic marker against the glass. I was following the story like a rope between house and barn; if I let go, the white wind would drown me. "Did Billy go back to the club?" I asked.

"Sure, after a couple days. Charlie wasn't going to lose an act that drew like the Range Riders. Billy could not do anything with the guitar, of course, but he sang and the boys backed him up. He was so full of pills by then he didn't half know what he was doing. Worst thing was, he could not get any sleep. If he laid on that bed, I guess he figured he would never get up alive."

That didn't make sense. Everybody slept, more if the giant unthinkables knocked at you when you were awake. I tuned in the bedroom, but there wasn't a murmur, and I pushed back my impulse to go check if he was alive. Of course he was. So was I.

Thin as he was, when Tweeter turned in the chair, it shook back and forth on its little wooden legs. He squinted at the snow against the sill, narrowing his eyes so much he must have been measuring its depth in his mind. "Lord," he said, and shook his head. Like a child, I wanted the rest of the story, could taste it on my tongue. His voice slid under my sensory explorations as he laid out the next words, speaking so slowly it was like he was picking them out of a box. Maybe this was the part he didn't tell everyone.

"Every night after the gig, Billy'd want to go right back to the apartment, no more partying. I thought he just did not feel right yet. Once I got him back there, though, he would bat around that place like he was lost. If he had it around, he would knock off a bottle of gin, whiskey, anything, but he would not even get normal drunk, just restless like some animal on the prowl. He said his hand hurt and he couldn't sleep, but he would not tell me anything more, Billy wouldn't. I would go home finally, dead tired out, but if I would call him, he'd be on that phone practically before it rang. I do not know how he kept on with the band, but he managed.

Every morning he would look worse, no shave, wouldn't even eat, and he was already one lean picker in those days."

The fire was getting low, with lots of smoke puffing out. I went and rolled on the next chunk of elm, glad to be able to take care of something that needed me. A crowd of sparks spurted up the chimney, then subsided as I walked back to my nest on the sofa, intending to check Tweeter's cup for him. But he had set it on the coffee table and was talking again, not even noticing as I held my knees steady and settled in. His voice was gravelly.

"After about a week of that, when he could not even sing right anymore, I finally went and called Jill. Traced her down to her folks in Georgia, but it sure took some doing. I told her I did not like to impose, but I was worried about Billy and could not seem to do a thing with him by myself. Jill and me, we did not get on any too well, but she heard me out from beginning to end and took the train on down to Dallas." Tweeter stopped and eyed me cautiously. "Billy tell you about Jill?"

"A little." Compulsively, I started to pile the pillows up again as carefully as I could, ladybug on top. I buried my cold hands halfway in the pile when I had finished.

"I picked her up at the station about two a.m. the next day and took her right to Billy's apartment. Thought he would be glad to see her, but he acted like she wasn't there, kept on rambling from the kitchen to the bedroom, then back to the kitchen, like somebody gone crazy. Jill sat there on the kitchen stool for about half an hour, looking at him every time he passed, and then she went into the bedroom. Turned down the bed real careful. She piled up pillows and stuff against the headboard, then went and made an ice bag and wrapped it in a bunch of towels. When Billy came through the kitchen again, she put one arm around him and followed him to the bedroom, where she just stood with him, kind of petting his back, till he sat down on the bed with her. Neither one said a word—it was so quiet in the place you could hear the cars on the freeway a mile down Frosden Road. She leaned herself up on the headboard and got him laying down against her with his head sort of in her lap, then she put his arm on a bunch of those rolled-up towels with the ice wrapped around above the cast. After that she just sat there holding him, smoothing his hair back with her hand until he went to sleep. When I came back to check on him in the morning, around ten or so, she was still sitting there holding him just like I left her, only now her eyes were shut too. She did that every night for a week. Cooked for him too, tacos and all those Tex-Mex things he likes. I didn't hear them say two dozen words to each other in that whole time, but after he had the next X-rays and the doctors said he was healing good, they started acting more like normal with each other. Or what was normal for them."

At first I thought it was the furnace, struggling to keep up with the storm. Tweeter was rubbing his eyes. Then when I heard it again, I pulled the afghan to one side so I could kick loose and check the thermostat. Were the kids waking up? Something didn't sound right.

It wasn't the furnace. The kids either. As I balanced on my feet, the afghan bundled in my arms, Billy plunged through the door of the bedroom. He staggered between us, head down, and into the hall. As we both caught our breath, he grabbed at the knob, lost it, then wrenched the door open. A gust of air swept the fireplace into brilliance, and then he was gone. And I was after him, no coat or mittens, though I did stop to thrust my feet into my boots in the hall as I tore past. Like a stupid southerner who didn't know about blizzards, I tore after him into the storm.

We both could have died. People did in North Dakota, when the visibility was down and the snow plugged the exhaust pipe of a stalled car. When they lost their way trying to walk home. I knew better; I was a northwoman born and bred. It was colder now too, with no moon and the streetlight dimmed by waves of white. Freezing.

From the porch, I could see where Billy's stockinged foot had skidded off the step, then where he'd caught himself on the sidewalk. Already the exposed cement was being covered, and I lost the trail. Where could he have run? I checked out to the street, the driveway. No sign. When the worst gusts came, I had to avert my face because the cold hurt too much. Tweeter was standing in the yellow rectangle of the open door, holding my red coat in front of him like a bullfighter's cape, but I barely registered his presence as I plunged into the drifts by the flower bed. Billy could *not* have disappeared. Tweeter started down the steps, absolute misery lining his face so deeply I could see it even in the half dark. I didn't feel any sympathy for him at all. He'd had Billy forever. Now it was my turn.

On the other side of the mounded flower bed, I thought I saw a mark in the snow. Girl Scout, Boy Scout, I was no good at this. I stood upright and shook the snow out of my turtleneck. If he wasn't on the sidewalk or in the driveway, he must have gone through the yard. I raced around the corner of the house, past Jake's tree, snow-coned and swirling in the wind. Then around the other corner. For a moment I couldn't pick out anything except the clothesline whipping out from the wall like a snake, but then I lowered my eyes and moved them along every foot of the yard. One ear was hot: frostbite, damn it. I'd had it before. It didn't scare me.

Billy was sitting on the edge of the sandbox, his head in his hands, shaking. But it was legitimate to shake when it was so cold. I took him in my arms, just like the movies, just like we were miles away from civilization and the light from the kitchen window wasn't cutting a hole twenty feet from us. I touched him and held him and rubbed his hands in mine, and kissed him every place I could reach, and even zipped up his jeans the rest of the way, like I did Jake's sometimes. Thank God he hadn't run out in his shorts.

"He ain't got no right. No right."

I knelt up against him and pushed his head into my sweater.

All my edges ached like I was trying to expand to take him inside. I was, too.

"She run out on me. Shit, I thought she come back 'cause she *wanted*. It was jest Tweeter then, fixin' things up."

"Oh, sweetheart." When I put my cheek against his, even his beard felt brittle with the cold. It was a good thing when Tweeter found us both a moment later, because I didn't have enough body temperature to get him thawed out or enough strength to pull him up. My face numb, my fingers like popsicles, we got Billy back into the house again, Tweeter patting and rubbing us both. When Billy reached the bed, he flopped across it, his back heaving. I took his hand. When I looked around for Tweeter, he was gone.

"She eased me so good, Jill did. Got my fingers in shape again with them exercises once the cast was off. Said she didn't want no crippled picker in her bed." He caught his breath. "I thought it was goin' t' work out, her and me, 'specially with the kid comin'. Stopped them goddamn lawyers too. But we jest went at it again once I started pickin'. I give 'em all the money they needed, still do, back in that goddamn Waycross. End of the world, that shithouse town." Under my hand, his fist clenched. "Don't even know my own daughter!"

"How old is she?" It was the only thing I could think of. I was shivering so hard he probably didn't understand me. But Tweeter had come back and he did.

"She's fourteen," he said, as he covered Billy up with the comforter and wrapped the afghan around my shoulders. "Just starting high school." We were back in the living room, the fireplace burning like a golden furnace, Tweeter folded back in the director's chair. Outside the wind was regular as breathing. There was a long pause, very long, while my lungs slowed back into rhythm and I stepped into the present. A Waycross, Georgia, girl, back before the beard. His one child not a lost spirit on the plains of Texas. When I could look at Tweeter again, peering up under his slanted face so I could catch his eyes, I realized they were closed.

He was a good man. I stepped toward him. "Tweeter, do you want to sleep here? It's a terrible night." My hair was still damp from the snow, but I could feel the blood moving around inside my body again.

"Oh no, ma'am!" Embarrassed, he jerked erect and blushed bright red. "I mean, it wouldn't be right. I can get back to a hotel downtown without too much trouble. These storms are never so bad in town."

"What do you know about snowstorms, Tweeter? I thought it was dust storms in West Texas."

"We had a blizzard when I was in high school," he said with assurance. "My daddy lost seventeen head." He got up and walked carefully to the front hall to put on his coat. "I will come by tomorrow if that's all right. After Billy wakes up."

"You may be trapped in your hotel for weeks, Tweeter. This is North Dakota. You could stay with Lisa's guinea pigs upstairs."

"I appreciate the offer, ma'am. But I had better not." He buttoned his coat over the fringes and pulled up the collar as high as he could around his neck. Then he focused on me hard.

"Ma'am?"

Why did I want to tie his shoes and dig out a neck scarf for him from the pile in the closet? "Out with it," I said. "No secrets between orphans of the storm."

"Ma'am, Billy said you had a gun. Guns are not a good idea for ladies who don't know much about them. He was worried you would hurt yourself."

"Is that why he took it?"

"He said he gave it back." In the most genteel, deferential way, Tweeter's voice had ice in it.

"He was right about that. He did give it back. It's here." I felt for the lump in my red coat pocket, hanging just slightly above my head on the rack. When I found it, I pulled it out and gave it to Tweeter.

"Would you mind if I kept this for a while, ma'am? This looks like a safe neighborhood, and I don't think you will need it. Especially during a blizzard." Once again his cheeks lifted just a little. Was that a smile?

Swinging around as if he had asked me to dance, I stood on tiptoe and put my arms around his neck. "You may keep it forever, Billy's friend. It isn't really mine anyway. The man I was married to bought it the year he died. In an awful way I just couldn't throw it out. Actually, Tweeter, I would appreciate not having it around anymore. It should be easier now, as they say in the country music trade."

"That was always a real good song, ma'am." With great delicacy, Tweeter kissed me on my forehead and turned out the door.

36

THERE WAS NO WAY I could have stayed on my side of the bed, because Billy already had most of it. Besides it was just too cold. Even when I put on my flannel nightgown, with the heat left up at sixty-five, the bedroom was like a refrigerator shelf when the wind blew. Above the headboard the window shifted and rattled with each gust, the tree moving in great sweeps across the glass. When I knelt on my pillow to look out, the streetlight was flinging itself from side to side, sending flashes through the snow like a signal. If it had soared loose and shattered on the pavement, I wouldn't have been surprised.

For a while I kept my light on and read, holding the Victorian poets over the edge so I would take up as little space as possible. Billy winced at the light at first, but kept on sleeping. His left hand was flung out across the bed, his right over his belly on top of the comforter. Both were twitching. What song, Billy? What song are you picking before what cheering crowd? Is Jill smiling up at you from the table nearest the stage? Are they all dancing in your dreams?

Of course I had to turn out the light eventually, because

even if the kids slept late in the morning, even if school for them was canceled as it must be, I would have to get up before noon and put the house together. And once the light was out, I had no way of knowing exactly where the edge of the bed was, did I? And it was awfully cold, the coldest night of the year so far, with the wind the loneliest voice on the prairie. Even if I had turned the heat up more, the bedroom was always the coldest place in the house when the wind blew. Even if I had turned the heat way up.

I really did think he was asleep. But when I pulled the comforter over his wandering arms, he shifted on his side toward me. He smelled of beer and cigarette smoke. With one hand he rubbed his forehead, grimacing, then his ears. No frostbite. "I ain't showered, Kay," he said, his eyes still shut. I was so stunned to hear my name I couldn't even be angry. Or sad.

"Are you all right?" It was stupid, childish to want to hold him. He wasn't mine. But maybe if I just held his hand.

Billy rubbed the top of his head as if it hurt him. It probably did. "I jest don't think I kin git it up tonight, Kay," he said. "You ain't mad?"

"No, I'm not mad." The first snowstorm, the first truth.

"Wouldn't mind if you took off that thing, though."

"I'll freeze, Billy." But I was already taking it off.

"Nobody's froze on me yet." Even though I was still snarled in the nightgown, he pulled me up against him. With one hand he tucked my face under his chin and held it there. His beard tickled. With the other hand he patted my rear.

"Nice 'n' firm. Like that in my wimmen." And he was asleep again.

37

"K A Y , what *are* you doing?"

"It's stuck, blast it."

"What's stuck?" Emily leaned against my door, holding a large pink heart-shaped cookie between her breasts like the Scarlet Letter. She was giggling.

"This file." I wrenched again. The drawer burst open, gouging my chair leg. I shot into the backrest.

"Not anymore." She broke off a piece of cookie and handed it to me. "Look what I got from my fans. A box of them actually, from the ten o'clock freshmen. I'm praying they didn't bake them themselves."

I chewed, contemplative. "Not too bad. They must love you."

"All beautiful young English teachers are loved by their freshmen." She stood by my desk, the cookie in one hand. "What do you need in that drawer bad enough to risk breaking an arm for it?"

What did I need? Last year's test on introductory paragraphs, I had thought. Was that right? I chewed and introspected.

"Are the kids OK?"

"Fine." All my papers were corrected, and I could go home. That test hadn't been any good anyway. The corner of the file drawer nudged my leg, a friendly nibble where my boot ended. I shifted and rubbed it with my toe, gently. Nice drawer.

"Kay." She waited until I looked at her. This must be serious if it had to be eye to eye. I focused and smiled. Sweet crumbs rimmed my molars like snowdrifts.

"Kay, there's a new visiting prof over in the History Department. I met him two nights ago at that crazy sleigh ride the Faculty Club gives. He's nice and not *too* scholarly. Would . . ." Emily rubbed her hair with the hand holding the cookie. It disintegrated.

"Good night!" She tossed her hair, sending crumbs onto her shoulders, then clapped her hands together. "Look what I get for my efforts!"

"Yes," I said.

"Yes what?"

"Yes, you can introduce him to me." The file slid shut almost as if I hadn't pushed it. Smiling again, I got up, slid into my red coat, silently thanking the janitor for having lowered the hook to where I could reach it easily, and hoisted my briefcase. On the way to the door, I gave Emily a quick hug before she could give me one.

Out in the parking lot, someone had written WASH ME in the grime on the side of the Trail Duster. Not a bad idea. Maybe Sunday, for Valentine's Day. And a pink ribbon on the aerial. The old machine had gotten me through three months of winter with no trauma, starting merrily, fording unplowed roads like an ox team. I climbed aboard, readying the rawhide reins. On for the Donner Pass! On to California! On to Fifth Street!

When I pulled through the last narrow trail and unloaded inside our front door, the house was quiet. Warm, though. Our gas bills would be phenomenal, but if I made tenure track in the spring, I could afford them. And if I didn't? But I would. Even Dennis would write a letter of recommendation for me if I asked him.

I nested down. Jake had stacked his Valentines-to-be-labeled in a pyramid on the dining room table. The list of his classmates sat by it. With a little dance step, more wiggle than walk, I headed for the kitchen and put on the teakettle, splotching the linoleum with water in a trail from the sink. It could drip dry. Ball-point triggered, I pulled out a chair and started to print names on Valentine envelopes, the first grade's finest. Merilee. Thomas. Joyce, Billy, Ethel. Ethel? She must have been named after a grandmother.

The door slammed. A swish of cold air rammed up under my skirt.

"Mom, are you home?"

"Yes indeed. Freshmen drawn and quartered, papers handed back, half Jake's Valentines labeled. A model of efficiency. Are *you* home?"

"You're *silly*." Lisa yanked me to the sofa and plopped down beside me. "Mom, guess what?"

"I am guessed out. Tell me what."

"Billy has a new forty-five record. I got it today after school when Rebecca and I went downtown. Want to hear it?"

"Of course. Our own private cowboy. Did you hear it already?"

"They played it on the radio in the lunchroom today. That's why I bought it. I couldn't hear all the words, though. About women, naturally." She sounded twenty-five.

"Well, put it on. Time the two of us learned something about women, especially from an expert like Billy. Then come here and sit with me. You can prop yourself on your favorite pillow."

Laughing, Lisa pushed the button on the stereo and bounced down next to me. Just before the needle took hold, she said, "He calls it 'Stormy Night,' but it sounds kind of like a letter. Listen, Mom."

I did just that, all of me concentrated in the present. No. But at least eighty percent. That was passing even on those modern grade scales. It was nice to be passing.

*"I woke up last night from my dreamin',
Still wish I had you again."*

"He always drops all his g's," laughed Lisa, as Billy's guitar made a quick transitional flurry.

*"Cowboys 'n' pickers, they run away.
Nobody catches the wind.*

*Baby, I weren't no store bargain,
Nothin' you'd shop for 'n' wear.
Your life's doin' jest fine without me.
We weren't no permanent pair."*

"Listen now, Mom, here's the chorus."

*"I was the first storm of the season,
Left when the new sun broke through,
Left like there was a good reason,
Can't stop rememberin' you."*

"Now he sings the whole thing over again," said Lisa, as she jumped up to take off the needle. "Did you like it?"

"It's a nice song, honey."

"Know what? I like it too." She gave me a hug. "That is, for a country-western song."

Mary Gardner was born in Wisconsin and lived in the upper tier of states until moving to Galveston, Texas, in 1984. Married, with three children, Ms. Gardner has taught English composition in various colleges and shares a love of country-western music with the protagonist of *Keeping Warm*, her first novel.